A MOST PROVOCATIVE PROPOSITION

Sophia settled back in her chair, trying to sort out her feelings. Could she possibly reconsider Lady Winwood's proposition and marry the Earl of Leyburn? If she became his wife, her sisters would meet suitors of the highest social standing. Her brother would be able to mingle with the kind of young men she wanted him to emulate.

As for herself, the thought of marriage to Joel Leyburn filled her suddenly with excitement and desire. From the first she had been attracted to him, she would not deny it. Against her will, she imagined herself pulled against his hard, muscular chest, her lips bruised by his sensual, devouring mouth. To be his wife, to share his bed . . . a shiver ran down her spine.

No, she rebuked herself. She had too much pride, too much integrity to allow a man who considered her beneath him in social class and character to make love to her.

Sophia drew a deep breath. Whatever her personal feelings toward Lord Leyburn, she had her family to consider first.

Perhaps she ought to at least speak with him again. She rose, walking to her writing desk.

"Dear Lord Leyburn . . ."

WATCH FOR THESE ZEBRA REGENCIES

LADY STEPHANIE   (0-8217-5341-X, $4.50)
by Jeanne Savery

Lady Stephanie Morris has only one true love: the family estate she has managed ever since her mother died. But then Lord Anthony Rider arrives on her estate, claiming he has plans for both the land and the woman. Stephanie soon realizes she's fallen in love with a man whose sensual caresses will plunge her into a world of peril and intrigue . . . a man as dangerous as he is irresistible.

BRIGHTON BEAUTY   (0-8217-5340-1, $4.50)
by Marilyn Clay

Chelsea Grant, pretty and poor, naively takes school friend Alayna Marchmont's place and spends a month in the country. The devastating man had sailed from Honduras to claim his promised bride, Miss Marchmont. An affair of the heart may lead to disaster . . . unless a resourceful Brighton beauty finds a way to stop a masquerade and keep a lord's love.

LORD DIABLO'S DEMISE   (0-8217-5338-X, $4.50)
by Meg-Lynn Roberts

The sinfully handsome Lord Harry Glendower was a gambler and the black sheep of his family. About to be forced into a marriage of convenience, the devilish fellow engineered his own demise, never having dreamed that faking his death would lead him to the heavenly refuge of spirited heiress Gwyn Morgan, the daughter of a physician.

A PERILOUS ATTRACTION   (0-8217-5339-8, $4.50)
by Dawn Aldridge Poore

Alissa Morgan is stunned when a frantic passenger thrusts her baby into Alissa's arms and flees, having heard rumors that a notorious highwayman posed a threat to their coach. Handsome stranger Hugh Sebastian secretly possesses the treasured necklace the highwayman seeks and volunteers to pose as Alissa's husband to save her reputation. With a lost baby and missing necklace in their care, the couple embarks on a journey into peril—and passion.

Available wherever paperbacks are sold, or order direct from the Publisher. Send cover price plus 50¢ per copy for mailing and handling to Penguin USA, P.O. Box 999, c/o Dept. 17109, Bergenfield, NJ 07621. Residents of New York and Tennessee must include sales tax. DO NOT SEND CASH.

A MARRIAGE OF CONVENIENCE

Lois Stewart

Zebra Books
Kensington Publishing Corp.

ZEBRA BOOKS are published by

Kensington Publishing Corp.
850 Third Avenue
New York, NY 10022

First Printing: October, 1996
10 9 8 7 6 5 4 3 2 1

Printed in the United States of America

One

She wasn't mistaken. The inebriated young gentleman sitting next to her in the coach was definitely pressing his knee against her leg.

Sophia edged as far away as she could. A moment later the coach lurched to the left, the movement throwing her against the young gentleman's shoulder. Hastily she scrambled back against the right hand side of the coach.

"The road's turned very slippery from the snow," the lady sitting opposite Sophia said fretfully. "It doesn't seem right, to have snow in the middle of March. I do hope we won't have an accident."

"Now, ma'am, don't ye worry," observed the elderly gentleman sharing the seat with the lady. "We had only a smattering o' snow, when all's said and done, and our coachman strikes me as a very reliable sort." He frowned. "I fear I can't say as much for the guard. Unless I miss my guess, the fellow's in his cups."

"Oh, that he is, sir," chortled the young man beside Sophia. "Half-seas over, I'd say. Heard the fellow boasting at our last post stop that he could put on and remove the skid pan without getting down from his seat. Well, we'll soon test his skills with the skid pan, won't we? I seem to remember a fair number of hills between here and Chester."

The young man flashed Sophia a confidential grin that made her think of nothing so much as the leer of an over-friendly wolf. She squeezed into the corner to put an extra fraction of an inch of distance between them, and huddled deeper into her fur trimmed pelisse against the dank March cold.

She'd mismanaged this journey, she thought darkly. She should have considered that a gentlewoman traveling alone in a public coach might be subject to the advances of drunken rakes. When her own coachman came down with the ague she should have hired a post chaise to take her and one of the household maids to Chester. However, the habits of economy ingrained during her impoverished childhood had been too strong for her. She'd resisted the expense of transporting herself and a servant by post chaise, especially since she would also be required to pay for accommodations for Edwina and Caroline on the return journey.

Edwina and Caroline. Frowning, Sophia removed her hands from her muff and reached into her reticule for the letter from Miss Beaton. She scanned the few brief lines in the schoolmistress's spidery handwriting.

"My dear Mrs. Ashley, it greaves me to inform you that the unseemly conduct of your young sisters forces me to request that you remove them forthwith from my academy."

Resisting the impulse to crumple the letter into an unrecognizable ball, Sophia replaced it in her reticule. She stared unseeingly out the window at the passing Cheshire scenery while she tried again to imagine the type of heinous behavior that might have brought her sixteen-year-old twin sisters to the point of expulsion from Miss Beaton's exclusive female academy. No, not sixteen. Next month Edwina and Caroline would turn seventeen. Whatever offense they'd committed, they should have known better, reflected Sophia angrily. Heaven knows, she'd done her best to instill the proper notions of propriety in her young sisters' minds.

She sighed, settling deeper into her corner. She was barely

eight years older than the twins, but sometimes, as in this instance, she felt positively ancient.

Her thoughts drifted back five years. Her father, Horace Dalton, an unsuccessful clergyman in a small village near Manchester, had just died, leaving his three daughters and his son with a pile of debts and little else. Sophia, a junior mistress at Miss Beaton's Academy at the time, had been faced with the heavy burden of supporting the twelve-year-old twins and their brother, Tristan, two years younger, on her meager salary. An offer of marriage from Bartholomew Ashley, a wealthy middle-aged mill owner who had been friendly with her father, had seemed to her a miraculous solution to her dilemma.

And indeed, thought Sophia, blinking away a tinge of moistness in her eyes, she had never regretted the marriage. True, she'd never deceived herself that she felt any sort of romantic love for Bartholomew, who had died the previous year, but she had been fond of her elderly husband. He had never been anything except kindly, affectionate, undemanding and considerate to her, and when he died his young widow became a woman of means.

A scream brought Sophia out of her reverie. The terrified lady on the opposite seat clutched at her companion as the coach began hurtling violently from side to side in its precipitous descent down a steep hill. Moments later the coach listed sharply to the left and crashed to a halt. The occupants of the carriage were thrown against each other on the left side of the vehicle.

For a few seconds Sophia remained dazed. Then, as she attempted to claw herself from her prone position atop her flirtatious seat mate, the right door of the coach opened, and a man she recognized as one of the outside passengers spoke reassuringly, extending his hand. "Here, ma'am, let me help ye out."

Feeling decidedly unsteady on her legs, Sophia stood in the roadway as her Good Samaritan assisted her fellow passengers out of the carriage. The left wheels of the coach were in a ditch, and the coachman, hatless, with his forehead marked by a streak of blood, was trying to calm the skittish team.

"It's a mercy no one was killed," said her rescuer cheerfully. "The roof passengers and the coachman an' the guard were thrown off, o'course, an' the guard has a broken head. And well he deserves it," the man added in a sudden burst of resentment. "The fellow didn't put the skid pan on when we started down t' hill."

"I understand the guard had been imbibing," Sophia murmured. She surveyed the overturned coach and the restless horses and the assortment of baggage strewn over the field next to the road. "What will happen now?"

"I reckon there's nothing much we can do except wait for help, ma'am. The coachman says as how the axletree is broke, an' as soon as he gets the team settled down he'll ride one o' the horses to the next posting stop—Davenham, I think it is— and fetch another carriage fer us."

"Oh," said Sophia hollowly. She was grateful—of course she was grateful—that she'd escaped the accident unhurt. Unfortunately, the snow had started again, and the temperature seemed to be plummeting by the minute.

"Thank you for being so helpful," she told her rescuer, and then, tucking her hands into her muff, she started off down the road, empty of traffic, hoping that the exercise would prevent her feet in her thin slippers from turning into blocks of ice.

"Where are you off to, lovely lady?" called a faintly slurred voice behind her. "Pray allow me to volunteer my services as your escort."

Sophia's heart sank. She shot an unfriendly look at her inebriated seat mate as he appeared beside her. "You're very kind, sir," she said coldly. "However, I don't require an escort, thank you. I have no destination in mind. I'm walking merely to keep warm until some transportation arrives."

"Ah, but one never knows what dangers a lady might encounter on the road," insisted the young man. "I won't hear of your walking alone. May I introduce myself? My name is Hayman, Caleb Hayman."

Sophia stole another look at her companion. He wasn't a bad

looking young man, only rather callow and faintly ridiculous in his aping of the latest fads of the dandies. His shirt points were so high they threatened to strangle him, his small flat hat was perched precariously on the top of his head, and he wore a spotted neckerchief in a bilious shade of yellow instead of a cravat.

"You'll understand, I trust, Mr. Hayman, that I can't give you my name, since we haven't been properly introduced."

"I beg you to reconsider, ma'am," the young man said earnestly. "You and I are no longer mere strangers. We've shared a journey, and now the dangers of the road." He stopped short in his tracks, giving her a toothy, cajoling smile as he placed a detaining hand on her arm. "Actually, I was convinced we were going to be friends from the first moment I saw you at the posting inn in Manchester."

As an affronted Sophia tried to wrest her arm from his grasp, Caleb Hayman swept her into a bearlike embrace and planted a clumsy kiss on her mouth.

For a moment Sophia was too surprised to move a muscle. Then, aroused to fury, she began to struggle, averting her head away from him and striking flailing blows to his chest with her fists. Hayman tightened his grip, and both he and Sophia were so absorbed in their contest that neither noticed the sound of wheels approaching from the direction of Chester.

A moment later, Sophia found herself released so suddenly that she staggered backwards and almost fell. She looked dazedly at Caleb Hayman, lying senseless on the ground, and then at the tall man in the beaver hat and many-caped, ankle-length greatcoat who had knocked Hayman down.

The tall man removed his hat, saying politely, "Are you all right, ma'am? The fellow didn't injure you?"

"No," she returned, a little out of breath. "I'm quite all right. That is . . . Thank you. Thank you so very much."

Blushing as she realized she sounded hopelessly disjointed, Sophia lifted her gaze to meet his. He was clearly one of the handsomest men she had ever met. He had curling tawny hair, eyes so intensely gray they were almost silver, an arrogant nose and a sensual mouth in a lean-planed face. Her heart seemed to turn over in her chest, a sensation so unusual for her she felt suddenly dizzy.

The stranger glanced down the road at the overturned stage-coach. "I gather you were a passenger in the coach, ma'am?"

"Yes. That's the Manchester to Chester coach. An axletree broke when we came down the hill too fast, they tell me. The other passengers and I are waiting for the coachman to ride to the next post stop for help."

The man raised an eyebrow. "You'll have a long wait, I fear. The coachman won't be able to return for some time, and heaven knows how long it will take to repair the coach. May I make a suggestion? From the next stop, Chester is only one stage. Will you allow me to take you there?"

Sophia hesitated, torn between decorum and discomfort. It would be most improper for her to accept a ride from a man to whom she hadn't been introduced. And as an unaccompanied female, she had already had one unfortunate encounter with a stranger today. On the other hand, the light snow had turned to an icy drizzle of rain. The fur on her bonnet brim was drooping, and she could feel the chilly damp penetrating through her pe-lisse. If she remained exposed to the elements for too much longer she risked coming down with the ague.

She glanced again at the stranger. He looked like a gentleman. And his elegant posting chariot, with its four horses and two postillions, looked like a positive haven of refuge.

Still hesitating, Sophia said, without much conviction, "But surely, sir, if you drive me to Chester you would be retracing your own journey?"

He shook his head. "Think nothing of it, ma'am. A slight detour, only. I'm on my way to Warrington, scarcely ten miles north of Debenham."

Sophia gave in without further argument. "Thank you, sir, you're most kind."

After all, she thought, even if the gentleman were so inclined, he would doubtless find it awkward to press unwanted attentions on her in the confined space of the chariot, with the postillions in plain sight through the front window. Not to speak of the two servants on the rumble behind.

"Not at all." He gave her a charming smile, extending his hand to help her into the chariot. Sophia breathed a sigh of relief to be out of the freezing rain as she settled into her seat. The gentleman carefully tucked a blanket over her lap and around her legs. Turning his head, he gave a brief order to one of the two servants on the rumble. A wiry youth jumped to the ground and trotted down the road toward the stagecoach. As the gentleman climbed into the chariot beside Sophia, he explained, "I sent my tiger to collect your luggage, ma'am."

"Oh, thank you," she replied with real gratitude. In the stress of the last few minutes Sophia had forgotten about the luggage strewn beside the road when the stagecoach overturned.

Shortly, the tiger returned with her portmanteau, which he deposited in a space between the front springs of the carriage. As soon as the tiger regained his perch the postillions turned the posting chariot around and drove off in the direction of Chester. From her window Sophia caught a glimpse of her erstwhile persecutor, Caleb Hayman, rising unsteadily to his feet. His expression was so completely befuddled that Sophia wanted to laugh. Did he have the faintest conception of what had happened after he had seized her in his arms?

It was the start of an almost two hours drive to Chester and Sophia was decidedly nervous. One part of her mind kept reminding her that gentlewomen did not accept invitations from strangers. The other part of her mind was very conscious of her companion, of his sheer size and good looks, of his superb grooming and of his air of quiet self-confidence. He was so different from her male acquaintances in the Manchester area that he might have been a creature from another world!

To her relief, her new acquaintance displayed not the slightest sign of flirtatiousness. In fact, he sounded almost diffident as he said, "May I introduce myself? I'm Leyburn. Er—actually,

I'm the Earl of Leyburn. Purely a courtesy title," he added hastily. "It's my father who sits in the Lords."

"Oh . . ." Sophia felt a momentary shock. She certainly hadn't been prepared to have the company of a lord—even a courtesy lord—as her escort! Recovering, she said, "How do you do, Lord Leyburn. I'm Mrs. Ashley."

"Mrs—Mrs. Ashley. How do you do?"

Had there been the slightest suggestion of disappointment in Lord Leyburn's voice when he hesitated over her name, Sophia wondered uneasily. He had thought—hoped?—that she was a single woman?

Leyburn quickly proved her suspicion incorrect. During the drive to Chester his conversation and manner was pleasant, well-bred and quite impersonal. He asked no intrusive questions, although his striking gray eyes were often warm and alight with interest when he looked at her, nor did he reveal anything of his own circumstances. Instead, he made small talk. He discussed the weather, inquired about the details of the stagecoach accident, mentioned the scenic attractions of Chester, and was solicitous of her comfort.

"Are you warm enough, Mrs. Ashley? Shall we stop at Debenham for tea and perhaps a bowl of hot soup?"

By the time the ancient red sandstone walls of Chester appeared on the horizon in the early spring twilight, Sophia's apprehensions about her escort had disappeared. He had made the journey so easy and comfortable for her that he might have been an old friend of the family, except that none of her friends were as worldly or as wickedly handsome as Lord Leyburn.

As the carriage passed under the arched portal of Eastgate Lord Leyburn inquired, "Where may I take you, Mrs. Ashley? Are you staying with friends?"

"No. I always stop at the Old King's Head in Lower Bridge Street."

A few minutes later, having helped her down from the carriage, Lord Leyburn stood beside Sophia on the pavement outside the Old King's Head. He motioned his tiger to carry her portmanteau into the hotel. Removing his hat, he said with a smile, "Goodbye, Mrs. Ashley. I trust you'll have a pleasant stay in Chester."

"Thank you. And thank you very much, too, for driving me here. But for you I'd doubtless be stranded in Debenham for the night."

"Not at all. It was my pleasure." Bowing, Leyburn put on his hat and turned to reenter his carriage.

As she walked into the hotel Sophia was conscious of a twinge of disappointment. Very properly, Lord Leyburn had refrained from pressing his acquaintance on her, but his good manners also had the effect of cutting off any future contact between them. As it should be, Sophia told herself firmly. She and the intriguing stranger had met by accident, for a brief time only, and that was the end of it.

Shown into a comfortable room, Sophia hung her still damp pelisse and bonnet in the wardrobe and tried to smooth her thick dark brown hair into its usual neat coil on the crown of her head. However, the damp had caused curling tendrils of hair to escape and cluster around her forehead and temples. About to scrape the curls mercilessly into submission, Sophia paused to examine her image in the mirror. The curls were curiously attractive, framing her deep blue eyes, creamy complexion and small even features. Perhaps she should take Edwina's oft-repeated advice and have her heavy long hair shorn into a more fashionable and youthful style.

Thoughts of Edwina caused her mouth to tighten. It was too late in the day, and she was too tired from her adventures on the turnpike, to look into her younger sisters' predicament tonight. She would visit the academy tomorrow. Meanwhile, she was ravenously hungry. She jammed a lacy cap on her head and headed down the stairs.

The landlord of the inn was politely regretful. "I'm very sorry, Mrs. Ashley, but I have no private dining parlor to offer you."

Disappointed, Sophia lingered in the hallway, gazing into the coffee room which was crowded with predominantly male, and very noisy, guests. Not the place, definitely, for a lone respectable female. Sighing, she said, "I'd prefer a private dining parlor, of course, but . . . please send a tray to my bedchamber, landlord."

A familiar voice behind her said, "Good evening, Mrs. Ashley. May I be of service?"

Sophia turned in surprise to see Lord Leyburn descending the last of the stairs. "But I thought—you told me you were traveling on to Warrington, my lord," she said, as he came up to her. She noted that he had changed from greatcoat, top boots and leather breeches to town dress of well-tailored coat, pantaloons and gleaming Hessians.

He bowed, smiling. "I'd scarcely gone a mile after I left you when the rain began pelting down, colder and harder than ever. So I took pity on myself, and more especially on my servants and the postillions, exposed so uncomfortably to the elements, and decided to remain in Chester for the night."

"Oh." Sophia felt oddly disconcerted, and at the same time very conscious of her plain dark blue gown, several seasons old and certainly never in the height of fashion.

"I overheard your conversation with the landlord," Leyburn went on. "Apparently I bespoke the only available private dining parlor. Shall we join forces? Will you do me the honor of dining with me?"

Sophia hesitated. Once again convention warred with inclination. It would be pleasant to dine with an agreeable companion. She took a deep breath. "Thank you. I'd like to dine with you."

"Splendid." He ushered her into the private parlor where he solicitously seated her in the chair nearest the fire and consulted with her over the menu. He ordered a wine, which from the landlord's reaction, she judged to be the most expensive vintage in his cellar.

Leaning back in his chair after the landlord left the room, Leyburn said with a quizzical smile, "I never thought I'd be grateful that bad weather had interrupted a journey, but I must confess I'm grateful for this storm."

Sophia ignored the implications of the remark. "You might well have had an accident if you'd continued your journey in such inclement weather," she said primly, feeling a slight glow of warmth on her cheeks. His gray eyes held an appreciative light she couldn't mistake. She felt certain he admired her, a sensation that caused her heart to skip a beat.

By degrees, slowly, gradually, as the inn servants deftly and unobtrusively served their dinner, Sophia realized the interplay between herself and Lord Leyburn had changed from the former impersonal quality of their drive to Chester to an easier, more casual relationship. Leyburn poured the wine freely and Sophia, though never much of a tippler, accepted a second glass without demur.

Leyburn spoke of his father, the Marquess of Kennington. "When he's not in London, he lives like a hermit in this vast old pile in Yorkshire," Leyburn said, grimacing. "Parts of the place date from shortly after the Conquest, and most of the rooms are as drafty and uncomfortable as they must have been during the Middle Ages. I've been trying to persuade Father to tear down the old hulk and build a new, modern house, but he won't hear of it, nor will he make improvements which would make the house more pleasant for everyone." He smiled bitterly, "The old man accuses me of being a traitor to the family traditions."

"You and your father don't sound very sympathetic to each other," ventured Sophia, as she took a sip of wine.

Leyburn laughed. "That we aren't. He was past forty when he married, so I've often felt more like a grandson than a son. But the real reason why we're at odds is politics. I left the Whigs a few years ago to join the Tories. Father was furious, of course. The Hilliard family, headed by the Marquesses of Kennington, has been Whig for over a century, more out of habit than anything else, I suspect. At any rate, Father refused to support me for a seat in the Commons. So, several years ago, I was elected to a Tory seat in Westminster, and Father hasn't spoken to me since."

Sophia watched him lower his eyes and she thought she detected a fleeting expression of sadness on his face as he sipped his wine. "Do you have other family members—brothers, sisters?" she asked.

He lifted inscrutable gray eyes. "My mother died within a year of my birth," he stated simply. "Father never remarried, though he had every opportunity to do so."

"Then he was quite particular in his tastes," she offered.

"Precisely so," Lord Leyburn responded. "Besides, Father became more interested in politics than love when mother died."

Sophia was frankly fascinated by this glimpse into his family as well as into their political affairs. She had never before encountered a Member of Parliament. However, she became mildly uneasy when the earl, refilling his glass, remarked, "That's enough of my not very interesting concerns. Now I'd like to know something about you." She still felt a certain reluctance to reveal details of her personal life to a man she had met for the first time today.

"Oh, there's nothing very remarkable about me," she said lightly.

Smiling, the earl said, "That's modesty talking, I daresay. I'm sure you're very remarkable. To start, tell me about your life in Manchester."

Sophia cleared her throat. "Actually, I don't live in Manchester. My home is in Woodbridge, a small village about seven miles from Manchester."

"With your husband, presumably?" There it was again, the faintly odd edge to his voice.

"My husband died a year ago," Sophia said quietly.

Leyburn's eyes narrowed. "I'm sorry to hear of your loss. You live alone, then?"

"No. I live with my younger sisters and our younger brother."

"I see. Do you prefer living in a small town, then, rather than in a large city like Manchester?"

"It's not a matter of preference. I live in Woodbridge because that's where my husband's mill is located, and I need to oversee the operation of the business. He was a cotton manufacturer by trade."

The earl looked at her curiously. "And you actually manage the mill yourself? Is it very large?"

Shrugging, Sophia replied, "Large enough, I suppose, considering that my husband began operations with a few looms in an outbuilding on his family's farm."

The earl nodded. "I understand that a myriad of small mills have sprung up in this area in recent years. And a good thing, too, with the war with Napoleon cutting into the textile trade."

Sophia forbore to correct Lord Leyburn about the size of her husband's cotton mill, which at the time of Bartholomew Ashley's death was one of the largest and most profitable spinning mills in all of Lancashire.

"Well, then you're obviously a very busy lady," observed the earl as he reached for a second wine bottle, the first being quite definitely empty, and refilled Sophia's glass. She looked at the glass with a slight feeling of surprise. Had she really consumed two large glasses of wine?

"You're also responsible for the care of your younger brother and sisters, I gather," Leyburn continued. "Why is that?"

"My mother died six years ago, and Papa died a year later. He was a clergyman in Woodbridge." Sophia smiled wryly. "Not a very successful one, I fear. He left nothing but debts!"

She fell into an embarrassed silence. Now, why did I say that, she asked herself. She had never talked to anyone—except to Bartholomew Ashley—about the desperate financial straits in which she'd found herself at her father's death. It must be the wine loosening her tongue, she decided, putting down her glass.

Lord Leyburn appeared not to notice her embarrassment. He began to chat easily about his life in London, mentioning the excitement of the debates in Parliament over the Regency Bills earlier in the year. "Prinny's Regent now, right enough, but it was a close-run thing. The Whigs almost defeated us." He then talked about the latest showing at the Royal Academy, and described his recent visit to the theater. "I saw Mrs. Siddons as Lady Macbeth just before I left London. It may have been my last opportunity to see her in the role. She's grown very fat, you know, and it's rumored she would like to retire."

The earl leaned across the table suddenly to clasp Sophia's wrist lightly in his hand. His voice was deep and resonant, his smile infinitely beguiling, as he said, "I'm positive you would enjoy a visit to London, Mrs. Ashley." He shook his head impatiently. "Oh, the devil, I can't continue calling you 'Mrs.' What's your given name?"

Startled, she replied, "Sophia." She lowered her gaze to look at his hand. It was a beautiful hand, graceful and long-fingered and well-kept. She found herself responding inexplicably to his touch. She felt dizzy and exhilarated all at once. Yet this should not be! The wine again, perhaps? In some confusion, she tried to pull her hand away.

"Sophia," the earl repeated dreamily, not permitting her to escape his hold on her wrist. "What a lovely name. And I'm Joel. Please call me Joel." He leaned closer, his silvery gray eyes almost diamond-like in brilliance as he held her gaze forcefully. "You're so very pretty. Come to London with me. I promise you a visit you'll always remember. I'll show you all the sights, and we'll go to the theater or the opera or Vauxhall Gardens or the Pantheon every night, if you wish for it. And if you don't care to stay with me in my rooms I'll reserve a suite for you at the Pulteney Hotel in Piccadilly. The *on dit* is that the Pulteney is the best hotel in London now—"

"What!" Sophia cried, arousing at last from the shock into which the earl's proposition had thrown her. She snatched her hand away. "You are suggesting I accompany you to London, for, for reasons I can't even give voice to? Oh, oh, how dare you?" She pushed back her chair so violently that it crashed to the floor. She jumped up and raced toward the door of the dining parlor.

For all her speed, Lord Leyburn was there before her, bracing his back against the door and preventing her from escaping. "What's the matter with you, Sophia?" he asked with a puzzled frown. "It's rather late in the day for you to be acting missish, isn't it? Besides, I've seen the look in your eyes. You're drawn to me, aren't you, just as I'm drawn to you. Don't deny it, for I won't believe you."

Sophia gaped at him in utter astonishment. She ignored the last part of his remarks and quickly addressed the former. "Are you implying that I'm a loose woman, open to any lure you care to cast out to me?"

The earl stared at her beneath drawn brows. "What else was I to think?" he asked. "Of course I know you're not a real Ladybird, perhaps, but I assure you that no gentlewoman of my acquaintance would have acted as you did today. When I met you, you were traveling alone by public transportation. No abigail, no companion of any kind. Well, that disregard for propriety may be common in your social circles, Sophia, but they aren't in mine! You coyly demurred at first when I offered to drive you to Chester, but in the end you accepted my offer. Again, hardly the mark of a gentlewoman. Then this evening you also accepted my invitation to dine with me in a private parlor. All in all, I had every reason to believe you would be receptive to my 'lures,' as you put it."

Sophia bristled with indignation, anger displacing the apprehension she felt at being restrained in the room against her will. "I'll have you know that I'm a respectable woman, my lord, even if I'm not a member of your aristocratic circle." A thought struck her. She glared at him accusingly. "You never had any intention of traveling on to Warrington tonight, did you? You deliberately took a room in this hotel, planning to coax me into your bed after you'd wined and dined me."

The earl's features relaxed into an amused smile. "Guilty as charged. I miscalculated, did I?"

"You most certainly did!" Sophia cried, lifting her chin. "Perhaps I did fail to observe all the conventions, but I beg you'll step aside from that door and allow me to pass, or I'll scream loudly enough to raise the rafters. Which will it be?"

The earl smiled more broadly still. "My dear Sophia, I assure you that I have never in my life forced a reluctant female to accept my favors." He opened the door, turning to her with a bow. "You're quite free to go, Mrs. Ashley. Thank you for a very enjoyable evening though I still wish it had ended differently."

"Oh . . . !" Too mortified and angry to think of a suitable retort, Sophia swept past him with her head held high.

Two

As Sophia emerged from the hotel the next morning, she glanced appreciatively up at the sky, where the sun shone brightly. The storm of the previous day was only a memory, and already the temperature was many degrees warmer. She decided against hiring the cab that waited in front of the hotel in favor of a brisk walk to Miss Beaton's Academy.

As she strolled north on Lower Bridge Street into Bridge Street itself, she encountered the first of the famous arcaded Rows that lined the streets in the old center of Chester. Feeling an instant glow of nostalgia, she slowed her walk to admire a number of the picturesque "black and white" timbered buildings that she remembered from her years as a schoolmistress in the city.

At the Cross marking the center of Chester she turned left on Watergate Street, passing the magnificent timbered building known as God's Providence House. Near the intersection with Weaver Street she paused momentarily in front of the large, substantial house that Miss Beaton had converted into a select academy for young females. Taking a deep breath, and gritting her teeth, she went up the steps and raised the door knocker.

She knew she would not enjoy her coming meeting with the headmistress.

A neatly dressed maid conducted her into the familiar office-sitting room where Miss Beaton conducted her interviews with parents, prospective assistant-mistresses, and recalcitrant pupils. After a brief interval the headmistress swept into the room.

Miss Beaton looked exactly as she always had—a tall commanding figure in a decorous high-necked black dress. Primly arranged dark hair was skinned back from small, neat expressionless features dominated by penetrating blue eyes.

"Pray sit down, Mrs. Ashley. I wish I could say I am happy to see you again, but, under the circumstances, I am not."

"You owe me an explanation, Miss Beaton," said Sophia coolly, as she took a seat on a stiffly upholstered settee opposite the headmistress. "You've asked me—no, ordered me—to come to Chester to remove my sisters from your school. I should like to know why."

A spark appeared in the headmistress's blue eyes. "My reason is quite simple, Mrs. Ashley. I do not tolerate gross immorality, either in my own private life, or in those of my pupils."

Sophia stiffened. "Gross immorality? Are you saying that my sisters have been guilty of immoral behavior?"

"I am. I have no wish to cause you pain, but I must be frank. I discovered one night that your sister Edwina was missing from her bed. I questioned her twin, Caroline, who denied any knowledge of Edwina's whereabouts. It was quite obvious Caroline was lying, that she knew perfectly well Edwina had slipped out in the dead of night for an illicit tryst with Signor Bernani, the young man who has been serving as music master to my pupils. Needless to say, he is no longer employed at the academy."

Feeling stupefied, almost as if someone had struck a hard blow in the pit of her stomach, knocking the breath out of her, Sophia stammered, "I can't believe . . . Edwina would never do such a thing . . ."

Miss Beaton fixed her with a steely eye. "Edwina has acknowledged her guilt. Caroline, too, has admitted she knew about her sister's tryst and withheld the information from me because she feared Edwina might 'get into trouble.' " The head-mistress's lip curled. "A misplaced sisterly loyalty, coupled with a total lack of moral sense, in my opinion." Miss Beaton rose. "Now that you have arrived, Mrs. Ashley, I wish your sisters to leave the premises immediately. I will send a housemaid to instruct Edwina and Caroline to pack their luggage and join you here in the parlor."

Bowing to the inevitable, Sophia said as calmly as she could, "Certainly. Neither my sisters nor I have any wish for them to remain in an establishment where they are not welcome."

"Thank you." Miss Beaton walked to the door of the parlor, pausing to say, "I am truly sorry matters have come to this pass, Mrs. Ashley. I have a great regard for you personally. I consider you one of the ablest assistant-mistresses I have ever employed. I also want you to know that I will be very close-mouthed about this affair, both to protect the good name of my academy and to save you from public embarrassment. It is truly a shame you should be obliged to suffer from your sisters' misdeeds."

Sophia bowed her head, too angry for the moment to reply. Angry at Edwina and Caroline, that went without saying. Angry, too, at Miss Beaton, who, though she undoubtedly meant to be kind, registered as insufferably patronizing.

As the headmistress opened the door, however, Sophia managed to say, "Thank you, Miss Beaton. I appreciate your thoughtfulness. Could I also ask you to have a servant hail a hackney cab for me?"

Miss Beaton inclined her head. "Of course. Goodbye, Mrs. Ashley."

Sophia waited impatiently in the parlor for a dragging half hour. Finally, Edwina and Caroline, dressed for the street in bonnets and pelisses, entered the room.

"Hello, Sophy," Edwina said in what for her was a rather subdued tone.

Caroline murmured an incoherent greeting.

The sisters were of the same height, with slender, graceful

figures, but there any resemblance ended. They were twins, but not identical twins.

Edwina had luxuriantly curling red-gold hair, more red than gold, and sparkling green eyes set in a pretty face in which every change of emotion registered in her animated features.

Caroline was pretty, too, although in a less striking way. She had Sophia's dark hair and blue eyes, and her quiet, reserved face rarely revealed what she was thinking or feeling.

Sophia remained seated. Her mouth set in a grim line, she stared at her sisters, not speaking, not returning their greeting. The two girls looked increasingly uneasy, shuffling their feet like errant children caught raiding the jam jar.

"Er, Sophy," Edwina began. "We're very sorry we put you to this trouble. We'd like to explain—"

Rising, Sophia said, "You may explain later. This is no place to talk about our personal affairs. Come along, now. A hackney cab is waiting outside the academy to take us to our hotel. And I might add that a cab is no place for personal conversation, either."

During the short drive to the hotel, Sophia chattered aimlessly about any topic that came into her head, including the accident to the stagecoach on the previous day. She did not, however, mention the Earl of Leyburn.

Her sisters listened, mute and dejected, until at one point, when Sophia was describing their hotel as an excellent example of early seventeenth century architecture, Caroline lifted her head and said, "Aren't you forgetting, Sophy, that Edwina and I are familiar with the Old King's Head? We stayed there when you enrolled us in Miss Beaton's academy."

"Oh," Sophia said, taken aback. There was a certain asperity in Caroline's tone which indicated the older sister—by a scant five minutes—was recovering her equilibrium.

Sophia had reserved a separate room for her sisters at the hotel. As they mounted the stairs she told them to come to her bedchamber as soon as they were settled in.

When Edwina and Caroline entered her chamber a little later

Sophia motioned to a tray on a side table. "I ordered tea for us. Would you like a cup? Are you hungry? The little cakes look delicious. Dinner won't be served for several hours."

After the girls had poured their tea, Sophia leaned back in her chair, saying, "Well? Shall we get to the bottom of this business? Miss Beaton told me, Edwina, that you stole out of the school to engage in a nocturnal tryst with a music master, and that Caroline denied any knowledge of your activity, although, in fact, she knew quite well what you were about. I found these accusations hard to believe, but of course I couldn't challenge Miss Beaton out of my own knowledge. So I ask you, are these charges true?"

A deep blush suffused Edwina's cheeks. She blushed easily and beautifully and the rosy color never seemed to clash with her red hair.

"Sophy!" she exclaimed. "You must know I'd never—Sophy, I see now I shouldn't have agreed to have a, that is, an assignation with Signor Bernani, but he was such a nice man, and he seemed to like me so much, and we never had an opportunity to talk for more than a minute or two, he only came to the academy twice a week, you understand, so . . . But nothing happened, I swear it!"

Sophia raised a skeptical eyebrow at this disjointed account. "What do you mean precisely, that nothing happened?"

Still blushing, Edwina replied, "Well, practically nothing. Signor Bernani had a hackney cab waiting around the corner of Weaver Street, and we just drove around the city for a time, talking, and getting to know each other. And I was enjoying myself so much, because you know, Sophy, or perhaps you don't know, that Miss Beaton's acadmy is such a boring place most of the time."

Eyeing Sophia's suddenly disapproving face, Edwina rushed on. "Well, as I was saying, it was such an interesting evening, and Signor Bernani was so pleasant and attentive, but . . . Then he tried to kiss me, and he said some things I didn't understand at all, and I was frightened, and I pushed him away, and I demanded he take me back to the academy. So he did, finally. Then, when I went to the dormitory I found Miss Beaton waiting for me. And I tried to tell her that I hadn't really done anything wrong, but she wouldn't listen to me. In fact, she as much as told me I was a loose woman, and poor Caroline, too, because she refused to betray me. And it's so unfair, Sophy, because you must see I haven't done anything so very bad."

Sophia gazed at her sister's flushed, indignant face and sighed. "Edwina, I know you're guilty of nothing except being exceptionally bird-witted and lacking in judgment. However, I must tell you that you may just have made micefeet of the rest of your life with your little escapade."

"But—"

"No buts. Listen to me. Supposing a prospective suitor should learn that you had been expelled from a select young ladies' academy for conducting a clandestine affair with your music master, and a foreigner, to boot. That suitor would never offer for you. What's more, he might very well spread the story, and then your reputation would be in ruins."

"Oh!" The rosy color faded from Edwina's pretty face. "I never thought—"

"You rarely do think before you act," Sophia retorted. "Fortunately, Miss Beaton has promised to keep your behavior confidential. And since I understand that none of your fellow pupils come from our area, I trust that nobody in our corner of Lancashire will ever learn about this distressing episode. But in the future, Edwina, I hope you'll be more discreet."

"Yes, Sophy," Edwina muttered. She seemed utterly crushed, quite unlike her usual bubbly self.

Caroline, who had been listening quietly to her sisters' conversation, now said unexpectedly, "Sophy, you're as much to blame for this foolish affair as Edwina. More so, actually."

Sophia stared at Caroline in astonishment. "What on earth does that mean?" she said frostily. "Pray explain yourself."

"Certainly. The fact is, Sophy, that you should never have enrolled Edwina in the academy. She begged you not to send her there. She was no scholar. She hated studying. She hated leaving Woodbridge where she knew everybody and where she'd always been happy. But no, you insisted she had to be educated. So she went to Miss Beaton's academy. She was miserable there. She was bored to tears. I'm not excusing her behavior, but I can understand why she wanted to spend an evening with Signor Bernani. He was young and handsome and interesting. I'm only sorry that he also turned out to be a rake."

Outraged, Sophia exclaimed, "You'll recall, Caroline, that you and your sister and your brother were left in my care when Papa died. When I enrolled Edwina in the academy I was only trying to do my duty by her, to the best of my ability. A young lady of quality requires a superior education if she hopes to make an exceptional match. I hoped Edwina would learn to be studious. You certainly did."

Caroline ignored the compliment. "Duty!" she snorted. "Tyranny is more like it. Tyranny in a velvet glove."

Sophia and Edwina gasped as one. Edwina exclaimed, "Caro! Mind what you're saying."

Recovering, Sophia said, "Hush, Edwina. I'd like to hear what Caroline has to say."

Caroline swallowed hard. Obviously she was beginning to regret her outburst. After a moment, however, she took a deep breath, saying, "We—Edwina and I—are very grateful to you for the care you've given us since Papa died. Without you, we'd have had no prospects. We might even have gone to the workhouse! We know that your plans for our welfare are always in our best interests. But we also resent the fact that those plans are your plans only, that you never ask us what we want, that you simply assume you always know best, because you're older and richer and more experienced. Sometimes it seems to us that you manage your family the same way you manage your mill!"

Sophia turned to the younger twin. "Caroline says 'we,' Edwina. Is she really speaking for you?"

In obvious discomfort, Edwina stared down at the floor.

"Well?" Sophia demanded.

Finally, Edwina muttered, "Sometimes I wish you'd listen to me a bit more, Sophy."

Sophia sat silent for a moment, surprised and stricken to learn that her sisters considered her a domestic tyrant. She'd been her siblings' caretaker for five years now and she believed she'd carried out her duties with love and responsibility, in the best way she knew how. And it was true that she was older and more experienced than the twins or Tristan, and she hoped, wiser. They had all been so young when their parents died. They were still so young. They needed someone to guide them.

Baffled, trying to stifle her aggrieved feelings, she said, "I'm sorry you believe I've been overbearing or dictatorial. I certainly didn't mean to be." She managed a smile. "Do you know what I think? I think we're all a trifle overset. Shall we simply put this whole unpleasant incident behind us?" At the relieved expressions that appeared on her sisters' faces, she added, "We'll say no more about the matter, then. And tomorrow we'll go home to Lancashire where I hope we'll all be merry as a grig."

Sophia looked up from her lengthy study of the diagrams on her desk to say to the sturdy bronzed man standing before her, "Of course I'm no architect, Mr. Walcot, but these plans appear quite satisfactory. You say the builder can begin construction immediately?"

Ned Walcot, her mill manager, nodded. "Yes, ma'am. By the autumn, if the weather stays clement, ye might have yer new power loom factory in operation."

"Splendid. And none too soon, in my opinion. I'm convinced that in the next few years no one will even consider building a spinning mill without attaching to it a power loom factory. It simply makes good business sense."

"Yes, ma'am, I agree." The manager added, "May I say, Mrs. Ashley, that I'm right glad ter see ye at home again?"

"Thank you, Mr. Walcot," Sophia replied with a laugh. "I'd remind you, however, that I was only absent for three days."

"Mebbe so, but I'm always easier in mind when ye'r ter home, seeing ter things, like."

When the manager took his respectful leave a few minutes later, Sophia gazed after his departing figure with a wry smile. Ned Walcot had been hard put to contain his disapproval when she'd first taken over the direction of the spinning mill during her husband's long terminal illness. Walcot had been convinced that a mere woman was incapable of managing such a large operation. To Walcot's credit, when he realized that Bartholomew Ashley had thoroughly indoctrinated his young wife into the day by day details of running a spinning mill, he had capitulated, holding no grudge. His loyalty was now complete.

Too restless to remain at her desk, Sophia walked to the window of her office, looking down at the valley below. Since her return several days previously from Chester she had found it difficult to keep her mind on business. Memories of the rakish Lord Leyburn kept creeping into her thoughts, first of the pleasant evening they had shared over dinner at the hotel and later of his horrid advances. How had he dared? Yet how much she had enjoyed the time she had spent with him. She felt so confused when she thought about him. He had been very right to suggest she was attracted to him, this much she would not deny, at least not to herself.

Her life had been so full of taking care of responsibilities that she had never really allowed herself to think in romantical terms. But whenever she turned to her encounter with Lord Leyburn her thoughts were nothing but romantical—how handsome he was, how his eyes crinkled at the corners when he laughed, how intense his gray eyes could appear when he was expressing a strident opinion, how much the mere touch of his fingers on her wrist had set her heart to fluttering.

But then he had ruined all by proposing she become his mistress!

A terrible thought occurred to her. She began to wonder what might have happened if he'd treated her with more respect, if he hadn't assumed she was no better than a common lightskirt. Would she have then given in to him, allowed herself to be seduced by him?

Sophia squared her shoulders as the upsetting thought brought hot blood rushing to her cheeks.

No, of course she wouldn't have succumbed to his lures. She was a respectable matron. The Earl of Leyburn wasn't important. She would never see him again and she would make every effort to keep his lordship out of her thoughts.

She drew in a deep breath and turned to something far more important—Caroline's accusation that she was unjust and dictatorial. It wasn't true. It couldn't be true. She'd tried so hard, she meant so well. If only her sisters would try to understand her point of view, but they were both very young. How could she then expect them to understand her sacrifices and her hopes that each of them would one day enjoy a good life? She couldn't, only time would give them maturity and with maturity a better understanding of the ways of the world.

Shaking her head to rid herself of her unsettling memories and ruminations, she stared down at the two long, multi-storied buildings, set at right angles to each other in the middle of the valley. Beside them flowed the little river Weirton, whose rushing water-power had prompted Bartholomew Ashley to construct his first small spinning mill on the site so many years before. The same mill had grown into the impressive textile enterprise of today, and would be more impressive shortly, when the new steam-loom factory began operations.

Sophia's office was on the ground floor of Woodbridge House, the large, square gray stone house of no particular style that Bartholomew Ashley had built on the hill above his spinning mill. He'd wanted to keep a close eye on his business, and Sophia had seen no reason to remove herself or her family from the proximity of the mill.

Perhaps because she'd been away, even only for so short a time, she found herself looking at the scene below her with a slightly different perspective. In some respects, the valley in the rolling hills south of Manchester, where she'd been born and reared, looked much the same as it had in her childhood, when her father had been the vicar of the parish of Woodbridge. The village still stood near the enlarged spinning mill, but in recent years had expanded to include the numerous workers' cottages, built of solid stone, of which her husband had been so proud.

However, it was not just size that marked the difference between the Weirton Valley of her childhood and the present. Long ago, before many of his competitors had seen fit to change, Bartholomew had converted his mill from water-power to coal. The smoking stacks, combined with the effluvium from the mills in the surrounding valleys, had deposited a grimy coat on every available surface—trees and grass, ponds and streams, cottages and shops. The trout stream flowing into the Weirton no longer held any fish because of the discharge from the dye vats, and in Sophia's well-managed household the chambermaids battled several times a day to remove the gray dust that settled on the floors and furniture. The change in the landscape had been so gradual that Sophia perceived it today almost with the eye of a stranger.

"Ho, Sophy, can I come in?"

Startled, Sophia turned away from the window to face her brother Tristan. "Of course you can come in, you goose."

Tristan Dalton was fifteen, large for his age, and giving promise of a tall rangy figure when he outgrew his present awkward coltishness. He had Edwina's red-gold hair and green eyes, with a sprinkling of freckles, and he shared her lively, outgoing disposition.

Glancing around her cluttered office, he said with an ingratiating smile, "I say, Sophy, it's very nice to have you back where you belong. I've missed you."

"Never mind that flummery," Sophia said tartly, but with a smile. "You want something, that's obvious. And what are you doing away from your studies at this hour of the day?"

Tristan grinned at the young man who had entered the room behind him. "Well, Mr. Ingram says I've been working so hard lately that I deserve a little holiday. With your permission, we're off to visit the new power-loom factory in Warrenton. I'd like to see how it operates, since we're about to install our own factory."

Sophia considered the request. "Oh, I daresay it's no great matter if you skip one day in the classroom. Go along with you. Be sure to tell me all about your visit when you get back! Oh, Mr. Ingram, could you stay behind for a moment?"

After Tristan had scampered off, Sophia smiled at the tutor, saying, "It just struck me that it's been some time since I talked to you about Tristan's progress. I trust he's continued to do well?"

"Very well, indeed, ma'am. He's a very bright lad, as you well know."

Mark Ingram was tall and well-built and brown-haired. He had intelligent brown eyes set in a plain though pleasant face. He was the son of a clergyman in modest circumstances, and had been Tristan's tutor since Sophia's marriage to Bartholomew Ashley had enabled her to remove her brother from the local school.

Sophia said, "Some time ago, Mr. Ingram, you spoke of the possibility that Tristan could enter Oxford early, perhaps when he's sixteen. Is that still your opinion?"

To her surprise, the tutor hesitated. "Well, I suppose I should tell you—though I'd intended to wait. That is, given a bit more time and thinking that Tristan might change his mind, I thought—"

Sophia cut through his floundering remarks. "I don't understand you, Mr. Ingram. What is it?"

"Oh, the devil—I beg your pardon, Mrs. Ashley—the fact is, Tristan has decided not to attend Oxford."

"Not attend Oxford? He'd rather study at Cambridge?"

"No. He doesn't wish to attend any university. He wants to go into the mill, become a sort of apprentice, if you will, to Mr. Walcot, your manager. Tristan hopes that eventually you'll allow him to join with you in running the business. Therefore, he would like to begin his training as soon as possible."

Shaken, Sophia said sharply, "I have no intention of allowing my brother to become just another cotton mill operator, as you should know quite well, Mr. Ingram. I've confided in you my hopes for Tristan. I plan soon to buy a suitable estate, so that when Tristan leaves university, he can take his place among the gentlemen in the county, and eventually, sit in Parliament."

The tutor gave her a sympathetic look. "I think Tristan could do anything he put his mind to. As I've said, he's very bright. He is not, however, a scholar. He much prefers mathematics and science to Greek and Latin, as you must have noticed."

Sophia squared her shoulders. "Regardless of his preferences, Mr. Ingram, I depend on you to discourage Tristan from these foolish notions. He's much too young to decide what he wants to do with the rest of his life."

"Yes, ma'am," Mark responded quietly but with a frown between his brows. "I will certainly do my best."

After the tutor left, Sophia brooded about her brother's feckless designs for his future. Fond as she had been of her husband, and grateful as she had been to him, she couldn't allow Tristan to become simply another mill operator like her late husband.

It was unfortunate that Tristan had attended the village school for a number of years. There he'd become friends with the children of the mill workers, and she knew that he still often slipped away from the big house to associate with these boys, most of whom were already mill workers themselves. Probably it had been inevitable that Tristan should develop such an interest in the spinning business. And now that she thought about it, she realized that Tristan had been spending entirely too much time at the spinning mill in the indulgent company of the mill manager, Ned Walcot.

"Could I see you for a moment, Sophy?"

Sophia smiled at Caroline who stood framed in the doorway. "Yes, of course. Come in."

As Caroline sat down next to her desk, Sophia reflected gratefully that the little spate of ill feeling between her and her sisters had seemed to evaporate during the journey from Chester.

Presently, however, Caroline appeared somewhat nervous. Her eyes cast down, she sat pleating the fabric of her skirt between restless fingers. Finally, looking up, she said, "Did you enjoy the assembly ball last night in Evanston?"

Sophia recognized a red herring when she heard one. "Yes, it was a pleasant affair," she responded.

"Edwina was very popular."

"Perhaps a little too popular. I noticed that she danced at least three dances with that young man Gates—Hugo Gates, I think his name was. His father is the manager of the Evanston spinning mill."

"Oh, yes," Caroline chuckled. "Mr. Gates seemed quite smitten with Edwina. He asked permission to call on her."

Sophia frowned. "Certainly not. Such an acquaintance won't do."

"Why not?"

"Because, although you and Edwina have just turned seventeen, it won't be long before suitors begin swarming around you, unless I miss my guess. And, if I allow Mr. Gates to call, he will naturally conclude that I consider him an eligible suitor. Which he isn't."

"Why isn't he? He seemed very presentable to me."

"Oh, for heaven's sake, Caroline, don't be obtuse. You know why not. He's a mill manager's son, far below Edwina in station."

Caroline burst out, "And what, pray, is Edwina's station? Or mine? Our sister owns a spinning mill. Our father was the village clergyman. Why is our station any higher than that of Mr. Gates, other than the fact that our older sister has pots of money? Your fortune, Sophy, doesn't make Edwina and me members of the gentry!"

Sophia stared indignantly at her sister. "You're forgetting that Papa's father—

"Grandfather Dalton was a clergyman, too, the younger son

of an obscure baronet. Mama's uncle was a baron, also very obscure and very poor. Hardly a distinguished ancestry!"

Sophia swallowed her angry resentment. She would not enter into a shouting match with Caroline about matters in which her younger sister, for whatever incomprehensible reason, was clearly so biased. Doubtless later Caroline would apologize for her disrespect. Sophia said coldly, "You wanted to see me about something in particular?"

"Oh." Caroline took a deep breath. "Yes. I came to ask you for permission to enroll in another academy. I understand the Tunbridge Wells Female Academy is excellent. You see, I want to become a schoolmistress and I need more education for that." Responding to Sophia's quick frown, she added, "Don't tell me you think the profession is beneath me. You were a schoolmistress once, if you remember."

"I was, yes, but only because Mama had died and Papa was in such dire financial straits, and I wanted to help the family. Caroline, there's no necessity for you to take a paying position. I'm positive that one day you'll make a very good marriage—"

Jumping up from her chair, Caroline exclaimed heatedly, "I might have known I couldn't speak rationally with you. I want to be a schoolmistress. I have no intention of getting married, not ever!"

Sophia stared at Caroline's back as her sister flounced out of the room. An idea that she realized had been lurking in a corner of her brain for several days, since her return from Chester, now surfaced. Unless she was prepared to let her family sink into the bourgeois confines of her South Lancashire village—unless she was prepared to sanction Edwina's eventual marriage to a social nobody, to allow Caroline to become a nonentity of a schoolmistress, and to see Tristan spending the rest of his life in a spinning mill, she must remove them, one and all, at least temporarily, from Woodbridge.

She walked to the window, gazing with disfavor at the billowing smoke stacks of the mill below. Nothing would do but to take her sisters and her brother to London. There she would launch Edwina and Caroline on the Marriage Mart, where, with their good looks and handsome portions, they would be certain to attract suitable *partis*. She would also make sure that Mark Ingram introduced Tristan into a more stimulating intellectual atmosphere, which would hopefully encourage him to enroll at Oxford.

An anticipatory smile curved Sophia's lips. Tristan Dalton, Member of Parliament. Or, better yet, Sir Tristan Dalton. It sounded so well.

Three

Sophia stood in the drawing room of her rented house in Brook Street, near its junction with Grosvenor Square, waiting for her sisters to join her for their daily carriage ride in Hyde Park.

It was a handsome room, she reflected, perhaps a little old-fashioned. Certainly there were no pieces of furniture in the Chinese or Egyptian mode, which she understood to be the *dernier cri*. But it was indeed a handsome room, just as the entire commodious house was both elegant and fashionable. Its owner, an elderly widow, had died recently, and her heirs had been happy to rent the house to Sophia for the Season for a substantial sum.

The household staff, too, had been willing to stay on, including an efficient and rather formidable butler named Osborne. Sophia quailed slightly at the thought of Osborne. His dignified mien and air of authority rather intimidated her. In Woodbridge her domestic help had consisted of a housekeeper and maids and men from the vicinity, all of whom, though properly respectful, had tended to treat Sophia and her family with cheerful familiarity.

Tristan appeared in the doorway. "Osborne said you wanted to see me when I returned to the house, Sophy."

"Yes, come, Tristan. How was your excursion to the Royal Institution?"

Tristan's green eyes ignited. "Oh, I'm so glad Mr. Ingram took me there!" he exclaimed. "We heard the most interesting lecture by a man named Small, who spoke about the use of gas to illuminate houses and streets. He told us that a company called—let me think—Gas-light and Coke has already been formed and he intends to petition the City of London for the right to light the streets of Westminster. Sophy, wouldn't that be wonderful to be able to read at night by bright light?"

Laughing, Sophia said, "Indeed it would. Did Caroline enjoy the lecture, too?"

"Oh, yes, she thought it was very interesting. She's gone up to her bedchamber to change her clothes for your drive in the park." He cocked his head at his sister. "I say, did you really mean it? You'll allow me to accompany you to Vauxhall Gardens tonight?"

Sophia laughed again. "Certainly I meant it. Your sisters and I require a male escort when we go out in the evening. Mr. Ingram has been most obliging, but I see no reason why we shouldn't have two escorts—even if one of them is very young—when there is an opportunity to see a gala display of fireworks!"

Grinning, Tristan said, "You're a great gun, Sophy, even if you are a female."

Sophia waved him off. "Go along with you. I know flummery when I hear it."

After her brother had scampered off, Sophia mused that the move to London had been beneficial to Tristan, at least. During the past two weeks Mark Ingram had taken him to the British Museum, the Tower, and the Royal Observatory, and to public lectures at such institutions as the Royal Society. Tristan had absorbed all the new facts and experiences like a sponge. Sophia well remembered how excited he had been after hearing the great Humphrey Davy speak about his early experiments with nitrous oxide. Round-eyed, Tristan had told her, "Sophy, a person could have his tooth drawn without pain if his dentist had allowed him to inhale some of this oxide."

Although Tristan was enjoying hugely his London stay, Sophia was growing dubious about the benefits to the rest of her family. After two weeks in Brook Street at the height of the Season, they had not made a single acquaintance, nor had any eligible suitors offered for either Edwina or Caroline.

Sophia now realized that she should never have come to London without knowing someone who could advance her social ambitions. Unfortunately, she had been relying on her godmother to introduce her to society. Her godmother was the Honorable Amelia Stafford, her mother's cousin and the daughter of a viscount, with whom Sophia had maintained an irregular correspondence since her childhood, though the two had seldom met.

Sophia well remembered the initial shock she had received, when, immediately after her arrival in London, she had gone to visit her godmother. Amelia, a vague-mannered, dowdily dressed, middle-aged lady, was living in a tiny house in an unfashionable corner of Knightsbridge.

"My dear Sophia, I am, of course, very happy to see you after all this time," Amelia had declared. "However, you really mustn't expect any help from me in launching your dear sisters into society. Heaven knows I am not acquainted with anyone in the ton. I've been living quietly retired here in Knightsbridge for many years. The vicar and several very old friends comprise my entire circle. What you require is an acquaintance with someone like Lady Jersey or another of the patronesses at Almack's, or a letter of introduction to one of them."

Well, thought Sophia resentfully as she waited for her sisters to join her for their drive, she didn't know the famous Lady Jersey, or the other patronesses at Almack's, and she had no hope of knowing them. Lacking such contacts, she had done the best she could to launch her sisters into society.

She had rented an expensive house in Mayfair, she had paid
for a box at the Italian Opera—better than two thousand pounds
for the Season, she recalled ruefully—she had taken Edwina
and Caroline to Covent Garden to see the great Kemble in *Co-
riolanus* and to Somerset House to view the latest paintings,
and she had faithfully driven every day with her sisters in the
five o'clock parade of the fashionable in Hyde Park. Nothing
had been of the slightest use. She and her family might have
been invisible as far as the ton was concerned.

She looked up as Edwina and Caroline entered the drawing
room.

"I'm sorry to keep you waiting, Sophy," Caroline said breath-
lessly. "Mark—Mr. Ingram—and I and Tristan were a little late
returning from the Royal Institution."

In one corner of her mind Sophia noticed Caroline's use of
Mr. Ingram's Christian name, and indulgently overlooked the
little slip. The tutor had been a member of the household for
so many years, and was so well-liked, that he was now almost
a member of the family.

Glancing at the watch pinned to her pelisse, Sophia said,
"We're in good time, Caroline. It's only half past the hour." She
noted with approval that both sisters looked very pretty, Edwina
in a green pelisse and a dashing Gypsy bonnet trimmed with
green feathers, Caroline in a blue pelisse and a bonnet wreathed
in white roses.

Osborne, with his usual formidable dignity, stood at the door
as Sophia and her sisters left the house for their afternoon drive.
Sophia felt a familiar sense of satisfaction at the sight of the
elegant landau drawn up in front of the house. She was glad
that the steep rental fee for the property had included the use
of the late owner's horses, carriages and stable hands. Alert to
Sophia's arrival, a groom in a smart dark blue livery jumped
down from his seat beside the coachman on the box to open
the door of the carriage for his passengers.

A few minutes later, as the landau rolled along Park Lane,

Sophia observed, "Tristan tells me that you enjoyed the lecture at the Royal Institution today, Caroline."

"I did, yes. Very much."

"I had no idea you were so interested in the properties of gas." There was a faintly questioning note in her voice.

Caroline shot Sophia a challenging look. "I thought the subject might have an educational value. In view of any future plans I might have, you know. Actually, I've asked M—Mr. Ingram to include me in any future such lectures."

Sophia stifled the objection that sprang to her lips. What was the harm if Caroline attended lectures with her brother and Mark Ingram? Sophia understood that a number of more serious-minded respectable females were interested in such matters. But she was disappointed. Caroline had been so calm, so reasonable these past weeks, so helpful in preparing for their stay in London, that Sophia had believed her sister had given up her ambition to become a schoolmistress. Now it seemed possible that Caroline might only have been biding her time.

It was a lovely bright day, ideal for driving. Hyde Park was crowded with elegant carriages occupied by fashionably dressed women and with superb horses ridden by equally fashionably dressed men. Many of the people appeared to know each other. The ladies smiled and waved at the occupants of the other carriages and sometimes halted their vehicles to allow a gentleman rider to greet them. But no one smiled, waved or bowed at the occupants of the landau from Brook Street.

Caroline murmured, "You know, Sophy, these drives are very pleasant, but sometimes I feel as though we're invisible!"

Edwina, sitting in the backward-facing seat, suddenly tittered. "There he is again."

Sophia glanced up at the rider who had slowed his horse to a walk as he approached their carriage from behind. He was a slender young man with attractive, slightly irregular features and dancing blue eyes. He handled the reins of his horse with a superb assurance, despite the fact that his left arm was confined in a sling. As he passed by the carriage he gave Edwina a long admiring look, a smile curving his lips, and almost imperceptibly, inclined his head.

"Edwina!" hissed Sophia. "Don't you dare bow to that man!"

Edwina lowered her shoulders with a resigned sigh as the young man rode past. "He seems so nice, Sophy. What would be the harm if he stopped to chat with us? We've seen him so often in the Park that I almost feel we know him. With any encouragement at all I think he might be our—our friend."

"Encouragement, indeed!" Sophia snorted. "How often must I tell you, Edwina, that you may not endanger your reputation by becoming friendly with a gentleman to whom you haven't been properly introduced?"

"Well, but Sophy, since we arrived in London we haven't been properly introduced to any gentlemen," Edwina protested. "And, correct me if I'm wrong, I thought we came here so that Caroline and I could meet some eligible suitors."

"Pray don't be indelicate," snapped Sophia, flustered and embarrassed that Edwina had voiced the unspoken reason for their trip to London. "We came here so that we could—er—extend our social circle beyond what was possible in a small Lancashire village."

"But—" Edwina lapsed into silence at Sophia's forbidding expression.

"Look at that lady in the pink hat with the peacock feathers," said Caroline suddenly. "Have you ever seen anything so droll?"

Sophia looked gratefully at Caroline for her diplomatic intervention. "Yes, it's hardly a hat that you would describe as prime and bang up to the mark, is it?"

As she was speaking a rider came alongside the landau. He slowed, removing his hat. "Sophia," he said in a pleased tone. "I had no idea you were in London."

Sophia looked up at the man on horseback and blinked several times. She was looking at a handsome, familiar face and her heart simply turned over in her breast. For a long moment she felt as though she was drowning in the ambiance of his amused, compelling gray gaze.

Lord Leyburn!

During the next fleeting moment, she recalled in quick succession her entire acquaintance with him—the snowy carriage ride to Chester, the warm, comfortable dinner, the sensation of his hand on her wrist just before he had made his horrid proposal and worse, how often he had been on her mind since she brought her sisters home from Chester.

Part of her wanted to acknowledge him, even to smile. But the sensible part of her which remembered that his opinion of her was wretchedly low, caused her to purse her lips tightly together, to avert her eyes, and to keep them fixed resolutely straight ahead.

"Still miffed, Sophia?" Laughter bubbled beneath the polite voice. "Well, that's your prerogative, certainly. Goodbye, then. Perhaps I'll find you in a more agreeable mood another time."

After a long, breathless moment as the hoofbeats of his horse faded away, Caroline said coolly, "He's gone, Sophy. You can look around."

Sophia turned her head to see the earl cantering slowly ahead of them. He didn't look back.

Giggling, Edwina exclaimed, "Who was he, Sophy? Such a handsome man. Someone of the first style of elegance, unless I'm sadly off the mark. I thought you didn't know anyone of consequence in London."

Sophia gave Edwina a stony look. "I certainly don't know that creature! He was an impertinent stranger. Let this be a lesson to you, girls, to avoid men who try to force their acquaintance on unwilling, respectable females."

After a surprised pause, Edwina blurted, "But Sophy, he couldn't have been a stranger. He knew your name."

"Pure guesswork," Sophia snapped. "Edwina, I don't wish to talk about him any further."

Edwina subsided, looking puzzled. Out of the corner of her eye, Sophia caught Caroline's mildly satiric look.

Ignoring her sister, Sophia maintained a dignified silence for the remainder of the drive, although her mind was seething. What infernal bad luck to encounter the Earl of Leyburn in Hyde Park, she fumed. She caught herself up. Was it really simply bad luck? Lord Leyburn was a prominent member of London society. He had told her so himself. She should have anticipated the possibility of encountering him at some fashionable place or other during the Season. Sophia mentally tossed her head. So be it. If the Earl of Leyburn accosted her again with his unwanted attentions she would again put him firmly in his place by refusing to acknowledge him. There was really no problem. She could manage Lord Leyburn and his insulting conduct toward her.

For all her confidence, she still felt ruffled and unsettled. She was drawn in a most disturbing way to the physical male beauty of his classically planed face and lean-limbed graceful body. Neither of which should matter a whit to a respectable matron with no taste for dalliance or romantic sensations! She was after all, a responsible widow, in charge of her brother and sisters. Thoughts of love were as superfluous as they were unhelpful and she would not give herself over to even the smallest daydream!

By the time she arrived in Brook Street she'd managed, with some difficulty to relegate the troublesome earl to the back of her mind, leaving her free to concentrate on the planned evening visit to Vauxhall Gardens.

She was pleased to observe that everyone in the household seemed to be looking forward to the excursion with pleasure. Caroline, in a gown of her favorite blue, had an anticipatory air about her, as did Mark Ingram, though he did his best to preserve his usual grave demeanor. Edwina—naturally, thought an amused Sophia—displayed the most excitement. Determined to appear at her best, she changed her gown three times, in the end choosing a dress of pink-orange crape embroidered in seed pearls, which should have clashed with her red-gold hair but did not. She looked entrancingly pretty.

For the sake of the promised fireworks display, Tristan had overcome his boyish aversion to fancy clothes and had consented to wear an embroidered waistcoat, tight black breeches, with silk stockings and slippers with silver buckles. Sophia thought he looked years older in his festive attire, almost instantly grown up, and felt an odd pang. In the not-too-distant future, Tristan would be a man, fully grown. How was that possible when it seemed only yesterday he would come into Woodbridge House muddy to the knees from hiking about the hills with his friends? She sensed that time had slipped by her while she wasn't looking.

Before she left her bedchamber Sophia took one last rather dissatisfied glance at her mirrored image as she adjusted her shawl over her arms. The white silk cap she had pinned across her smoothly arranged dark brown hair suddenly seemed very plain, as did her gown of rose-colored sprigged muslin, which it now occurred to her she had worn entirely too often of late. While she was buying new clothes for her sisters why hadn't she replenished her own wardrobe?

The coach was a beautiful sight with its elaborate metal work and burnished dark blue paint which matched the liveries of the two grooms on the red platform and the bewigged coachman on his hammer cloth covered box. But it was a rather tight fit for five passengers, though Tristan managed to wedge himself fairly comfortably between his two slim younger sisters on the backward facing seat.

At shortly after seven, in the clear light of a developing spring twilight, the carriage rolled smoothly over Westminster Bridge and along the Kennington Road, stopping in front of the unobtrusive little porched entrance in Kennington Lane.

The greatest days of Vauxhall may have been in the near past, but to Sophia's unjaded eyes, fresh from the northern county of Lancashire, a first view of the famous pleasure gardens was pure magic. The pavilions and shady groves lit by thousands of lamps, the elaborately decorated arcades, the walks terminating in the center of the gardens in a large Gothic orchestra surrounded by handsome dining alcoves adorned with paintings—all seemed to her like a modern version of a fairyland.

An attentive waiter showed them to a supper box facing the orchestra, where their meal included the famous thin-sliced Vauxhall ham and even a sip of Arrack punch for the younger members of the party.

"Sophy," hissed Caroline, after hastily swallowing a bite of ham. "Look across to that box opposite us."

Edwina stifled a giggle as Sophia's affronted gaze took in the occupants of the box to which Caroline had directed her. The Earl of Leyburn, in exquisitely tailored evening clothes, was entering the box in the company of a familiar figure, equally elegantly dressed, with the exception of the silken sling that confined his left arm. As Sophia watched the two men, the earl turned his head, meeting her eyes. He bowed to her, a pleased smile curling his lips. His companion, his eyes lighting up at the sight of Edwina, bowed in turn.

Sophia returned her gaze to Edwina and between clenched teeth said, "Pay those gentlemen no mind. In fact, I think we should go home now, before they actually try to speak to us."

"Sophy!" Tristan exclaimed indignantly. "I don't know why you're so angry with those men, but we can't go home now. It's not full dark. The fireworks display hasn't started."

"Oh." Sophia's brow furrowed. "Well . . . I did promise we'd watch the fireworks, didn't I?" She lifted her head as the musicians struck up in the orchestra. "The concert is just beginning, too," she added wistfully. "I was so looking forward to hearing John Braham sing."

"There you are, Sophy. You mustn't miss the concert. We can't leave yet." Tristan's eyes brightened. "Er—would you mind if Mr. Ingram and I went off to view the Cascade?"

"I'd like to see the Cascade, too," Edwina added, her green eyes alive with excitement.

Sophia laughed. "Oh, very well, be off with you. Obviously I'm the only real music lover in the family. Caroline?"

"I think I should keep you company," she replied, her glance shifting to the box opposite them, where the Earl of Leyburn and his companion were having supper.

"Oh, yes, of course," Sophia agreed hastily. The earl and his friend seemed absorbed in their own concerns at the moment, but Caroline's presence would provide a measure of safety if Leyburn attempted to further their acquaintance. "Thank you, Caroline. That was very thoughtful of you."

Sophia waved Edwina, Tristan and the tutor off as the glorious voice of the great English tenor floated out from the box, in the midsection of the orchestra, singing the familiar popular air, "Cherry Ripe." Operatic selections Braham had sung on stages all over Europe followed and soon Sophia was immersed in the flow of melody. She had a natural love of music that she had never had time to indulge. For years she'd been promising herself—when she had more leisure, when the children were grown, when the business was secure—that she would resume lessons on the pianoforte she'd begun as a child, perhaps even take voice lessons.

The music faded away and Sophia looked away from the orchestra, feeling almost dazed, as if she'd been lost in a spell. She stared rather blankly at Caroline, who smiled, saying, "I was watching you while the music played, Sophy. A part of you was here, but another part of you was somewhere else."

"I daresay I was somewhere else, in a sense," she responded dreamily. She was oddly touched by Caroline's understanding remark.

"I suspect that man isn't as appreciative of music as you are," Caroline observed.

Sophia lifted her brows. "What? Whatever do you mean?"

"That man you seem to dislike so much. You needn't worry about him any more. He and his friend left when they finished their supper."

Sophia glanced at the box opposite them. Leyburn and his companion were no longer there, to her relief. She decided to ignore the amused twinkle in Caroline's eye.

"Oh, look," said Caroline.

Sophia raised her eyes skyward as a fiery rocket exploded into the air in the middle area of the gardens behind the orchestra kiosk. "Tristan, Edwina and Mr. Ingram should be here now that the fireworks have started," she said, frowning.

Shaking her head, Caroline said, "Don't expect them back just yet. Tristan has probably persuaded Mark—that is, Mr. Ingram—to allow him to watch the workmen operating the display."

Sophia laughed. She had no doubt Caroline was right. Settling back relaxed in her chair, she sipped a glass of wine as she watched the rockets, squibs, Catherine wheels and cascades spangle the dark with glittering torrents of multi-colored fire.

Shortly after the display ended Sophia looked up with a smile to greet Tristan and his tutor. "Well, Tristan, did the fireworks live up to your expectations? Though I daresay—" She broke off. "Where is Edwina?"

The tutor looked confused. "Why, I thought she was with you. She told me she wanted to return to the box where she could sit down in comfort to watch the fireworks."

"She never came back here. Where could she be?" Panic seized her as she jumped up exclaiming, "She might have fallen, or someone might have attacked her! We must find her. We should separate so that we can make as thorough a search as possible. Mark, I think you should cover the farthest reaches of the grounds. Tristan, you and Caroline search the area around the orchestra pavilion and the arcades. I'll look in the middle section of the grounds."

"Mrs. Ashley, you shouldn't go wandering about by yourself," Ingram protested. "It's not safe. All manner of folk, many of them not very respectable, have access to the gardens. Let me come with you."

"No. I want as complete a search as possible. If someone tries to interfere with me, he'll be sorry."

Sophia hoped she sounded more confident than she actually was. When she parted from Ingram beyond the more illuminated area behind the orchestra and the attendant pavilions she had to suppress a qualm of anxiety as she watched his sturdy figure march down the path toward the far end of the gardens. She sternly resisted the impulse to call him back.

The principal walks in the gardens were adequately illuminated by a myriad of swaying lanterns hanging from the trees, but the curving shady alleys leading off the walks were in near darkness. The alleys were a haven, Sophia had heard, for courting couples and for others with less virtuous aims in mind.

Her hands clenched tightly together, her eyes shifting nervously from side to side, Sophia proceeded along a walk behind the orchestra complex, calling out Edwina's name as she went. She shrank back when an unsteady figure lurched around a corner of an intersecting walk and nearly caromed into her.

The man stopped, leering at Sophia. "Looking for someone, m'dear? Well, I'm lonely, too, so here I am, very much at your service." He was young and fashionably dressed, although his gallantry was considerably spoiled by badly slurred speech punctuated with hiccoughs. "Shall we join forces?" He put out his hand to grab her arm, drawing her to him.

Jerking her arm away, Sophia aimed a clumsy kick at a sensitive part of the stranger's anatomy. Unfortunately, her foot merely grazed his breeches. Grasping her shoulders, he growled, "No you don't, my poppet. I see I'll just have to give you a lesson—show you how to treat a gentleman properly." Wrapping sinewy arms around her, he pressed wet lips to her mouth, sickening her with the sour stench of wine on his breath.

Pushing frantically against his chest, Sophia struggled vainly to free herself. Her attacker's suffocating grip only seemed to grow stronger. Then, abruptly, he staggered back, gazing with an expression of sheer astonishment at the tall man who had forced him to break away from her. He exclaimed indignantly, "Here sir! What the devil do y'mean interfering—" An expert blow to his chin ended his protest.

"Really, Sophia," the Earl of Leyburn drawled as he surveyed the limp form sprawled in front of them. "You should avoid strolling the walks of Vauxhall without an escort. You seem to have a penchant for being attacked by predatory males and having to be rescued. Think what might have happened if I hadn't chanced to come along in time to take this fellow off your hands." He bent down to pick up Sophia's shawl, which had fallen to the ground during her struggle, and draped it over her shoulders. Then he reached out to straighten the cap on her head, which had also come askew.

Sophia gritted her teeth, torn between gratitude to the earl and a burning anger at his condescending manner. Backing away from him, she said stiffly, "I thank you, my lord, for coming to my rescue. I agree with you that it was foolhardy of me to walk alone in this part of the gardens. However, I had good reason. My younger sister is missing. I was hoping to find her."

In the swaying light of the lanterns, Sophia observed his expression change from careless amusement to concern. "I'm sorry," he said. "Will you let me help you in your search? At the very least, I could fend off any other unwelcome attentions."

Sophia hesitated. She would certainly feel safer with an escort. But wouldn't she then risk receiving unwelcome attentions from Leyburn himself? On the other hand, she knew from past experience of him that, although he undoubtedly wanted to seduce her, he was no rapist. She drew a deep breath. Edwina's welfare had to come first. "Thank you," she said. "I'd appreciate your help."

"Then let's be going." He extended his arm. Rather tentatively, she slipped her arm about his, placing her hand on his sleeve. She became acutely aware of the firm, muscled arm beneath the broadcloth fabric and the faint scent of expensive shaving soap as together they moved out of the shadows. It had been a long time, she realized, since she had walked beside a man with her arm entwined about his. Because her thoughts were full of concern for Edwina's safety, she was deeply conscious that Leyburn's presence was providing her with a warmth and comfort she had not known in many years.

"Tell me," he said, as they began walking along the path. "What makes you think your sister might be in this part of the gardens? Didn't you warn her not to go wandering off alone, away from the bright lights and the crowds?"

Swallowing her resentment at the implied rebuke, Sophia said, "I don't think she wandered off. I think someone may have made off with her. She left my brother and his tutor at the site of the fireworks display to return to our box, only a very short distance. That was the last anyone has seen of her."

"I see. Yes, I agree. If your sister has been abducted she might well be in one of these secluded areas."

Sophia began calling Edwina's name again, and the earl suddenly raised a warning hand. He lifted his head, listening intently. From a darkened patch to the right came the sound of scuffling and muted cries. Leyburn plunged down a leafy path and Sophia followed at his heels.

" 'ere, now. Wotcher fink ye're doing wi' my Rosie?" an outraged voice demanded as Leyburn erupted into a tiny ill-lit clearing and dragged a young woman from a bench she was occupying with an amorous male companion.

"Lord Leyburn!" Sophia cried, peering at the girl in consternation. "We've made a mistake! That's not Edwina."

The earl released the young woman, who, having scuttled back to the safety of her lover's arms, glared at Leyburn and Sophia accusingly.

His color heightened, Leyburn muttered, "Pray accept my apologies for disturbing you."

"Apologies, is it?" the young man repeated with a venomous scowl. "Tha' ain't enough, by George! I've a mind ter 'ave the law on ye fer assault, or some such."

Taking Sophia's hand and moving backwards with her, Leyburn said hastily, "You're quite right, my man. I owe you more than an apology. Perhaps this will help." He tossed a coin to the pair, who gleefully leaped from the bench to retrieve it when it fell to the ground, and then pulled Sophia back down the path to the lighted walk. There he turned away from her, his shoulders shaking.

"My lord, are you ill?"

He turned back to her, wiping the tears of laughter from his eyes. "Not ill, merely chagrined. I've never before been accused of tampering with *true love.*"

"Oh." Sophia lifted her chin. "You'll excuse me, I trust, if I don't find the situation amusing. My sister is still missing."

The laughter left his face. "Yes, of course. Shall we resume the search?"

More than once, during the next half hour, as Sophia and the earl roamed the walks of the pleasure gardens, continually calling Edwina's name, they disturbed another courting couple in a sequestered nook making profuse apologies to the lovers, but failing to find Edwina. Then, as they approached the farther end of the gardens, they heard a surprised voice respond to her call. "Sophy?"

Racing down a curved path, Sophia came to an abrupt halt as her affronted gaze absorbed the sight of Edwina sitting in a cozy tête-à-tête with the dashing young horseman from Hyde Park, his left arm still in a sling.

"Edwina!" she cried. "How could you? I've been frantic with worry, wondering where you were! I've been searching for you everywhere."

An expression of guilt suffusing her face, Edwina jumped to her feet. "I'm sorry. I didn't realize—"

The young man rose, seemingly unembarrassed. "There was no need for you to worry, ma'am," he told Sophia. "Miss Edwina was quite safe. I chanced to meet her near the fireworks display and suggested a leisurely stroll of the grounds—so that we might become a little better acquainted, don't you know."

Exploding in rage, Sophia exclaimed, "Yes, I do know—all too well, sir, what you had in mind! Edwina, come with me." Grabbing her sister's arm, she marched Edwina toward the exit of the secluded alcove.

The Earl of Leyburn reached out his hand to slow her progress. "Sophia, wait a moment. I think you have the wrong idea about the situation. I assure you, my friend, Captain Royce, had no intention of harming your sister. He was merely trying to be friendly—"

Sophia brushed his hand from her arm. "My idea of friendship is totally different from yours, my lord. Mine doesn't include seducing an innocent girl!"

"Seducing—" The earl raised his eyebrow. "Aren't you being a trifle melodramatic, Sophia?"

"Not at all," she retorted. "Recall, you and I have met before. I've no reason to think your friend's morals or intentions any better than your own. Good night, my lord."

Dragging Edwina with her, Sophia walked past the earl, head high.

Four

As she glanced at the clock on the mantel Sophia's lips tightened. At the breakfast table she had told Edwina to attend her at nine o'clock in the morning room, which had become Sophia's makeshift office. It was already a quarter past.

Edwina appeared in the doorway, plainly reluctant to enter.

"Come in, Edwina. Sit down."

Seated opposite Sophia at her desk, Edwina fixed an apprehensive gaze on her sister, saying, "I've been wanting to explain to you what happened at Vauxhall, Sophy, but last night and this morning at breakfast, you wouldn't allow me to speak—"

Sophia shook her head. "I was so angry last night I didn't think it was right to talk to you then. And this morning I presumed you wouldn't care to talk about your affairs in front of Caroline or Tristan not to mention Mr. Ingram, at breakfast."

Edwina blinked. "I guess not. Thank you, Sophy."

"However, now—" Sophia gave her sister a direct, serious look, "I should like to know why you risked your reputation, and for all you might have known, your life, by agreeing to an assignation with a man who was a complete stranger to you."

"My life!" Edwina gasped. "How can you talk so, Sophy? My life was never in danger. And Captain Royce wasn't really a stranger. We'd seen him so often in the Park that I almost believed I knew him. So when I met him, quite by chance, near the fireworks, I saw no harm in accepting his invitation to stroll in the gardens."

At Sophia's quick frown, Edwina hurried on. "As for you worrying that Captain Royce had become—er—familiar, he did no such thing. All we did was talk." Her eyes sparkled. "He's such an interesting person. His father is an earl! Fancy that!"

"Are you saying he's Lord Royce?" Sophia asked, raising a skeptical eyebrow. She was of the opinion that the dashing captain would say anything to impress her gullible younger sister.

Edwina missed the sarcasm. "No, he's not a lord. I asked him that. He's the younger son of the Earl of Middleton, so he's Captain the Honorable Nevil Royce. He's an officer in the Household Troops. The Coldstream Guards. They're the 2nd Foot Guards, you know. Captain Royce was wounded last spring in the Peninsula, during the French retreat from a place called— let me think—from Santarem." Edwina's brow clouded. "He says his arm is mending, but I think he's a little worried that he still needs to wear a sling, weeks after the battle."

"I sincerely hope the captain's arm does mend. However, you must accept the fact that his medical condition is no concern of yours. You've seen the last of the honorable captain."

"Sophy!" Edwina wailed. "He asked permission to call on me."

"If he does presume to call, the butler will inform him that we are not at home."

"How can you be so cruel?" Edwina glared at Sophia. "My first opportunity to meet an eligible man here in London—and such a distinguished one, the son of an earl!—and you won't allow me to make his acquaintance. Don't you want me to be happy, Sophy? Don't you want me to marry and have a family?"

Sophia breathed an exasperated sigh. "Edwina, don't talk fustian. Listen to me. Supposing this Captain Royce is indeed an officer in the Coldstream Guards, and he really is the son of an earl. You may be sure the intentions of such a man toward a girl like you can't be honorable."

"A girl like me? What do you mean? I told you, he didn't say or do anything the least improper—"

"Not yet," Sophia snapped. "Why can't you understand this one simple fact; if Captain Royce is the sprig of the aristocracy he claims to be, he'll have little reason to respect a girl, to whom he hasn't been properly introduced, who accepted his invitation to stroll unchaperoned with him in Vauxhall Gardens. No young woman in his own social circle would risk her reputation by behaving in that fashion. I'm sure the captain thinks of you as a light-minded young woman who is fair game for his advances. I don't intend to let you be his prey. I can't allow you to see him again."

Tears filled Edwina's eyes, and Sophia's expression softened. Gently, she added, "I want you to be happy more than anything else in the world. If I thought Captain Royce would make you happy, I'd withdraw my objections in a trice. However, I can't believe he has anything more in mind than an amorous interlude. I'm afraid you must accept my guidance in this matter."

Brushing the tears from her eyes Edwina said mutinously, "Do I have any choice, Sophy?"

That afternoon, as Sophia sat in the drawing room with Caroline and Edwina, the latter looking subdued to the point of sullenness, the butler, Osborne, brought in a tray containing a calling card. Not a flicker of expression crossed his austere face to indicate his opinion of this card, which represented the first person to call at the house in Brook Street since the arrival of Sophia with her family.

Sophia glanced at the card. "Tell Captain Royce we are not at home," she said calmly.

Osborne bowed. "Yes, Mrs. Ashley." He left the drawing room with his customary stately tread.

"Sophy, how could you?" choked Edwina.

"I told you I wouldn't receive him, remember?" Sophia paused, frowning. "Tell me, Edwina, while Captain Royce was being so talkative last night, did he tell you where he lived?"

"N-no. Why do you ask?"

"No matter. Well, then did he mention his club? I understand every fashionable member of the ton belongs to a club or clubs."

Sounding puzzled, Edwina said, "He mentioned meeting his friends at—let me think—a place called White's. Is that a club?"

"Oh, indeed. A very prestigious club. Captain Royce obviously moves in the very best circles."

"Sophy—what are you planning to do?"

"I'm going to nip this problem in the bud before it becomes a weed," Sophia responded grimly.

Later that same afternoon, Sophia's carriage stopped in front of a building, 37 St. James's Street. The footman who opened the door of the carriage and let down the steps looked at her with such a painfully embarrassed expression that she said, "Is something wrong, Trant?"

"No, ma'am—it's jist that Coachman—he says ter ask ye, do ye know No. 37 is a gentleman's club, ma'am?"

"Certainly. I'm well aware that this is White's Club." She extended her hand to the footman, who, with his face an impassive mask, helped her down from the carriage.

Sophia walked up the steps of the classically designed, pillared building, the famous bow window to the left of the door—the window with which even she, living in the wilds of Lancashire, was familiar—and lifted the knocker. A liveried porter answered her knock, gazing at her with eyes that bulged with astonishment.

"Yes, ma'am?"

"I wish to see a Captain Royce, if he is present in the club."

"Er—I fear that's not possible, ma'am. Ladies are not permitted in the club."

"I don't wish to visit White's," Sophia stated impatiently. "I merely wish to talk to Captain Royce." She swept past the porter and into the foyer before the man could stop her. "Pray inform the captain that I'm here."

Sorely agitated, the porter exclaimed, "Ma'am! Ma'am, I must ask you to leave. I told you, females are not permitted in the club."

"I'll leave as soon as I've talked to Captain Royce and not before. Now, my man, will you go notify the captain that I wish to see him, or must I find him myself?"

As Sophia took a step forward, the porter actually turned pale. He put his arms up in front of him in a warding-off gesture, saying, "Ma'am, please, I beg of you—"

A familiar voice intruded. "Is there a problem, Smithson?"

The porter turned in almost palpable relief to the tall figure descending the staircase. "Perhaps you could make the lady understand, my lord, that we do not welcome females at White's."

Sophia drew in a deep breath at the sight of Lord Leyburn. She had left him in less than happy circumstances on the night before, but for the barest moment all that was forgotten as she watched him move easily down the stairs. He wore day-dress, his blue coat fitted snugly to his broad shoulders, his buff pantaloons encasing muscular thighs. In the afternoon light, he was as handsome as ever and her pulse quickened at the mere sight of him. If only they had met in better circumstances and with less of a social discrepancy between them. Perhaps then, their acquaintance would not have been so rocky. As it was, his face as he caught her gaze bore a familiar arrogant expression that instantly put her on her mettle.

"That's all right, Smithson," the earl said, sauntering up to Sophia. "I'll take care of this." Bowing, he said in formal tones he would have used to address a stranger, "If you'll come with me, ma'am, perhaps I can help you."

In a small waiting room off the foyer the earl, relaxing his formality, said, "I hardly expected to see you again so soon, Sophia, and here of all places. How did you know where to find me? In any case, the porter was quite right, you know. White's does not allow females on the premises. Actually, though I'm sure you're unaware of the fact, no lady would risk her reputation by being seen in any part of St. James's Street in the afternoon."

Sophia felt her face grow hot with embarrassment. She was coming to understand this truth. The coachman had tried to warn her. Then the porter. How ironic that she had committed the very same error of which she had accused her sister only a few hours ago.

At the same time, she resented the earl's condescending tone combined with his several careless assumptions. "First of all, my lord, I did not come here in search of you," she retorted, "nor am I interested in prying into the secrets of your precious club. As I told the porter, I came here to speak to your friend, Captain Royce."

A faintly surprised expression crossed his face. "Captain Royce isn't here today, to my knowledge. May I give him a message?"

"You may. Please ask him not to call again in Brook Street. We will never receive him. Tell him, also, that my sister Edwina wishes to have nothing more to do with him."

Leyburn's eyebrows drew together in a frown. "At the risk of seeming overly inquisitive, could I ask you why you object so strongly to your sister's friendship with Captain Royce? Many people think of him as a—well, a very suitable acquaintance. After all, his father is an—"

"His father is an earl. Yes, I know that. He, too, has a title of sorts, I'm told. He's an Honorable. Give me your honest opinion, Lord Leyburn. Would you consider it likely that Captain Royce has any intention, now or in the future, of making my sister the Honorable Mrs. Royce?"

"I certainly hope not!" the earl blurted. He paused, looking slightly ruffled. Evidently the words had slipped involuntarily from beneath his mask of well-bred indifference. "I do beg your pardon," he hurriedly added.

"Enough said," she responded quietly. "Please give my message to Captain Royce."

Leyburn looked at her curiously. "Tell me, Sophia—"

"Another thing, I never gave you permission to use my Christian name," Sophia flared. "You will please address me as Mrs. Ashley if we meet again, which I trust is unlikely."

The curious look deepened. "Tell me, Mrs. Ashley, why did you come to London, with apparently, your whole family? For a sightseeing holiday? Not to live here permanently, I imagine. From what you told me at our first meeting, you seemed to be very well situated in, er, in your own social niche in Lancashire."

The unconscious arrogance of the question infuriated Sophia. She exclaimed, "I came here for the same reason your sisters, if you had had any, or the daughters of your aristocratic friends, come to London during the Season. I wish to establish my younger sisters in respectable marriages." She paused, biting her lip. She hadn't meant to reveal to the earl any part of her private affairs.

Leyburn raised an eyebrow. "A laudable ambition, certainly. I presume you have friends here, people of standing who might introduce eligible partis to your sisters?"

"I do not. Unless I count you among my acquaintances, which would surely be counter-productive. Your interest in me and my sisters is the opposite of respectable! Good-day, my lord. Please convey my message to Captain Royce." Head high, Sophia swept past the earl into the foyer and out the door of White's Club. If he seemed disconcerted and even wishful of apologizing when she brushed past him, she ignored him. They lived in two very different worlds—she was having difficulty navigating his and he seemed inescapable of respecting hers.

* * *

As they rode together in her landau in Hyde Park, on a perfect May afternoon bathed in benign sunshine, the countess of Winwood smiled affectionately at Lord Leyburn. "My dear Joel, I know very well that you'd much prefer to be astride one of your elegant bits of blood today, rather than to be riding tamely in your decrepit old aunt's carriage."

Leyburn laughed outright. "What a fraud you are, Aunt Georgina. Old and decrepit? All my eye and Betty Martin! There's not a gray hair on that handsome head of yours, and you look at least twenty years younger than any other female of your generation."

Trying not to look pleased, Lady Winwood said severely, "I see what you're about, my dear. You'll please to stop talking such fustian." Georgina Winwood was a pretty, slender woman in her sixties, with much of her nephew's incisive personality and his cool gray eyes. She was his father's only sister, and had always been like a second mother to him since the early death of his own mother.

"I'm so glad you decided to come to London for the Season, Aunt Georgina. How did you persuade Uncle Horace to come? I know he hates leaving the country."

Lady Winwood made a face. "It was touch and go. I had to bribe Horace by promising him that he needn't play host at any entertainment I planned to give." She paused to give a smile and a wave to a passing acquaintance.

"Is there anyone in London society you don't know, Aunt Georgina?"

"Probably not. After all, I've had more than forty years to become acquainted with people!" The countess glanced at the occupants of the landau that was about to pass them. "I've just proved myself wrong. I don't know those young women."

Leyburn turned his head to meet Sophia's gaze as her carriage moved past. He lifted his hat politely. She ignored the gesture, turning away from him coldly as if she had never seen him before in her life.

"Well!" Lady Winwood said. "Who was that? It's not every

day the Earl of Leyburn gets snubbed in public! Or, rather, who were they? A trio of uncommonly pretty girls. Should I know them? Or shouldn't I ask?"

"Ask away," retorted Leyburn. "I thought you knew where my interest lay."

"Indeed, I do." The countess looked meaningfully at the stolid figure of the coachman on his box. She was far too well-bred to discuss Leyburn's relationship with his actress mistress in front of her servants.

"That young woman who snubbed me—it's a habit with her!—is a Mrs. Ashley, the widow of a mill owner in Lancashire," Leyburn told his aunt.

"A mill owner's widow? How did you make her acquaintance?"

"Purely by chance, on a journey to Chester. I was able to, er, do her a slight favor."

"What sort of a favor?"

The earl grinned at his aunt. "Actually, the stage coach in which she was traveling broke down, so I drove her to her hotel in Chester. I never thought to see her again, to tell the truth, but recently I discovered she had arrived in London with the object of finding suitable husbands for her two younger sisters."

Sounding puzzled, the countess inquired, "What is the family background of this Mrs. Ashley?"

"None, that I'm aware of."

"Humph," snorted Lady Winwood. "I wish the young woman luck, then, in her husband hunting." Dismissing Sophia from her mind, she turned her attention to the many friends and acquaintances who thronged the drives of the Park. At the end of their drive, when she and Leyburn arrived back at her large, substantial house in Hanover Square, she said, "Are you in a tearing rush, Joel? Come drink a dish of tea with me."

A little later, eyeing her nephew over the rim of her cup in her richly furnished but old-fashioned drawing room, the countess said abruptly, "Out with it, my dear. I've known you since you were birthed. Perhaps you can deceive other folk, but I cut my wisdoms before you were out of short coats."

The earl flashed his aunt a crooked grin. "I've sometimes thought you were a witch. You can always read my mind." He shrugged. "The fact is, Aunt Georgina, my next lodging may very well be debtors' prison in Newgate."

"What in heaven's name does that mean?" she asked, shocked.

"It's quite simple. A few months ago I co-signed a promissory note with Jack Adkins. You remember him. Younger son of Lord Middlemarch. We were in the same form at Eton, and later we were students together at Oxford. Jack was a gambler, a very unlucky gambler. He owed thousands when he asked me to co-sign his note to the cents-per-cent. He thought his problems were only temporary. His brother George had just succeeded to the earldom, and Jack counted on George to pay his debts. George refused. Last week Jack blew out his brains. Now the moneylenders are after me for the debt Jack owed."

"And how much is that?"

"Fifty thousand pounds."

Georgina winced. "Oh, Joel. Can you—?"

"No, I can't raise a half, a quarter, of that sum. You know my situation. Greatuncle Augustus's legacy gives me a fairly comfortable income of five thousand a year. I live up to every shilling of it."

"Your father?" The countess sighed at Leyburn's quick grimace. "I know," she said. "My brother Philip has never changed his mind about anything since he was in his cradle."

"And never will. He disowned me when I left the Whigs, or abandoned them, as he put it. As far as he's concerned, I don't exist."

"And you, of course, are as stubborn as he is! You won't even ask him for the money." Lady Winwood shook her head. "He was much too old when you were born, you know. He might have been your grandfather, and you've never understood each other." She paused. "Perhaps if I went to Philip . . ."

"I'd rather you didn't."

"Oh, very well. Joel, I'd like to help. Though Horace and I don't have an extremely large sum at our disposal, we can certainly raise a few thousand."

"Thank you, Aunt Georgina. Other friends have offered, too. Perhaps I can scrape enough rhino together to keep the jackals at bay for a spell, at least."

"I'm sure you will," the countess said, unable to keep a dubious note out of her voice. "But this subject is too dispiriting. Let's talk about something else. This Lancashire widow of yours, for example. Mrs. Ashley, is that her name? She intrigues me. Tell me more about her. Is she wealthy?"

Leyburn gave his aunt a wary look. "Well-to-do at any rate it would seem if she can bring her family to London. She said her late husband owned a spinning mill in England."

"My goodness. I understand some of these new mill owners in the Midlands and the North are very prosperous." The countess cleared her throat. "Ah—is Mrs. Ashley presentable? She and her sisters are handsome girls, and they were dressed well enough, not in the first style of elegance, perhaps, but well enough."

"Yes, I'd say that Sophia is presentable. Quite charming, in fact, when she cares to be, and obviously well-educated." Leyburn stared curiously at his aunt. "Why this sudden interest in her?"

"As I said, she rather intrigues me. Well, her sisters shouldn't have any difficulty snaring husbands, then, if their portions are large enough. I presume, with Mrs. Ashley's lack of family background, that she isn't aiming too high beyond her station?"

"I have no idea. Sophia hasn't confided in me. As you probably gathered from the cut direct she gave me today, she's out of all charity with me."

"I daresay it wouldn't be seemly of me to inquire why," Lady Winwood said dryly. "Well, enough of the mill owner's widow. Will you dine with us, Joel? Horace always enjoys your company."

* * *

Sophia looked up from the letter she was writing to her mill manager as her butler appeared in the doorway of the morning room.

"Yes, Osborne?"

The butler presented her with a tray. "Are you at home, Mrs. Ashley? Her ladyship is waiting in her carriage."

Sophia took the card from the tray. "The Countess of Winwood," she murmured. "I don't believe I know . . ." She came to a sudden decision. "Show Lady Winwood into the drawing room. Tell her I'll be with her shortly."

After the butler had left Sophia remained at her desk for a moment, furrowing her brow. Who was Lady Winwood, and why had she come calling? There was little point in conjecturing. She would soon find out the identity of this woman, since she'd agreed to receive her, the first person, with the exception of the rakish Captain Royce, to call at the house in Brook Street. Before leaving the morning room Sophia paused at the small mirror over a side table to adjust her lace cap and smooth the lace inserted into the bodice of her figured muslin gown.

As she entered the drawing room her visitor rose from the settee with a smile. "Good afternoon, Mrs. Ashley. How kind of you to see me."

Lady Winwood was a slender, attractive woman, seeming neither young nor old, wearing a modish pelisse in maroon crape and a dashing straw bonnet trimmed with matching ribbons. She was not unfamiliar. She was the lady who had been driving with the Earl of Leyburn in the park yesterday.

Taking a deep breath, Sophia said, "Good afternoon, Lady Winwood. Won't you sit down?"

"Thank you." Her eyes crinkling with amusement, the countess added, "You're being very polite and patient to an old lady, my dear. You're wondering how I came to call on you, are you not?"

"Well . . ."

"Of course you are. I'm a perfect stranger to you. Let me tell you, it wasn't easy to find you. I didn't know where you lived. Fortunately, I have an old butler who can find out everything there is to know about the residents of Mayfair."

Sophia said quietly, "May I ask why you went to so much trouble, Lady Winwood? As you said, we're perfect strangers to each other."

The countess gave her a long, thoughtful, rather unnerving look, as if she was examining Sophia, not only from head to toe, but inwardly as well. At length she said, nodding her head, "My nephew was right. You're a very charming woman."

"Your nephew?"

"My nephew Joel, the Earl of Leyburn. You are acquainted with him?"

Sophia stiffened. "More so, frankly, than I care to be, with all respect to you as his aunt."

Chuckling, the countess said, "Oh, that wretched boy. How did he manage to put himself out of favor with you?"

Sophia put up her chin. "I would prefer not to discuss it, Lady Winwood."

"Certainly, my dear. I'd much rather talk about you. Tell me, are you enjoying your stay in London?"

Thrown off balance at first by this unexpected visit from Lord Leyburn's aunt, Sophia was rapidly recovering her equilibrium, even as her temper was rising. She said pointedly, "Why did you come here, Lady Winwood? Did Lord Leyburn send you? And if so, why? I thought I'd made it clear to him that I wanted nothing more to do with him."

Lady Winwood smiled. "No, Joel didn't send me. And I really don't know or care what your personal relationship might be with him. However, what Joel told me about you interested me so much that I decided I wanted to know you."

Sophia stared at the countess. "You want to know me? Why?"

"Well, I admire independence in a woman, and I see all too little of that trait in the namby-pamby young females of today.

Joel tells me that you've taken complete charge of your family, for example, that you've come to London to find husbands for your two sisters. Is that true?"

"It is. Though I fail to see why it should be of any concern to Lord Leyburn, or to you."

Lady Winwood ignored the warning note of anger in Sophia's voice. "Oh, I agree. But please bear with me. Your efforts in the Marriage Mart regarding your sisters, have they been successful?"

Too angry now to care whether she revealed the details of her personal affairs, or whether she was offending Lady Winwood, Sophia snapped, "No, my efforts have not been successful. We came here without knowing anyone, without having a patron who might have introduced us to society. As a result, my sisters and I have met no one of consequence, nor are we likely to. Frankly, I've about decided to leave London and the Marriage Mart, as you put it, and return to Lancashire."

Lady Winwood said coolly, "You misstated your position, Mrs. Ashley. You do know people of consequence. You know my nephew. You know me."

Sophia was too thunderstruck to speak.

Lady Winwood continued, "I suggest you make use of your acquaintance with me. Come dine with me and my husband tonight. We live at Number 23, Hanover Square."

Five

"Hold still, Sophy," Edwina said, as she stood behind her sister at the dressing table, arranging Sophia's thick brown hair into a smooth coil on the crown of her head. "I do wish you'd change your mind and let me curl your hair in the front. It's all the crack, you know."

"No, thank you, I like my hair the way it is."

"Well, will you at least let me wind Mama's pearls around your topknot? There, see? Admit the pearls look pretty."

Sophia gazed at her image in the mirror. The pearls did soften her severe hair style. She liked the way she looked, too, in the gown of silk crepe in a shade of deep rose, with its short Spanish shoulder sleeves and its vandyked hem. It was the only evening gown she had bought from Madame Fleurette at the time she was ordering the twins' new wardrobes. She hoped Lady Winwood would approve of her appearance.

Lady Winwood. Sophia still felt bewildered by the countess's dinner invitation. She still found it hard to believe that a prominent hostess of the ton would really want to become friendly with an unknown widow from the hinterlands. And yet it was undeniable that Lady Winwood had invited her to dinner. What's more, the lady had implied she could be of help in introducing Edwina and Caroline to eligible suitors. Wouldn't Sophia have been foolish to refuse the invitation, even though she was thoroughly puzzled by it? Even though she suspected that, for some dark and devious reason of his own, the Earl of Leyburn might have had a hand in the situation?

She roused to hear Edwina saying, "It's so exciting, Sophy, to be helping you dress for an evening at the home of a countess! How did you happen to meet this Lady Winwood?"

"Yes, that's what I would like to know," Caroline chimed in. She was sitting on the bed watching Edwina assist Sophia with her coiffure. "You've remarked often enough that we didn't know a soul of any consequence in London. Here, all of a sudden, you're hobnobbing with the swells!"

"Don't be ridiculous, Caroline! Or vulgar, either."

"No, but really, how did you meet this woman?" Caroline persisted. "It must have happened very recently, or you'd surely have called on her, or she on you, when we arrived in London."

Uncomfortably, Sophia resorted to a lie. The last thing in the world she intended to do was to reveal to her younger sisters her humiliating experiences with the rakehell Earl of Leyburn.

"Edwina, Caroline, do you remember Mama's cousin

Amelia, the baron's daughter, who I had hoped would introduce us to society? Unfortunately, I discovered that she lives retired in Knightsbridge now, and doesn't have any acquaintance in the ton. But recently she remembered that she'd known Lady Winwood many years ago, and wrote to the countess about us."

"How nice of Cousin Amelia," Edwina said, pleased, Caroline nodding as well. Apparently they had no difficulty accepting the tale. Sophia felt relieved, but guilty. She was a naturally truthful person and hated telling whiskers, even if her reasons were good.

A knock sounded, and a moment later Tristan poked his nose around the door of the bedchamber. "Are you decent, Sophy? Can I come in?" Without waiting for an answer he walked into the room. "Well, don't you look top of the trees, Sophy," he said admiringly. "What a pretty gown. I just had to see how you looked before you set out to visit a nobleman's house. I've never met a nobleman."

Sophia smiled. "Peers aren't much different from the rest of us, at least to look at. They're human, after all. So what did you and Mr. Ingram do today?"

Tristan's face lighted up with a familiar enthusiasm. "We went to the Pool of London and the West India Docks. Sophy, there must be millions of ships in the Pool of London. Well, hundreds, thousands, at least. And Mr. Ingram says that the construction of the docks has made it possible for merchantmen to unload their cargo in four days, instead of four weeks!"

"So, are you thinking about trying a sailor's life?" Sophia teased.

"Of course not," Tristan exclaimed indignantly. "I'm a Lancashire man, born and bred. Why would I want to go to sea?"

Sophia laughed. "Why, indeed? Lancashire is such a superior place."

"Will you be very late tonight, Sophy?" Caroline asked.

"I'm not sure. Why?"

"Oh, you know, if you don't return too late, and you're not too tired, we'd like to hear everything that happened at your dinner party. What kind of food was served, what the ladies wore, whether any duchesses were present, that sort of thing."

"I promise," Sophia said, amused at the excited, curious expressions on her sisters' faces. "If it isn't too late when I come back, I'll tell you all about my evening."

She was still feeling amused at her family's reaction to her unexpected invitation when she stepped into the town carriage for the ride to Winwood House. Minutes into the journey, however, her amusement began to fade. By the time the carriage stopped in front of Number 23, Hanover Square, she was a mass of nerves. She swallowed the anxious lump in her throat and breathed deeply as the groom opened the door of the carriage and extended his hand to help her down the steps. A butler of imposing dignity greeted her at the door of the mansion and conducted her to the drawing room. "Mrs. Ashley, I'm so pleased you could come to us," Lady Winwood said as Sophia entered the room. "Allow me to introduce my husband."

Sophia bowed to Lord Winwood, a stout, balding, elderly gentleman with a kindly smile.

"I believe you already know my nephew," Lady Winwood continued.

With a sinking feeling, Sophia turned her head to greet the Earl of Leyburn, who had risen from his chair to stand beside his aunt. He bowed. "Mrs. Ashley. A pleasure to see you again."

He spoke politely, almost indifferently, but beneath the formal mask of his face Sophia thought she could detect the faintest shade of surprise. She suspected that, more likely than not, Lady Winwood had neglected to inform her nephew who one of his fellow guests would be just as she had neglected to inform Sophia.

"What a pretty gown, my dear," Lady Winwood observed. "That rosy color suits you. Don't you agree, Horace, Joel?"

"What? Oh, indeed," replied her husband, who seemed to be a pleasantly well-meaning if rather vague old gentleman.

"Mrs. Ashley always looks charming," the earl said. "No matter what the occasion."

The remark was quite unexceptional, but as Leyburn looked directly into her eyes, an uncomfortable warmth rose to Sophia's cheeks. She sensed he was remembering their cozy supper at the hotel in Chester and that he wished her to recall the evening to mind as well. She lifted her chin ever so slightly and turned her gaze away from his.

The countess commented on the weather and the latest doings of the Prince Regent, the minutes passed and just as Sophia was beginning to wonder where the other guests were, dinner was announced. Stunned, she realized that the occasion was dinner for four. There would be no other guests. Her perplexity grew. Why had the countess invited her to such an intimate evening? Surely she had not done so to forward her nephew's lascivious designs. Surely not. Lady Winwood did not strike her as such an immoral person. But why, then?

At the dinner table she suppressed her doubts, trying for an outward poise that would give the impression that dining with members of the peerage was an everyday occurrence in her life. Because of her training, the magnificent silver and china and the elaborate meal, failed to overawe her. Her mother, and later Miss Beaton at the academy in Chester, had drilled her and her sisters for hours on end in the proper deportment of young ladies so that each might be equal to even the most elegantly appointed situations.

"Georgina tells me you operate a cotton spinning mill, Mrs. Ashley," Lord Winwood said, gazing at Sophia over the rim of his wine glass. "A rather unusual occupation for a female, what?"

"I suppose it is," Sophia said composedly. "My late husband had no male heirs, so he decided that I should learn how to run his business."

"Good for you, my dear. The cotton business is prosperous, I take it?"

"Well . . ."

Leyburn looked up from his venison. "I presume by your hesitation that you're having difficulties, Mrs. Ashley, similar to so many in the textile trades in the Midlands and in the north? For the past year or so we in Parliament have been inundated by petitions for relief from the cotton districts. The Home Secretary was telling me the other day that unless matters improve soon there will be no more than half work in the cotton trade."

"I think that's an overly gloomy forecast," Sophia responded, frowning. "In my own case my sales haven't suffered too much, and I've been able to hold down unemployment among our local people. Of course," Sophia lifted her chin, "the product of my Woodbridge mill is a superior one."

Leyburn smiled faintly. "I'm sure it is, Mrs. Ashley."

"It's certainly true, however, that our foreign markets have been disrupted by the war with Napoleon, and this year we've lost our American trade because of the United States's nonintercourse acts." Sophia gave the earl a belligerent look. "Might I suggest that you and your fellow members of Parliament help the textile trade by improving relations with the United States so that Americans would buy more English cottons and woolens?"

After a startled moment, Lord Winwood chuckled, saying, "Well, Joel, there you are. Mrs. Ashley's problems are all your fault."

Leyburn raised his glass to Sophia. *"Touché,* Mrs. Ashley." His eyes narrowed. "Or should I call it *first blood?"*

Sophia kept her calm. "Surely not," she responded with a faint smile. "I wasn't aware you and I were in some kind of contest, Lord Leyburn."

"Quite right, my dear," Lady Winwood interjected. "Put Joel in his place, where he belongs. This is a dinner party, not a debate in the House of Commons! We've had enough talk about serious topics. Let's talk of something else. I hear the Regent is planning a great fete at Carlton House next month in honor of the Bourbon princes."

Leyburn laughed. "Prinny originally intended to host the fete to celebrate his ascension to the Regency, Aunt Georgina. But now His Royal Highness isn't positive he'll remain Regent for very long. The old king's health has been improving of late—he was actually seen enjoying a stroll on the terrace at Windsor the other day!—so the Regent decided he should invent another reason for his fete."

"Oh, well, I daresay I'll enjoy the fete—if I'm invited, that is!—no matter what purpose the Regent has in mind for giving it."

During the rest of the dinner Lady Winwood made sure that the conversation avoided any subject that wasn't light to the point of frothiness. After the dessert course she said to her husband, "Horace, tonight you must drink your port alone. I wish to talk to Joel and Mrs. Ashley about an important matter."

Lord Winwood looked vaguely surprised. "Very well, my dear. I'll join you later."

Wondering why Lady Winwood wanted to speak privately to her and the earl, Sophia followed her hostess into the drawing room. She suspected, from the intent look Leyburn was giving his aunt, that he was just as puzzled as she was. Lady Winwood busied herself with pouring their coffee from the tray the footman had brought in.

"Now, then," the countess began, taking a sip of her coffee and setting down her cup. "I have a proposition for both of you." She addressed her nephew. "You, Joel, have a serious problem. You owe fifty thousand pounds. If you don't pay up, you run the risk of rotting in debtors' prison."

Sophia turned to the earl and blinked rapidly. Was this true?

Leyburn's complexion became heightened. "Aunt Georgina, I see no reason to discuss my private affairs in front of a stranger.

The countess disregarded his protest. To Sophia, she said, "Mrs. Ashley, you have a problem, too. You came to London to arrange advantageous marriages for your sisters. Unfortunately you had no influential friends here who could sponsor your introduction to society. Your sisters are still without husbands. I suggest it would be to both your advantages if you were to join forces with my nephew."

Sophia frowned. "What do you mean, Lady Winwood?"

"It's quite simple. I think you two should get married. Joel has social position, but no money—which he badly needs to keep himself from moldering away in Newgate Prison. You have money—or so I presume—but no position. Could you comfortably spare fifty thousand pounds, by the way?"

"Fifty thou—" Sophia turned to stare at Leyburn. "May I ask how you've come to owe such a sum? Are you a gambler, by any chance?"

The earl scowled. "No, I am not, no more than most. I wouldn't want you, or anyone, to think I was stupid enough to squander fifty thousand pounds at the gaming tables. Beyond that, you may not ask, Mrs. Ashley. My financial situation is of no concern of yours, or of my Aunt Georgina's either. And, I might add, I have no present intention of getting married!"

"Nor have I," Sophia retorted. She turned to her hostess, her lip curling slightly. "If you invited me here solely to arrange a matrimonial alliance between your nephew and me, then I see no reason why I should stay." She rose and shook out her rose silk skirts. "Good night, Lady Winwood."

Leyburn rose in his turn. "Mrs. Ashley and I agree on that point, at least. Good night, Aunt Georgina."

Remaining in her chair, the countess snapped, "Stop behaving like children and sit down—both of you!"

Two pairs of eyes stared at her reproachfully.

"Lady Winwood!"

"Aunt Georgina!"

Looking ruffled, rather like an agitated pouter pigeon, the countess said, "I'm sorry, I should have said 'please sit down.' Pray do me the courtesy of listening to me for five minutes more, then feel free to leave."

Sophia exchanged a glance with the earl. She hesitated for a moment, as did he, then as if consenting together for the sake of propriety, they resumed their seats.

"Thank you," Lady Winwood said. "I think I should say, first, Mrs. Ashley, that Joel is in the pickle he's in out of the goodness of his heart. He foolishly co-signed a bad promissory note for a friend—a friend he trusted."

Leyburn protested. "As before, I don't think my affairs—"

Lady Winwood lifted a hand, but not unkindly. "Please let me continue." Her supplicating expression had its effect and Joel shrugged his shoulders. The countess addressed him, "You just informed us before Mrs. Ashley arrived that you had no intention of marrying. What then do you intend to do about your future?"

"Well—some day I'll be obliged to marry, naturally. There's the succession . . ."

"Precisely. Some day you'll be Marquess of Kennington, and you'll need an heir. Can I assume, however, that you have no particular candidate in mind for you future marchioness?"

"I—no. Aunt Georgina, this is ridiculous!"

Lady Winwood again lifted her hand, waving her nephew to silence. This time, she turned to address Sophia. "Mrs. Ashley, you have also said that you had no intention of marrying. So I can also assume that you have no devoted suitor waiting in the wings?"

Sophia shot the countess a repressive look. "You may. However, I fail to see the signifi—"

"Well, then," Lady Winwood interrupted triumphantly, "I fail to see why it wouldn't be a good idea for the two of you to marry. Neither of you has a heart-interest you would be obliged to give up. Both of you would achieve what you want most from life. Joel, you would be able to pay your debts and stay out of prison, free to pursue your political career. Mrs. Ashley, you would have the position you need to find suitable husbands for your sisters. I have known many marriages arranged for even less exalted reasons than these. Do think on it!"

She paused, gazing at the earl and at Sophia with the air of one who has made a suggestion with which there could be no possible disagreement.

Leyburn moved swiftly to the attack. "I know you mean well, my dear aunt, but in making this outlandish proposal you've overlooked some very important points. I think you'd be the first to agree that people in our station of life need not, and often do not, marry for romantic reason. I think you would also agree, however, that a successful marriage demands a reasonable amount of affection and respect."

"Which in our case is totally lacking," Sophia cut in. She glanced at the earl. She then addressed him, "You and I neither like nor respect each other."

Leyburn spread his hands. "You see, Aunt Georgina? I might add that the partners in a good marriage should also have a certain comparability in taste, background and—" he broke off, looking faintly embarrassed.

"Don't bother to spare my feelings, Lord Leyburn," Sophia assured him. "I know exactly what you meant to say. The word you didn't bring yourself to say was 'class.' I'm a middle-class woman engaged in trade. We met under informal circumstances and you assumed I was a person of loose morals. You don't think I'm good enough to marry into your aristocratic family. Isn't that so?"

Leyburn stared at her in silence. A muscle twitched in his cheek. After a moment, he murmured, "You have expressed the opinion more harshly than I would have."

Sophia turned to the countess. "There you have it. Lord Leyburn would rather rot in debtors' prison than marry an inferior woman. I would cheerfully accept the devil himself as my husband than marry your nephew. It would seem you failed to persuade either of us. Good night, Lady Winwood."

"You've mistaken my nephew," Lady Winwood began.

But Sophia had heard enough. Rising quickly to her feet, she bowed to the countess and left the drawing room without a glance at the Earl of Leyburn. In the hall, she instructed the butler to order her carriage.

Lady Winwood rushed into the hall. "Please don't leave, Mrs. Ashley. I'm sure you have given voice to an opinion that is more yours than Joel's. If you will only try, I'm sure you can come to an understanding with my nephew. He is not quite the monster you believe him to be."

"I fear we have differences too great to set aside lightly," Sophia returned, "even if I was of a mind to do so, which I assure you I am not. If ever I should marry again, it certainly won't be to a husband who's ashamed of me."

"I say again, you've misunderstood Joel, at least in part. He doesn't really mean—" Lady Winwood's voice faded away as Sophia lifted her brows meaningfully. After a moment, the countess shrugged. "Have it as you will, then, but I believe you are making a mistake and that neither you nor my nephew are as indifferent to each other as you pretend." With that, she retreated to the drawing room.

A few minutes later, as Sophia was about to enter her carriage, Leyburn emerged from the door of his aunt's house, calling to her. "Sophia, wait," he said, as he came up to her. "For just a moment, please. I do apologize. I was angry just now—and yes, embarrassed—when my aunt revealed the nature of my difficulties and not less so when she tried to force my hand. But what I inplied about the disparity in our circumstances was inexcusable. I like to think of myself as a gentleman but in this case my behavior has been insufferable."

"Yes, it has been and not tonight only," she said quietly. "But I'd rather not discuss it. Goodnight, Lord Leyburn." Sophia turned to enter her carriage.

"Please stay a moment," he said, sounding urgent. He caught her arm at the elbow and restrained her from climbing the steps.

She turned back to him, frowning up at him. "Yes?"

The earl's expression in the dim light of the carriage lamps was oddly ambivalent, totally lacking in his usual air of cool poise. "I've been thinking these past few minutes," he said haltingly. "My aunt didn't exaggerate my predicament. Sooner or later, unless I can produce the required amount, I will suffer the consequences we discussed. I don't relish the thought. You, I think, would rather not go back to Lancashire without establishing your sisters in good marriages, unless I much mistake the matter. Is there—is there any chance, would you say, that you and I could—*discuss* Lady Winwood's proposal?"

"I have no interest in it, my lord," Sophia responded truthfully. "And now, if you don't mind, I should like to leave." She glanced down at his hand which was still hooked about her elbow.

He released her slowly, a frown between his brows. "Good night then," he murmured. His face was impassive as he extended his hand to help her into the carriage. A hard snap of the door separated them.

As the vehicle moved off, Sophia wrapped her shawl more closely around her. She felt chilled, even though the evening was warm. Her nerves were fairly shredded. She shook her head and quick tears sprang to her eyes. From the moment she had come to understand that she had been invited to Hanover Square merely to serve as a means of extricating the earl from his financial difficulties, she had expended great energy in maintaining her composure. Lady Winwood would never know how acute her humiliation had been. She felt secure that she had succeeded in hiding her hurt and her embarrassment, which was her only consolation. Doubtless she would never see the countess or her nephew again, and good riddance.

Admitted by the indefatigable Osborne to the house in Brook Street, Sophia walked quietly up the stairs. As she passed Edwina's bedchamber, which was next to her own, she noticed a light beneath the door. So Edwina was still awake, and Sophia had promised she would tell her sisters all about Lady Winwood's dinner party when she returned tonight.

Pressing her lips tightly together, Sophia walked past her sister's room. She was in no mood to pretend that she'd taken part in a great social event. And yet . . . She slowed her steps as she approached her door. Wasn't she simply putting off an unpleasant task? Tomorrow her sisters would be just as curious. It might be better to go to Edwina and Caroline now, to explain briefly that the occasion had been a very small dinner party—no duchesses, no grand array of fashionable gowns, no exciting gossip about the ton—and then, pleading fatigue, make her escape. By the morning her sisters' interest might well have evaporated so that she would be able to avoid any penetrating questions as to the actual purpose of the dinner.

Sophia went back to Edwina's bedchamber, gave a cursory knock at the door and entered the room. Edwina wasn't there. She was probably in Caroline's bedchamber, waiting for Sophia to return. As Sophia was about to leave she observed an extravagantly large bouquet of hothouse camellias on Edwina's dressing table. Her curiosity piqued, Sophia walked over to the dressing table to look at the flowers. They were beautiful. And probably very expensive. Had the bouquet arrived that evening? Yet, if it had arrived earlier, why hadn't Edwina mentioned it? And who had sent it?

Belatedly, Sophia noticed the note lying on the dressing table. She hesitated. She had never been in the habit of prying into her younger sisters' rooms or possessions. Then, succumbing to temptation, she picked up the note.

"My beautiful Edwina, I hope these posies will remind you of me. I live in hope that the Gorgon will relent and allow me to visit you. Nevil Royce."

Dropping the note as if it were a burning coal, Sophia whirled about and left the bedchamber. She fled to her own room, shutting the door behind her. She threw herself into a chair, chaotic thoughts torturing her. She was the Gorgon who Captain Royce hoped would relent and allow him to call on Edwina. There could be no two opinions on that score. She knew her younger sister. Another bouquet, romantic note, and Edwina would soon agree to meet her eager suitor secretly. In no time at all she would be compromised.

Short of giving permission to the captain to openly pursue his campaign of seduction, Sophia thought tiredly, her only recourse was to remove her family from London. And if she did that, she would forever narrow their horizons to the confines of a tiny Lancashire village. Beyond doubt, Edwina would lose her heart to the handsome son of a neighboring mill owner. Caroline would persist in her feckless ambition to become a schoolmistress Tristan, who had blossomed in the exhilarating mental stimulus of London, would revert to his resolve not to attend Oxford in favor of training to manage the Woodbridge cotton spinning mill.

Sophia settled back in her chair, trying to sort out her thoughts. She realized she had been more influenced by her mother than her siblings had, who were so much younger. Her mother, Olivia Weare, had been the daughter of a baronet. She was also a baron's niece. Sophia surmised now, in retrospect, that Olivia had probably always nursed a grievance that she had married beneath her in accepting an obscure clergyman as her husband. Sophia remembered how often her mother had said, "You must always be polite to the people of Woodbridge, my dear, but don't ever be like them. My children must be ladies and gentlemen!"

Well, for better or worse, Olivia had influenced her eldest daughter, Sophia reflected ironically. More than anything she wanted her sisters and her brother away from the stifling atmosphere of Woodbridge. She wanted the best for them that life could offer and right now, life had presented her with an unparalleled opportunity for social advancement for them all.

Could she possibly reconsider Lady Winwood's proposition? If she married the Earl of Leyburn, Edwina and Caroline would meet suitors of the highest social standing. Tristan would be able to mingle with the kind of young men she wanted him to emulate.

As for herself, the thought of marriage to Joel Leyburn filled her suddenly with a sensation that startled her, of excitement and desire. From the first she had been attracted to him, she would not deny that much. Against her will, she imagined herself strained against his taut, hard chest, her lips bruised by his sensual, devouring mouth. To be his wife, to share his bed . . . a shiver ran down her spine.

No, she rebuked herself, bringing her senses to order. She pushed the insidiously beguiling images out of her mind. She had too much pride, too much integrity, to allow a man to make love to her who considered her beneath him in social class and in character.

Sophia drew a deep breath. Whatever her personal feelings toward Lord Leyburn, either her attraction to him or her dislike of his opinions, she had her family to consider first.

Perhaps she ought to at least speak with him again. She rose, walking to her writing desk.

"Dear Lord Leyburn . . ."

Six

"Sophy, you're not listening!"

Sophia looked up from her breakfast plate at Edwina's reproachful remark. "I'm sorry. I must have been woolgathering. What did you say?"

"I said, you promised to tell us about your dinner party, and Caroline and I waited and waited for you last night, but you never came to talk to us."

Sophia tried to gather her thoughts. She glanced at her plate and realized she had consumed several pieces of bacon and a slice of toast without remembering what she'd eaten. She was finding it hard to concentrate. Her mind was entirely on the letter she'd despatched early this morning to Lord Leyburn at his aunt's house in Hanover Square. She wondered if Lady Winwood would send the letter on immediately to the earl's lodging. She wondered when—or—if she might expect a reply.

She wondered . . .

"Sophy!" Edwina called to her again.

Sophia blinked several times then sighed. "You must take me for a perfect ninnyhammer," she apologized. "I can't seem to think straight this morning. Perhaps I didn't get enough sleep last night. I returned home very late. That's why I didn't come to chat with you and Caroline as I promised. I was too tired."

"You're forgiven," Caroline said, smiling. "Tell us about your evening now."

"There's nothing much to tell. It was a very small dinner party. I was one of only two guests."

"Oh," Edwina said, obviously disappointed. "Well, who was the other guest?"

"Lord Leyburn. The Earl of Leyburn. He's Lady Winwood's nephew."

"An earl!" Edwina sounded impressed. "What was he like? Old? Young? Handsome?" Her eyes twinkled. "Wealthy?"

"He was . . ." Sophia paused. She had to be careful. She couldn't very well describe Leyburn as a stranger. If she later had occasion to introduce him to her family—which was by no means certain—Edwina would certainly wonder why Sophia hadn't identified her fellow dinner guest as the flirtatious rider in the Park and as the gentleman who had helped her search for Edwina in Vauxhall Gardens.

Clearing her throat, Sophia said, "Actually, you already know Lord Leyburn, in a sense. You've seen him several times. In the Park and with Captain Royce at Vauxhall Gardens."

Edwina's eyes grew round. "He's Captain Royce's friend?"

"Yes."

Edwina's eyes grew even rounder.

Looking puzzled, Caroline said, "Do you think this Lord Leyburn asked his aunt to make your acquaintance?"

"I don't know," Sophia said shortly. She rose, setting down her napkin. "Excuse me, girls. I have a great deal of work to do this morning."

In the morning room, however, she sat at her desk, pen in hand, without putting ink to paper. She was too much on edge to reply to her mill manager's letter. The minutes ticked by with a maddening slowness. It was only ten o'clock in the morning. She could hardly expect to hear from Leyburn—if she heard at all—until midafternoon.

"I beg your pardon for interrupting you, Mrs. Ashley."

Sophia turned her head to look at her butler, who came into the room with a tray containing a calling card. She glanced at the card, drew in a deep breath, then said, "Ask Lord Leyburn to wait."

A few moments later, Sophia, her heart feeling as if a giant fist were squeezing it, entered the drawing room on legs that felt rubbery. "Good morning, Lord Leyburn."

"Good morning." He was superbly turned out, as usual, in a perfectly fitted coat, tight pantaloons and glossily shined Hessians. He also appeared slightly less assured than usual as he said, "Aunt Georgina forwarded your letter on to me as soon as she received it. You wrote that you had changed your mind about my aunt's proposal. I take it, then, that we're to be married?"

"Provided we come to an agreement, yes. Please sit down, won't you?"

"An agreement?" he questioned, as he took a chair opposite her. "I assumed that the lawyers would negotiate the settlements—"

"Oh, I think we can agree on a number of points without lawyers. To begin, I'll authorize my bankers immediately to pay you fifty thousand pounds. That was the sum you needed, was it not?"

"Yes," he murmured. "Thank you." He hesitated. "It's a great deal of money. Are you sure—?"

Raising an eyebrow, Sophia replied, "Do I have that much I can spare? Yes. When he died, my late husband was reputed to be a very well-to-do man." She paused for a moment before continuing, "Next, I would prefer to live in this house after we're married. I've already paid a substantial rent for the Season and I'm comfortable with the arrangements."

Leyburn nodded. "I have no objections. I'm living in lodgings at the moment. As I think I once told you, my father and I are estranged. I can't offer you the hospitality of the family town house in Hanover Square."

"That takes care of two points, then. However, you may not be willing to accept my third point—everything I own, in real property and ready cash, is to remain in my hands, to manage as I see fit. As my husband you will have no access to my assets."

Leyburn frowned. "You badly need legal advice. I'm no lawyer, but I do know that, as regards to your property, my position as your husband is clear; as soon as we marry, everything you own belongs to me. That may seem unfair to you, but it happens to be the common law of England."

"That may be the law governing a wife's property rights in the vast majority of marriages. It doesn't need apply in our case. You may not be familiar with the principle of separate estate, that is, property settled on a wife for her separate use, independently of her husband. My late husband, Bartholomew Ashley, left me his entire fortune, which included his real estate holdings and a substantial amount of cash. In his will he stipulated that my inheritance was to go into a separate estate which, if I married again, would remain strictly my own property, untouchable by my new husband."

Leyburn gazed at her in taut silence, his lips set in a straight, uncompromising line. After a moment, he bit off each word, saying, "I can't accept such a financial arrangement."

"Oh? You don't wish to marry me unless you also control my money?"

His eyes blazing with fury, Leyburn exploded. "I don't care a damn about your money, other than the sum you agreed to give me to keep me out of debtors' prison. I have a perfectly adequate income, and at some time in the future, when I succeed my father, I'll be a wealthy man, because the bulk of the family estate is entailed. I had no intention of taking over your fortune, on our marriage, or of making you merely my chattel, which I believe most English husbands have a legal right to do. What I do care about is the prospect of being the laughingstock of London when my friends and acquaintances learn that I'm about to become my wife's pensioner!"

"So it's a matter of your pride?"

The earl gritted his teeth. "I—yes. Call it that if you like."

"I understand your feelings."

He cast her a look of surprise.

"You see," she went on, "I have some pride myself. I don't relish being known as a woman whose husband married her solely for her money. Supposing, if we decide to marry, we make a covenant that we keep our personal affairs private? For instance, I could engage not to reveal to anyone that my property is held in separate estate. Your friends could assume that you married an heiress whose fortune is entirely at your disposal. You, on the other hand . . ."

Leyburn visibly relaxed. "I, on the other hand," he continued for her, "could let it be known, very tactfully, that I was pleased to discover, though I played no part at all in my courtship, that the charming and beautiful lady to whom I had become affianced was also a very wealthy woman."

Sophia said coolly, "Exactly. Providing we're both properly reticent, the public will think what we want them to think. There's no reason for anyone to know that our marriage will be purely a business arrangement, or perhaps less crudely, a marriage of convenience."

She thought the earl looked slightly taken aback at her directness. However, he said merely, "I agree. Is there anything else to be settled? Then may I send a notice of our engagement to the newspapers?"

"Wait until tomorrow, please. Will you come for dinner tonight? I want to introduce you to my sisters and my brother. They should know about our betrothal before the public does."

"Of course. What time?"

"Come at six."

He bowed. "Until this evening, Sophia." And almost as an afterthought, he reached down and took her hand ever so gently in his and placed a kiss on her wrist. The gesture, so thoughtful, stunned her. He smiled faintly, then turned on his heel. She watched him leave and wondered suddenly what marriage to such a man would be like. He carried himself with supreme confidence as though he owned the world. He was handsome and in every way exactly the kind of man a young girl dreamed of marrying.

Only she wasn't a young girl, but a widow with many responsibilities.

When his footsteps faded away, Sophia felt the tension drain out of her. She believed she had accomplished what she'd started out to do in this interview that she had been anticipating with such dread. She had wanted to make it clear to the earl that, no matter what his opinion of her social status and character might be, she thought reasonably well of herself and didn't feel inferior in her social standing or embarrassed to be known as a cotton mill operator. Thus, she had no need to be grateful to him for marrying her, nor need she be a meek, subservient wife. Her separate estate, which had come as such a shock to him, would preserve her independence. She'd also made it clear, she hoped, by her reference to their marriage as "purely a business arrangement," that she didn't expect him to play the romantic lover.

Then he had kissed her wrist, dutifully perhaps, but the attention was not lost on her. That her heart still seemed a little unsteady because of the unexpected salute, was something of a mystery.

"Tell me about the balloon ascent, Tristan."

Sophia's brother stared at her. "I've already told you about the balloon ascent, Sophy, don't you remember?"

"Oh, yes." Sophia felt her face redden with chagrin. She had been speaking aimlessly, trying to fill the void of silence in the drawing room, where five pairs of eyes, including her own, had been fixed expectantly on the door for a sight of the invited guest.

She was nervous, she admitted it. She didn't know how Leyburn would react to her siblings, or they to him.

Earlier in the day, when she'd announced that the earl was coming to dinner, her family's reactions had varied. Edwina had blurted, "Does this mean that Lord Leyburn is courting you, Sophy?"

"Edwina, you goose, what a silly question," Caroline had retorted. "Recall, Sophy has just met the man."

Tristan had remarked with interest, "I'd like to meet an earl."

As Sophia waited for Leyburn to arrive she hoped she hadn't committed a grave *faux pas* in inviting Mark Ingram to be a member of the party. What would the earl think when he discovered that he was expected to dine with Tristan's tutor? But she'd wanted Tristan to meet Leyburn, even though her brother was too young to mingle in society, and she'd refused to injure the tutor's feelings by banishing him to a solitary supper. Mark, though he was technically a hired employee, was almost a member of the family.

Fortunately for her frayed nerves, the butler soon appeared in the doorway to announce, "Lord Leyburn."

He entered the room, smiling, self-possessed, elegant in his superbly tailored evening clothes. Sophia rose to greet him. "Good evening, Lord Leyburn."

"Mrs. Ashley," he bowed. "A pleasure." He glanced inquiringly at the other occupants of the room, blandly pretending that they were all perfect strangers to each other.

Sophia made the introductions. "My sisters, Caroline Dalton and Edwina Dalton. My brother, Tristan. Mr. Ingram."

Leyburn bowed again. To the girls he said with a teasing smile, "I presume I should call the elder of you Miss Dalton, and the younger, Miss Edwina or Miss Caroline, as the case may be. However, I'm dashed if I can tell which of you is the elder!"

Always literal-minded, Caroline replied seriously, "Unless you have the ability to read minds, you really couldn't be expected to tell which of us is the elder. We're twins, even though we don't look alike. Actually, I'm older than Edwina by five minutes."

Leyburn laughed. "Thank you for clearing up my uncertainty, Miss Dalton. I always like to observe the convenances."

As he sat with the family in the drawing room before dinner was announced, Leyburn appeared perfectly at ease, speaking to everyone in turn.

"Are you from Lancashire, too, Mr. Ingram?" he inquired at one point.

"Not originally. I was born and reared in Kent." The tutor cleared his throat. "Presently, however I am living in Lancashire. I'm Tristan's tutor."

Leyburn didn't turn a hair. "I trust Tristan is an apt pupil?" he inquired pleasantly.

"Very much so, my lord."

To Tristan, the earl said, grinning, "I wish I could say that my own tutor considered me an apt pupil worth his efforts. Alas, I wasn't." He added with mock dismay, "Do you object to the way I tied my cravat, Tristan? You're staring at me as if something is wrong."

Reddening, Tristan muttered, "Sorry, sir. I was just wondering—you see, Sophy told us you were a member of the House of Commons. She also said you were an earl, which makes you a peer, as I understand it, and I always thought that peers sat in the House of Lords."

"Oh, that's easy to explain. I'm not a real earl, only a courtesy one. I simply use my father's secondary title. He's the one who's entitled to sit in the House of Lords, though I must say he very seldom does so."

Tristan gravely considered the earl's explanation. "Thank you, sir—Lord Leyburn. I do like to know why things are the way they are."

"Good for you. There's nothing wrong with a little healthy curiosity."

During the remaining interval before dinner, and during the meal itself, Leyburn continued his easy, informal manner of speaking, and soon everyone had lost his or her awe of him. Mark Ingram engaged in an intelligent conversation on the war in the Peninsula. Tristan asked if the earl had a favorite for the Derby. Carefully avoiding Sophia's eyes, Edwina said, "I be-

lieve you were at Vauxhall Gardens with a gentleman I recently
met, Lord Leyburn. A Captain Royce?"

"Why, yes." Giving not the slightest indication that he had
witnessed Edwina's cozy tête-à-tête with the captain in the secluded arbor in Vauxhall, Leyburn said, "I'm sure you'll like
Nevil Royce when you know him better, Miss Edwina. He's an
old friend of mine, a very good sort of fellow. We were at Eton
together."

Edwina beamed. Sophia could cheerfully have strangled both
of them.

After the dessert course, Leyburn said to the tutor, "I suggest
we gentlemen dispense with our port on this occasion, Mr. Ingram. I'm sure Tristan won't object."

Tristan flashed the earl a grin. "I hate the stuff, frankly. Anyway, Sophy won't let me drink it."

"Very wise of your sister. Plenty of time for you to learn to
tipple, young Tristan. Well, then shall we go with the ladies?"

In the drawing room, Leyburn waited until Sophia had poured
the coffee, and the footman had passed around the cups. Then,
when the servant left the room, the earl said, "Don't you think
we've waited long enough to make our announcement, Sophia?"

Sophia gulped. She could feel the warm color creeping into
her cheeks. "Yes, of course," she murmured. Steeling herself,
she looked in turn at her sisters, her brother and Ingram, who
all gazed back at her with blank expressions.

"I daresay this will come as a great surprise to all of you,"
she began. "The fact is that Lord Leyburn and I have decided
that we, er, suit, and we plan to be married in the near future."

The members of her household continued to stare at her in
sheer befuddlement. Finally, Tristan blurted, "Does this mean
you'll be an earless Sophy? No, that can't be right."

"Idiot boy," Caroline pronounced with a scathing look.
"There's no such thing as an earless. Sophy will be a countess.
The Countess of Leyburn."

The earl smiled. "A very charming Countess of Leyburn, too."

Edwina wandered into the morning room, where Sophia was trying to total a column of figures that annoyingly added up to a different sum every time she made the attempt.

"Yes, what is it, Edwina?"

"I can't belive it, Sophy."

Sophia put down her pen in resignation. "You can't believe what?"

"I just passed by the salver in the hall. It's positively overflowing with calling cards. It's incredible. The first several weeks we were in London not a soul called on us. Now callers are descending on us in a deluge. Of course, it's really not incredible at all, I know that. The moment the announcement of your betrothal appeared in all the newspapers, the ton began calling on you." Edwina cocked her head at Sophia. "When you marry Lord Leyburn you'll be a very important person, won't you, Sophy?"

"Of course not, silly. I'll be the same person I always was."

Despite her light-hearted disclaimer, Sophia was secretly as bemused as Edwina by the change in their social life since the fateful announcement had appeared a little over a week ago in all the London newspapers. ". . . Joel Adam Hilliard, Earl of Leyburn, son of Philip Richard Hilliard, 7th Marquess of Kennington, to Sophia Elizabeth Ashley, daughter of the late Horace William Dalton, D.D., of Woodbridge, Lancashire."

So few words, yet what a difference they had made. Callers, as Edwina had said, had descended on the house in Brook Street in a deluge. Letters offering their custom poured in from tailors, hatters, modistes, milliners, haberdashers, wine merchants and grocers.

Sophia and her sisters spent every afternoon now greeting guests in a crowded drawing room. Many of the guests had familiar names; Lady Jersey, the famous patroness of Almack, had arrived with Lady Winwood, and those well-known Corinthians, Lords Alvanley and Sefton had also called. The sisters had already received invitations to soirees, dinners and balls. Tonight they were to attend a ball given by a famous London hostess.

What had most struck Sophia about her changed social standing was Leyburn's part in it. She had to give him credit for living up to the terms of their compact. He was playing the attentive fiancé to the hilt, with never any suggestion that his engagement was a matter of expedience. He was at the house in Brook Street at all hours, he accompanied Sophia and her sisters on their drives in the Park, introducing his friends to them with every evidence of pleasure.

He had even interested himself in her appearance. On an occasion shortly after their betrothal, when he and Sophia were taking tea with his aunt, Lady Winwood had observed, "Could I make a suggestion, Sophia? I think you need a much larger wardrobe. Soon you'll be receiving invitations for every day— and evening—of the week."

"Oh, I agree. I've been taking my sisters to Madame Fleurette. Would you recommend someone else?"

"Well, I've given my custom for many years to a Mrs. Armbruster in Leicester Square."

To Sophia's surprise, Leyburn had cut in. "Dear Aunt Georgina, you're the top of the trees yourself when it comes to fashion, but wouldn't you say that Mrs. Armbruster caters to an older, more conservative clientele? Sophia is neither plain nor dowdy—quite the contrary! I think she should go to a modiste who would reflect her youth and good looks." He'd smiled then at Sophia. "You and your sisters always look charming. Why don't you continue patronizing Madame Fleurette?"

So, gradually, Sophia had begun to lose her qualms about this strange arranged marriage. She thought that Leyburn, too, now that he was more acquainted with her and her family, had become reconciled to a match that he previously wouldn't have considered under any circumstances. Well, perhaps more than forbearance. Unless he was simply acting the part, he appeared to enjoy being in her company and that of her sisters, and he seemed to be developing a special kind of wry liking for Tristan. Was it possible that she and Leyburn could achieve, not merely a civilized forbearance, but even—something of a miracle?—a real friendship?

"Sophy," Edwina said, breaking into her sister's thoughts, "do you object to my visiting Lady Middleton this afternoon? Captain Royce said he would be happy to call for me and bring me to his mother's house. Lady Middleton has said she would like to know me better."

Sophia clamped her mouth shut against the retort she had been about to make. She'd felt unable to refuse to receive Nevil Royce when he called in Brook Street in the company of his charming and eminently respectable mother, the Countess of Middleton, a famous beauty and influential society hostess, according to Leyburn's Aunt Georgina.

"Nevil is Daphne Middleton's favorite, even though he's the younger son," Lady Winwood had informed Sophia. "Daphne will do anything for Nevil."

As far as Sophia knew, Captain Royce had made no attempt to entice Edwina into an improper secret tryst. He had merely been a frequent caller, gazing at Edwina with admiring eyes from an inconspicuous position at the rear of the drawing room.

Reluctantly, Sophia said, "No, I see no reason why you shouldn't visit Lady Middleton, provided Caroline goes with you."

"Oh, I'm sure Caroline will be delighted to accompany us." Edwina scampered away before Sophia could register any further objection.

That evening, Sophia stood before her cheval glass, trying to display the pleasure she felt in seeing herself in the three-quarter tunic of sheerest silk crepe in a deep blue over a white sarsenet slip, a gown delivered only that afternoon from her modiste. Tonight, along with her sisters, she would be making her entrance into London society, at a ball given by Lady Winwood's good friend, Lady Alender.

Sophia's eyes sparkled beneath the curls framing her face—she'd finally given in to Edwina's pleas to cut her hair. A much-recommended hairdresser had come to the house to clip short her locks in front and to show her abigail how to arrange the rest of her hair into a high knot at the back of her head, ending in trailing ringlets.

Around her neck . . . Sophia put up her finger to touch the necklace of diamonds and sapphires, the gleaming azure stones almost exactly matching the blue of her tunic. The necklace had arrived that afternoon with a note in what she was coming to recognize as Leyburn's bold slashing handwriting. "Dear Sophia, this belonged to my mother. From what you told me of your ball gown, the necklace should go well with it."

Remaining in front of the cheval glass, Sophia continued to stare at the necklace. Why had Leyburn made the gesture of presenting her with a family heirloom? He'd promised to present a polite and attentive exterior to the world during their engagement, and he'd done that. He was under no obligation to do anything of a more personal nature.

"Ma'am?" Her abigail stood beside her, holding out her shawl.

Sophia shook herself out of her thoughts. "Thank you, Rose."

After the abigail had arranged her shawl over her shoulders, Sophia took one last look into the cheval glass before she left the bedchamber and went down the stairs to the drawing room, where Leyburn and her sisters were waiting for her.

Before Sophia could greet Leyburn, Edwina exclaimed, "Oh, Sophy, the necklace looks even more beautiful draped around your neck than it did in the box." She turned to the earl. "Sophy says the necklace belonged to your mother."

"Yes," Leyburn smiled. "And now it belongs to the next Marchioness of Kennington."

Sophia opened her mouth and closed it again before she committed a *faux pas*. She had been about to thank Leyburn for the loan of the necklace, and to tell him she would take very good care of it. Now it seemed she was the new owner of the family heirloom. She felt a little light-headed.

Still gazing at the necklace, Edwina sighed, saying, "It's so lovely. I'm not jealous, you understand, Sophy. I just like to look at beautiful things. Beautiful jewelry, especially."

His eyes twinkling, Leyburn said, "I think I should introduce you to an old friend of mine, Lady Saltire, who has the most fabulous jewelry collection in London. She's very old now, a semi-invalid, and doesn't go out into society, but she likes visitors, reminiscing to them about the days when her husband was the ambassador to the court of Louis XV and she was the toast of Versailles. I'm sure she'd enjoy showing you her jewelry, Edwina, even though she never wears the pieces now. It will bring back her youth." He turned to Sophia. "I think you might like to know Lady Saltire. She was a woman of action, someone who accomplished things, like yourself. Many people thought she was the real ambassador to France, not her husband."

It was an unmistakable compliment, perhaps the highest one Sophia had ever received. She colored faintly and remained silent, not knowing what to say.

Gazing from one girl to the other—Edwina in a new gown of green silk and Caroline in a glowing shade of pink—Leyburn said with a grin, "Beyond doubt I'm the luckiest man in London tonight. Never in my wildest dreams did I think I'd be the escort of three beautiful women all in the same evening!"

Edwina giggled, giving Leyburn a mock curtsy. "Thank you, my lord. It's good to know that we look well. This is our first London ball, you know." A stricken look crossed her face. "Sophy, I wasn't thinking. We won't know a soul at the ball. What if no one asks us to dance?"

Leyburn laughed. "I will positively guarantee that you have nothing to worry about on that score."

However, Edwina was unusually subdued during the carriage drive to the house of Lady Alender in Cavendish Square. When they arrived at Number 6, she gazed at the canopy that had been erected over the entrance, and at the footmen in liveries and powdered wigs who lined the steps. "Oh, my," she breathed in a small voice. "I feel almost like royalty. Or a duchess, at the very least."

Walking up the long flight of stairs leading to the ballroom, Sophia glanced sideways at Edwina and Caroline beside her, and hoped no one would realize that all of them were self-conscious to the point of panic. A footman's powerful voice rang out in introduction: "Mrs. Ashley. Miss Dalton. Miss Edwina Dalton. Lord Leyburn."

At the entrance to the ballroom, taking a deep breath, Sophia curtsied to her smiling gray-haired hostess. This was the beginning of the new life she'd chosen for herself and her sisters.

Seven

From the moment she and her sisters set foot in Lady Alender's ballroom that evening, it was an enchanted occasion. Every now and then, Sophia felt like Cinderella at the ball, wondering when she'd wake up to reality. But never at any time during the evening did she encounter any slights or any other indication that the guests at the ball regarded her and her sisters as interlopers from the hinterlands.

Lady Winwood set the tone when she bustled up to Sophia to say, beaming, "My dear, you and your sisters look uncommonly handsome. No one in this room can hold a candle to you." She fixed her eyes on Sophia's necklace. "Those are Sybilla's sapphires. I'd recognize them anywhere." She patted Sophia's shoulder. "Sybilla would be pleased to see them worn by Joel's intended bride."

During the evening Edwina and Caroline were never without partners, which delighted Sophia, although she had to resign herself to the fact that Nevil Royce was among the guests. After all, he did belong to the inner circle of the ton. The moment he arrived he sought out Edwina.

She greeted him with a delighted smile. "You're not wearing your sling. Is your arm better, then?"

"Much better. In any event, I had no intention of coming to a ball without being able to dance. May I have the next cotillion?"

As Sophia watched her sister go off on the captain's arm, she understood perfectly how Nevil Royce had managed to captivate Edwina's inexperienced, seventeen-year-old heart. His laughing eyes and smile of pure charm animated his rather nondescript features so that he appeared positively handsome. Nor did his colorful Guards uniform detract from his dashing appearance. And the fact that he had been wounded in the service of his country appealed to Edwina's sensibilities.

When she came off the floor after the dance, however, Sophia drew her aside to hiss, "Don't you dare dance more than two dances with Captain Royce, and not in succession!"

Somewhat to her surprise, Sophia had to repeat the same stricture to Caroline when a certain Lord Sanditon repeatedly asked her to dance. He was a pleasant-looking, attractive young man with exquisite manners.

"Robert Sanditon's a viscount," Lady Winwood informed Sophia. "Not an especially old title, but he has a snug estate in Berkshire. A Whig, of course. Into reform, and all that." Georgina's eyes twinkled. "Caroline might do worse."

Sophia protested, "But Caroline just met the man!" She did notice, however, that Caroline appeared to like Lord Sanditon.

Also to her surprise, and not a little shock, Sophia, too, danced every dance. She reflected with a wry amusement that she'd grown used to thinking of herself as a settled old matron. Well, perhaps she wasn't quite on the shelf, judging by some of the admiring glances and comments she'd received.

At one point Leyburn sent a faint glow of color to her cheeks by saying in mock despair, "I'm thinking of calling out some of your eager partners. They're not allowing me to have any dances with my own fiancée!"

Trying to emulate his bantering tone, Sophia said, "Oh, I hardly think you need go to the extreme of challenging anyone to a duel in order to obtain a dance with me, Lord Leyburn."

He raised an eyebrow. "Which reminds me, do you think you could bring yourself to use my Christian name? We'll soon be married, and I must tell you that I've long disapproved of the practice I've observed in so many married couples, to speak to each other in public as "Mr." or "Mrs." or "Lord" or "Lady Something or other." I find it hard to believe that they address each other so formally in—er—more intimate circumstances."

Sophia looked away, feeling a warmth in her cheeks. "Oh, I quite agree. I always spoke to my husband as Bartholomew."

"Then—"

"Then I'll of course call you Joel, if that's what you wish. Especially—" she added with a note of asperity, "—especially since you always refer to me as Sophia."

He smiled, a warm light in his silvery gray eyes. "It's always seemed natural to call you that."

Sophia felt obscurely pleased, although, when she thought about it, she conceded the irrationality of her feelings. During her first meetings with Leyburn she'd been indignant at his cavalier use of her Christian name. Yet now they were to be married. Why shouldn't she feel a little pleasure when he called her Sophia? On the other hand, theirs was a marriage of convenience and to begin allowing herself to believe otherwise would be a foolhardly act. But as she looked up at him and saw that his eyes still held a warm expression, she realized that had she been permitted to engage in schoolgirl daydreams, Joel was precisely the sort of man she would have chosen to act as her knight in shining armor.

After the ball, during the drive back to Brook Street, Edwina and Caroline chattered excitedly about their experiences of the evening, with Edwina declaring at one point, "I think this is the happiest night of my life. Thank you, Sophy, for bringing us to London!"

Joel laughed. "I hope you won't be feeling jaded by the end of the Season, Edwina. This was only the first of many balls you'll be attending, you know."

To Sophia a little later, as he accompanied her into the foyer of the house, he said quietly, "I think you were a little nervous at the beginning of the evening, wondering how you and your sisters would be received. I hope you know now that you have nothing to fear from the ton. Aunt Georgina informed me that you, Edwina and Caroline were a *succes fou* tonight."

Sophia smiled. "Oh, I think Lady Winwood exaggerated. But it was a lovely evening. Thank you, Joel."

She went up the stairs to her bedchamber with her heart singing. She was sure now that Edwina and Caroline, at the very least, would have many opportunities to meet eligible suitors. And it had been a lovely evening. She thought Joel had genuinely enjoyed it.

Joel. During the next few days, as she and her sisters plunged into a dizzying succession of balls and routs, dinners and soirees, it became easier to think of, and speak to him as Joel. In fact, as the days went by, Sophia found it increasingly hard to remember that she had once viewed the arrogant Earl of Leyburn with aversion and distrust.

As she walked out of the imposing Tudor gatehouse of St. James's Palace with Lady Winwood, trailed by Edwina and Caroline, Sophia turned a glowing face to Georgina. "I'm so glad you invited us to go with you to Sunday morning service at the Chapel Royal. The music was beautiful."

Georgina smiled in gratification. "My dear Sophia, I know how much you love music, and you will never hear more exquisite ecclesiastical music anywhere else. The Chapel Royal employs the most eminent church musicians in England." She glanced at the watch pinned to her pelisse. "Oh, dear. The service lasted longer than usual. Horace will be ravenous for his luncheon. Joel, too, no doubt. Come along, then," she said, as she headed for her carriage. "We mustn't keep the gentlemen waiting."

As she entered the drawing room of Winwood House in Hanover Square, Sophia had to suppress a smile at the sight of Lord Winwood, pausing in his impatient pacing of the carpet to pull out a large, old-fashioned watch.

"Well, now I'm sorry we're late, Horace," Lady Winwood said. "I know you like your meals served on time. Of course," she added with an accusing glance at her husband and her nephew, "if you two had seen fit to accompany us you might have been so uplifted by the service that you'd have forgotten all about your stomachs."

"My dear, I trust I'm as faithful a member of the established church as you are," Lord Winwood said with an injured dignity. "A man does get hungry, however."

Joel burst out laughing. "Come, now Uncle Horace, you know very well Aunt Georgina isn't accusing us of being heathens."

A little later, as the party sat at table, Joel inquired of Sophia, "Tristan didn't go with you to the service at the Chapel Royal?"

"No," she said demurely. "Like you, he had better things to do this morning."

Joel tossed her an appreciative grin. "Touché. Where are Tristan and Mark today?"

Smiling, Caroline broke in to say, "Oh, Sophy did her best to persuade Tristan to come to church with us, for the sake of his soul, you know, but he and Mark had other plans. They were going to a fair, they said."

"A fair?" Joel frowned. "I'm not aware of any major fair scheduled for this time. There's Peckham—but no, their fair takes place at the end of July. Did Tristan mention where this fair was being held?"

"I think he did. A place spelled with a 'b,' as I recall." Caroline knit her brows. "I have it! Batt-Battersea Fields."

Joel's frown deepened, and Sophia said quickly, "What is it, Joel? Shouldn't Tristan have gone to this place?"

"I'd have advised against it. It's a lonely area along the Thames, principally used for market gardening. An ideal place for duels, I'm told. In recent years it's acquired a very unsavory reputation, primarily because of the Red House Tavern, which attracts the riff-raff and criminal elements of London. There are other places of entertainment and refreshment on the river, too. Gypsies camp in the fields during the summers. And every Sunday informal fairs are held there. Horse and donkey racing, gambling and drinking booths, popular entertainments, vendors selling every manner of merchandise, that sort of thing. I'm told the fairs are very popular, especially among the lower classes."

"It doesn't sound very respectable. I wonder that Mark would take Tristan to such a place," Sophia remarked with a frown.

"Probably Mark didn't realize that Battersea Fields has a bad reputation," Caroline observed. "I'm sure he'll take good care of Tristan. Mark is very conscientious."

"So he is. In broad daylight, too, what could really happen?" Sophia's face brightened, and she resumed her lunch.

As the footman was serving the dessert course, Sophia looked up from her plate at the sound of racing feet in the hallway and Mark Ingram's voice shouting, "Mrs. Ashley! Mrs. Ashley!"

She jumped up from the table and ran to the door of the dining room. "Mark, I'm in here. What's the matter?" She glanced behind him. "Tristan isn't with you?"

Ingram, his expression panicky, blurted, "Mrs. Ashley, I'm so sorry to disturb your luncheon, but I couldn't see any alternative. I—I don't know how to tell you about Tristan. I've lost him. He's disappeared in those cursed Battersea Fields."

Joel emerged from the dining room. "What's this? Tristan's lost? How did it happen, man?"

Appearing close to shock, Mark said tightly, "I should never have taken him there but I didn't know. I realized almost at once after we arrived that the place was swarming with the scum of London. I told Tristan we should leave."

Mark ran a hand through his hair. "You know Tristan, how

insatiably curious he is, how he always wants to explore every corner. He begged to stay just a few minutes more. He was fascinated with the tricks of a strolling conjuror, and he promised a Gypsy woman he would let her tell his fortune, and later he wanted to watch the donkey races—"

His voice trailed away. A moment later he mumbled, "I swear I had him in sight for all but a few seconds. I turned my head to glance—only to glance!—at knives in one of the booths. When I looked up again he was gone. I searched all through the place for over an hour, calling his name, asking everyone I met if they'd seen him."

"Honor among thieves," Joel said grimly. "Even if they knew where Tristan had gone, those villains wouldn't inform on their friends."

"I daresay," Mark muttered dispiritedly. He flexed his shoulders wearily. "I wasn't accomplishing anything in Battersea. I decided to return here to tell Mrs. Ashley what had happened."

"Joel, what should we do?" Sophia asked, her hands clenched together at her breast as she instinctively turned to her betrothed for help and counsel.

"I'll tell you what we're going to do. We're going into Battersea Fields with a posse of sorts and tear it apart. Give me a moment, first, to write notes to Nevil and Saintsbury and several other friends, and to Sir Nathaniel Conant at the Bow Street Magistrates' Court, asking for the hire of any available Runners."

Lord Winwood appeared in the hallway. "Is something wrong? Can I help?"

After explaining the situation briefly, Joel added, "With your permission, I'm going to commandeer your household, Uncle Horace."

"Of course, my boy. Anything at all that Georgina and I can do. Poor child, Tristan. Such a nice lad."

Joel turned to Mark. "Ingram, go to the butler. Inform him that Lord Winwood has given you permission to round up every male servant in the house, including the boot boy, if necessary.

Tell the butler to supply the servants with cab fare. I'm sending them out with notes to my friends, asking for help. Meanwhile, you and I will go straight to Battersea Fields and resume the search. The others will join us there. Oh, and order a carriage from the stables."

"Yes, my lord." Mark went off, looking as if a mountain had been removed from his shoulders. Sophia understood how he felt. A strong hand was at the helm and she was deeply grateful.

Joel shot an apologetic look at Lord Winwood. "Sorry, Uncle Horace. I've taken over your house."

"Not at all, not at all. Do whatever you think best. Naturally, I'm going with you to help with the search."

Ten minutes later, when Joel emerged from the library, a sheaf of letters in his hand, Sophia was waiting for him along with Mark and Lord Winwood and the male staff of the house. She was dressed for the street in pelisse and bonnet.

Joel distributed the letters to the footmen, quietly giving them instructions. They scattered like sparrows.

Joel gave Sophia a piercing look. He drew her aside, saying, "The answer is no, in case you had any ideas about coming with us."

"I must go. I can't just wait, wondering if Tristan is alive or dead. I've sent Edwina and Caroline home to Brook Street. They'll stay there, waiting for messages—"

"Messages?"

"If Tristan's been abducted, won't the kidnappers send a ransom note?"

"Yes, I suppose so. But Sophia—" Joel broke off.

"What?" She gazed up at him anxiously. "You don't think he's been kidnapped, do you? You think something even more terrible has happened to him."

Spreading his hands, Joel said, "Sophia, I simply don't know. Yes, there's the possibility Tristan was the victim of purely random violence. Someone might have tried to rob him, thinking so well-dressed a boy must have a fat purse, and then when he resisted the thief might have struck at him to silence him."

"So he might be lying in a ditch somewhere, bleeding to death, or already dead," Sophia said in a choked voice.

"Yes, we can't rule that out. He could also have wandered away and become lost. I told you Battersea Fields is a very lonely area. Ingram and Uncle Horace and I and my friends, together with the Bow Street Runners, will explore every possibility, I promise you. I want to make one thing clear, however. You are not going with us."

"Joel, I beg you. I can't wait here in such suspense. I already feel guilty enough. Tristan was in my care. I should have questioned Mark more carefully about what kind of a place this Battersea Fields was before I allowed Tristan to go there. If anything should happen to my brother it will be my fault."

"That's nonsense. No one could accuse you of neglecting Tristan. But I can't allow you to go with us. Battersea Fields is one of the hellholes of London. You could be accosted, insulted. You might even be in danger if we're forced to use violent means to rescue Tristan."

She said mutinously, "If you won't take me with you I'll go to Battersea Fields on my own."

For a moment he stared at her, his eyes narrowed. "I believe you would," he returned, tight-lipped. "You're the most stubborn woman I ever met." He threw up his hands. "Very well. You can come with us, provided you agree to stay close to me at all times and to do whatever I tell you, without argument, if any violence should develop."

"I promise. Thank you, Joel."

"Don't thank me," he retorted. "I'm acting against my better judgment." He turned to Mark and Lord Winwood. "Let's go."

Huddled beside Joel as the carriage rolled down Park Lane into Knightsbridge and Sloane Street, Sophia's concern for Tristan grew more acute. She glanced at her watch. "It's so late," she fretted. "Well past noon."

"It will be daylight for many hours yet at this time of year," Joel assured her. "The crowds will stay until dusk starts to fall."

They rattled across the arched wooden bridge at Battersea

and drove to the bare, lonely area beyond, a place of marshy fields intersected by streams and ditches, and separated from the river itself by a narrow raised causeway.

"There's the fair," Joel said as they approached one of the larger fields, and signaled the coachman to stop. Leaving the carriage, they walked to the fairground, swarming with people and animals amid a maze of booths and tents.

Instinctively Sophia edged closer to Joel. In all her life she had never taken part in such a scene, so unlike the bustling little country fairs she had attended in Lancashire. Comic actors, dancers, conjurors, fortune tellers, hawkers and vendors roamed through the crowds, which comprised to some extent respectably dressed family groups. The majority of the people, however, even to Sophia's unsophisticated eyes, were the dregs of the lower classes, ill-clad, dirty, either drunken themselves or preying on inebriated victims. She winced at the sight of the many drab, hopeless-looking prostitutes plying their trade, and she was even more appalled by the number of ragged, emaciated children she saw, begging for small coins and obviously without family.

"Most of these children have either been deserted or neglected by their parents," Joel said in a low voice. "The authorities say there are thousands of them in greater London, many of them living by thievery. See?"

Sophia's eyes widened as she observed a small child slipping his hand into the pocket of a drunken fairgoer. Suddenly her throat closed up at the thought of Tristan, whose entire life had been surrounded by love and care.

Joel, with Sophia by his side, along with Mark and Lord Winwood, fanned out among the crowds, their eyes alert for any glimpse of Tristan, asking entertainers and vendors and fairgoers if they had seen anyone of Tristan's description. Within the hour Nevil Royce and Saintsbury, and a number of other men Sophia recognized as parliamentary friends of Joel, arrived to join in the search. Shortly afterwards, two stern-looking men, wearing striking red waistcoats, came up to Joel.

"Lord Leyburn? Sir Nathaniel sent us. We're from Bow Street Magistrates' Court. How can we help you?"

Quickly Joel gave the Runners a description of Tristan, and they merged into the crowd to join the search.

The minutes passed, then an hour, and another, with no sign of Tristan. At intervals the searchers gathered to compare notes. In late afternoon, when they came together again they looked hot, tired and discouraged.

"Joel, we've scoured the entire fairground and the area all around it," Nevil Royce declared, "including the pigeon and sparrow shooting grounds and the Gypsy encampment. If the boy is still here, I don't think we could have missed him."

"O'course, there's the river, my lord," began the older of the two Bow Street Runners, only to clamp his mouth tightly together at Joel's warning glare.

"Joel," Sophia faltered, clutching his arm with a desperate grip. "You don't think—"

"I think we should search the grounds one last time, foot by foot, inch by inch, before we conclude that Tristan isn't here," Joel stated firmly. "Come, Sophia."

Feeling little hope, Sophia walked with Joel along the main avenue of the fair. Her eye was caught by a booth displaying a hodgepodge of items—cheap jewelry, ribbons, bits of lace, used clothing, pins and needles, second-hand cutlery, everything tattered and used. A sense of despair mounted within her.

"Yes, m'lady? Ye like one o' these necklaces, mebbe, or p'raps this 'ere beautiful ring?" the booth's swarthy proprietor called to her ingratiatingly, holding up for Sophia's inspection a ring containing a lifeless piece of glass.

Sophia looked at his worn, dirty face but couldn't bring herself to respond. Her gaze slid past him, landing on an object toward the rear of the booth. "Joel!" she said in a choked voice. "That's Tristan's watch. There, next to that old knife. I'd know it anywhere. It belonged to my father."

Joel entered the booth and snatched up the watch. "Where

did you get this?" he cried harshly. "You stole it, didn't you, from a young boy of about fifteen? Where is he now?"

The man shrank back, his face growing pale beneath the layer of filth. "I never stole nuffink," he whined. "I bought this 'ere watch from a gent jist passing by, like."

Turning, Joel shouted, "Nevil, Saintsbury, Ingram, Uncle Horace, here to me!" His voice thundered above the murmurings of the curious crowd that now began to gather around the booth. In a few seconds Lord Winwood came running into view, followed shortly by Royce and Mark.

Still holding the watch in his hand, a grim-faced Joel exclaimed to the proprietor, "Either you produce the boy you robbed, or I and my friends will tear apart that tent behind your booth."

"I don't know nuffink about any boy, nor any thievery, neither," the booth owner protested. "And ye can't search me booth, that's private propity, that is."

Joel slammed his fist in the man's face, knocking him into a senseless heap.

"Good for you, Joel," Nevil crowed. "I'd say you gave the fellow a proper facer."

Ignoring his friend, Joel plunged into the tent behind the booth. In a few moments he emerged, carrying Tristan's inert body in his arms. A shabbily-dressed, dark-visaged woman stumbled out of the tent behind Joel to stare in dismay at the unconscious figure of the booth proprietor.

Joel deposited Tristan on the ground next to the booth. The boy's limbs were fastened with rope, and a grimy cloth had been tied around his mouth as a gag.

"Oh, God, Tristan," Sophia wailed, throwing herself down beside her brother's body. She snatched at the rag covering his mouth.

Kneeling beside her, Joel said, "I don't think he's injured. Look, he's breathing normally. I think he was drugged." He leaned forward, tearing the knots that bound Tristan's limbs.

The rest of Joel's informal posse converged on the booth,

pushing aside the curious spectators. One of the Bow Street Runners dragged the body of the booth proprietor, who was just recovering consciousness, to his feet. "Ye're coming wi' us, mate," the Runner growled. "Like as not, ye're bound fer the nubbing cheat. Kidnapping, an' theft, an' attempted murder, too, like as not."

Her face distorted with grief and rage, the shabby woman, who had been standing in stunned immobility, screamed in protest. "I won't let ye tak 'im. Josh didn't mean ter 'arm the boy. 'E jist wanted ter git a bit o'rhino out o'the lad's family. 'E don't deserve the gallows, nor deportashun. An' what'll 'appen ter me, all alone?" Wild-eyed, her glance fell on Sophia. "It's all yer fault," she cried. "If ye hadn't spotted that damned watch—"

Before anyone could stop her, the woman dragged Sophia to her feet then fastened sinewy hands around her throat. The cruel grip tightened until Sophia's lungs were in agony and her sight began to darken. Dimly she realized that Joel was working frantically to pry loose the woman's clutching fingers. Finally, the grip loosened and Sophia staggered back, coughing and gulping for air.

"Are you all right, Sophia?" Joel inquired anxiously, putting out his hand to steady her.

"Yes. My throat's a little painful, but it's no matter. What about Tristan?"

To her relief, Tristan's eyes had opened, although he appeared quite dazed. In a few moments, however, his eyes cleared and he jumped to his feet. "Sophy—Joel!" he gasped. "You found me!"

Sophia hugged him tightly. Then, placing her hands on his shoulders, she held him away from her, looking at him searchingly. "Did those dreadful people hurt you?" she asked.

Pale, disheveled, his face marred by streaks of dirt, Tristan shook his head. "I'm fine, Sophy." His attention was distracted momentarily by the sight of the booth proprietor and his wife being led away by the Bow Street Runners. "I say," he exclaimed, the familiar look of alert curiosity spreading over his face, "Are those men the Robin Redbreasts I've heard so much about?"

Joel laughed. "They are, indeed, young Tristan." He put his arm around the boy's shoulder, saying, "Do you think you can walk a short distance? Good. Come along, I want to get you and your sister home as soon as possible."

They walked slowly through the fairground, the object of gaping stares from all sides, followed by their "posse" of searchers. At one point Tristan stopped abruptly. "My watch. Papa's watch. My purse!"

"Joel has your watch," Sophia said. "The purse isn't important. Forget about recovering it. I don't want to stay here another moment."

Arriving at the carriage, Lord Winwood said, "I'll ask your friend Saintsbury to drive me home, Joel. You go along now with Mrs. Ashley and the boy and Ingram."

As they began their return journey across the Thames, Mark Ingram, still pale and strained, said to Tristan, "Now tell us what happened. As I told Mrs. Ashley, I had you in my sights save for a few seconds, and then you were gone."

Tristan looked sheepish. "Well, I followed along after that conjuror. I had to know how he changed those colored balls into live chicks. I felt a hand in the pocket of my coat where I kept my purse, and before I could turn around something hit me on the head."

Tristan rubbed the back of his head with a rueful grimace. "Next thing I knew I was in some kind of tent, trussed up like a Christmas goose. That greasy-looking fellow, the one the Robin Redbreasts arrested, told me he wouldn't hurt me. All he wanted he said, was my name and direction, and he would send a ransom note to my family. Of course, I refused to tell him my name or where I lived. What's more, I started to yell for help. So then he held my mouth open and poured some vile tasting liquid down my throat, and that's all I remember."

"Oh, Tristan," Sophia said with a catch in her voice. "Why didn't you give that terrible man the information he wanted. I would have been happy to pay any sum he demanded to get you back safely."

Tristan looked at her indignantly. "Don't talk fustian, Sophy. Surely you wouldn't wish me to surrender to that kind of blackmail?"

"Spoken like a true-blood free Englishman," Joel observed.

Sophia threw up her hands. "Men!" she exclaimed.

Tristan gave her an affectionate grin.

When they arrived at the house in Brook Street, Edwina and Caroline rushed into the hall to greet them, their faces alight with relief. The sisters embraced Tristan demanding excitedly to know what had caused his disappearance at the fair in Battersea Fields. Before he could answer, Sophia suddenly drooped and clutched at Joel's arm. "I feel a little faint," she murmured.

"I don't wonder," Joel said crisply. He swept her up into his arms. To her sisters he explained, "Sophia has been under an enormous strain. She was attacked and almost strangled to death by one of the kidnappers. She needs rest. Show me to her bedchamber."

After Joel deposited her carefully on her bed, Sophia sank back gratefully against her pillows. She still felt light-headed. She heard herself saying, in a tremulous voice, "Thank you, Joel. No one else could have saved Tristan. I owe you his life. I'll never be able to repay you."

"Nonsense," he said gruffly. He placed the tip of his forefinger over each of her eyelids in turn, forcing them gently to close. "Go to sleep. Tristan is home. You've nothing more to worry about."

Eight

On the following afternoon Sophia walked into the drawing room, dressed for her customary drive in the Park. "Did I keep you waiting?" she asked, with an inquiring glance at her sisters and Joel.

Joel came over to her, his face concerned. "I was surprised when Edwina and Caroline told me that you intended to drive with us today. Do you think that's wise? You narrowly escaped being strangled yesterday. Do you feel well enough to leave the house?"

"I'm quite all right, really," Sophia smiled. "Oh, my throat is still a little painful, and I must admit I still have some rather ugly bruise marks. But this lacy scarf takes care of that."

She felt a warm glow spreading within her at the tone of solicitude in Joel's voice. She had a sudden conviction that they had entered into an entirely different, more intimate relationship. They knew each other far better now, after sharing those moments of genuine danger in the Battersea Fields. She, especially, knew how strong and resourceful he could be in an emergency, and, yes, how caring. He'd been as distressed about Tristan's disappearance as she had been.

"Well, let's be going, then," Joel said, offering his arm. "Mind, if you begin to feel tired, or ill, we'll return here immediately."

As they drove in the landau along Park Lane, Joel remarked, "Caroline tells me that Tristan is completely recovered from his experience at the fairgrounds."

"Yes," Sophia said with considerable asperity. "He actually had the gall to say he'd like to return to the Battersea Fields fair. He hadn't seen all the attractions, he said. If only I would allow him to go, he would promise faithfully not to stray away from Mark's side!"

Joel chuckled. "That sounds like Tristan."

"Needless to say, he won't be returning to Battersea Fields," Caroline observed mischievously. "Sophy informed him that from now on he was to attend only the most respectable events!"

Joel shook his head. "Poor Tristan," he said in mock condolence.

The sunny day in late May was perfect for driving in the

Park. Sophia once again reflected about how different this drive was from those other excursions when she and her family had first come to London. Then she and her sisters had driven through the Park every afternoon as if they were invisible. Today, they could scarcely drive a yard without a wave and a bow from the occupants of a passing carriage, and often, as now, their coachman was forced to halt the landau to allow gentlemen to dismount and pay their respects.

There was an unusually large number of gentlemen visitors today. Nevil Royce was the first to arrive. "I say, Mrs. Ashley, how are you feeling after your horrific experience yesterday? You look top of the trees, I'm happy to say."

"I'm very well, Captain. Quite recovered."

"I'm delighted to hear it."

Royce was again wearing his sling, and Edwina eyed it anxiously. "Did you hurt your arm again, Captain?"

"No, no, nothing like that," Royce said quickly. "Only a twinge, a mere ache. I've been told I must wear the confounded sling more often. Though I refuse to do so when I'm dancing with beautiful ladies," he added, with a meaningful look at Edwina.

"Or when you're helping to rescue my missing brother, I suppose," Edwina retorted. "Joel told me you weren't wearing your sling yesterday at the fair."

"Well, you can't expect me to foil villains with only one arm, now, can you? Actually, I played practically no part in the rescue. Joel was the hero of the day."

"Oh, but you helped. Joel said he couldn't have managed without his posse." Edwina gave the captain a radiant smile.

Sophia pursed her lips. She'd hoped, once Edwina had been exposed to a number of eligible men, that her tendre for Nevil Royce would diminish. Unfortunately, her attraction to the Guards officer showed no sign of diminishing.

Other gentlemen crowded around the landau to inquire about Sophia's health. Doubtless the news of Tristan's kidnapping and rescue had already spread to everyone in the ton, she reflected.

Lord Sanditon, the young man who had seemed so impressed with Caroline at her first ball, came by. "I was so relieved to hear, Mrs. Ashley, that you and your brother had been spared serious harm," he said earnestly. Then he plunged into an absorbed, animated conversation with Caroline.

Under his breath Joel observed to Sophia as he stood beside the landau, "Young Sanditon looks smitten with our Caroline."

"It's too soon to tell, don't you think? Caroline met Lord Sanditon only recently though he seems a pleasant sort of man."

"I daresay he is." Joel's eyes twinkled. "I should point out, however, that he belongs to the wrong political party!"

He smiled at her, inviting her to share his little joke. She smiled back, although she added a tart observation of her own. "I must tell you that I'm not political, Joel. I hardly know one political party from the other. In spite of that, I presume you'll expect me to become a rabid Tory as soon as we're married!"

"Why not? Perhaps you could become a great political hostess like Lady Melbourne, or Lady Holland." He added with a teasing grin, "You're certainly prettier than either of them!"

Joel was still looking amused when an elegant landau passed beside their carriage. Its occupant, a beautiful auburn-haired woman dressed in the height of fashion, inclined her head, saying, "Good afternoon, Lord Leyburn. How delightful to see you again."

Joel lifted his hat a fraction of an inch. "A pleasure, ma'am." His voice was clipped, his face completely without expression.

After pausing a moment, as if to allow Joel to add to his brief comment, the red-haired woman said with a dazzling smile, "No doubt, we'll meet again soon. Goodbye." She motioned to her coachman to drive on.

Joel didn't explain who the woman was. Normally, when people unknown to Sophia approached them when they were together, he made a prompt introduction. He consulted his watch, saying, "If you really feel equal to attending the opera tonight, perhaps we'd best be returning to Brook Street. I think you should rest before the performance. Also, I know how much time you ladies need to primp for your public appearances."

Joel's words were light, but he seemed distracted, almost somber. Sophia eyed him curiously.

Sophia gazed around her at the great horseshoe-shaped auditorium with its five tiers of boxes, gallery and pit, feeling a by now familiar sense of satisfaction that she was actually a spectator in this place about which she'd heard so many anecdotes during the years when she lived in Lancashire. The King's Theatre in the Haymarket was the home of London's Italian opera and ballet, and it was also very probably the city's most fashionable place of entertainment.

Tonight all the boxes were occupied. Someone had once told Sophia that the theater could seat over three thousand spectators. She could not believe it. The gallery and the pit were also packed, not necessarily with music lovers like herself, she reflected dryly. The rakish dandies in the pit seemed more intent on showing off their modish clothes and ogling the pretty girls in the boxes. She spotted Nevil Royce in the pit, smiling and waving to Edwina, who inclined her head decorously.

"Why, there's Lord Sanditon," Sophia remarked to Caroline, sitting beside her on her left in the front of the box. "Over there, not far from Captain Royce in the pit. "Did you know he would attend the opera?"

"I thought he might," Caroline replied demurely. "He told me today in the Park that he was very fond of Mozart."

Sophia studied her sister. "Do you like him, Caroline?"

"Why, yes, I think I do. He's a very serious person, you know. Today he talked to me about the possibility of establishing a school for his tenants' children in his home village. Fancy that, those poor children have never had the opportunity to learn their letters!"

Sophia lifted a mental eyebrow. Although Caroline seemed to be enjoying the social whirl into which she'd been plunged since Sophia's engagement to Joel, she had not, unlike Edwina, appeared to have developed a special liking for any of the young men to whom she had been introduced. It was premature to speculate, of course, the two had met so recently, but could Lord Sanditon be the eligible parti Sophia had been seeking for Caroline? He certainly seemed to share her sister's intellectual interests.

"What a gala evening," Lady Winwood remarked appreciatively. She sat on Sophia's right in the first row of the box. Joel and Edwina were together in the second row. Georgina was a guest in Sophia's box tonight, without her husband. "Horace positively hates opera," she'd informed Sophia. "He says the caterwauling hurts his ears."

Lady Winwood gazed at Sophia. "And how gala-looking you appear, my dear. Not a sign that yesterday you were in danger of your life."

"This black ribbon around my throat conceals all the damage, thank goodness."

"I'm so grateful you escaped so lightly. Horace tells me that the woman who attacked you seemed almost diabolical." Georgina shivered. She turned her gaze back to the audience. "There's Lady Melbourne," she said. "I'm so glad to see her. I'd heard her health wasn't good. And Lady Jersey. Look she's bowing to you."

Lowering her voice, Georgina said to Sophia, out of earshot of the others, "My dear, I haven't had much opportunity to speak to you privately of late, but I do want you to know how happy I am that your engagement has been received so enthusiastically. Any number of people have told me recently that you and Joel are an ideal couple."

Sophia said lightly, "Really? That rather confounds me. After all, I'm still a mill owner's widow from Lancashire."

Lady Winwood looked shocked. "Whatever possessed you to say that, my dear? Has someone been unkind?"

"No," Sophia responded hastily. "Not at all."

"I'm grateful to hear as much. Personally, I've never heard

a disparaging word about your origins. I assure you, no one would ever take you for a mill owner's widow!"

Sophia felt a momentary shock. She was convinced that Georgina liked her for herself, and not merely because she had saved Joel from debtors' prison. Nevertheless, and doubtless without in the least meaning to do so, Georgina had just made a very patronizing remark, reminding Sophia that, if she had looked and acted like the popular image of a rather crude, lower class female, she would not have been accepted by the ton.

Positive that Lady Winwood hadn't meant to be hurtful, Sophia dismissed the remark from her mind and surrendered to the magic of Mozart. The famous soprano Catalani was singing the role of Susanna in 'Le Nozze di Figaro.' The diva was in her best voice tonight. So also, Sophia soon realized, was the auburn-haired beauty who was singing the role of the countess. The same auburn-haired beauty who had greeted Joel in the Park this afternoon.

When the red-haired singer made her entrance, Georgina audibly gasped.

"What is it, Lady Winwood? Are you ill?"

"Oh, no. No, indeed. It was just that—I was a little surprised, that's all. I thought Fannie Price was no longer singing at the Italian Opera. I'd heard she was acting in burlettas with the company at Sadler's Wells."

"You sound as if you know the lady personally."

"Oh, my, no. I've never met her. Well, one doesn't socialize with professional entertainers, naturally. However, I've always admired Fannie Price's singing, and I've followed her career."

"Miss Price does have a lovely voice," Sophia agreed. She turned her attention back to the stage. Lingering in the back of her mind, though, was an impression that Lady Winwood had been distinctly overset by the appearance of Fannie Price on stage. Why? Why should she care where the singer performed?

The answer to Sophia's question, or at least a glimmering, came at the end of the first act, when the principals took their bows. As she acknowledged the applause, Fannie Price ignored the rest of the audience and directed all her attention to Sophia's box. And, in view of the encounter earlier today in the Park, Sophia was under no illusions that Miss Price was expending her seductive smiles and grateful bows on the female occupants of the box. Sophia flashed a glance behind her to Joel. He was gazing at the stage, clapping politely, his face a blank. Beside her, Georgina Winwood sat like a marble garden statue, her features equally blank.

Even before the singers had left the stage for the interval, gentlemen began arriving in the box to pay their compliments. Nevil Royce was the first, sitting down beside Edwina and totally monopolizing her attention. Lord Sanditon promptly put in an appearance, doing the same to Caroline. Other gentlemen followed. An usher came to the box with a note for Joel, who glanced at it briefly and tucked it into an inner pocket.

As the orchestra filed in and began tuning their instruments the visitors started to leave. Another usher came to the box with a second note for Joel. This time he leaned over to speak to Sophia. "Will you excuse me? When Jack Saintsbury was visiting with us a bit ago I forgot to remind him to see me before he speaks tomorrow in the house."

"Of course." Sophia hoped her expression matched the calm of her voice. She was trying very hard to curb her annoyance. Joel must think she was a country-bred ninnyhammer, unable to reason between cause and effect. His excuse to leave the box was transparently thin, coming as it did so soon after the arrival of that second note.

As the opera progressed during the next few minutes she glanced frequently down at Jack Saintsbury, plainly visible in the pit, chatting with Lord Sanditon. Joel didn't join him, nor had she expected him to. He'd gone off to see Fannie Price, who had made a second peremptory summons when he hadn't responded to the first one. He returned to the box shortly after the auburn-haired countess made her second act entrance.

Turning her head, Sophia smiled sweetly, saying to Joel as

he sat down behind her, "Did you conclude your business with Mr. Saintsbury satisfactorily?"

For a moment he looked blank. Then he said, "Oh, yes, thank you. Actually, the matter wasn't very important."

Wasn't it, though, Sophia thought spitefully. Miss Price's demands don't rank as high as a political emergency? How nice to know. She bit her lip. She'd come perilously close to expressing her thoughts aloud.

By the end of the fourth act of the opera she was still simmering with resentment. In the darkness of the carriage on the return drive to Brook Street after the opera, her mind was so distracted that she had to force herself to pay attention to the conversation of her companions.

Edwina chattered excitedly, ecstatic about a scheme Captain Royce had broached. "Sophy, the most exciting news. Nevil's mama"—now when had the captain become Nevil?—"would like to organize a day-long barge trip on the Thames, perhaps as far as Kew. We'd picnic on the river bank, and Lady Middleton thinks it would be a grand touch if we had musicians aboard during the voyage."

Sophia roused herself. "Really? That sounds like an interesting excursion."

"Isn't it, though? So I can tell Lady Middleton, then, that you approve?"

Sophia's brain was too occupied to think of a convincing excuse. "Why not?"

Caroline said, "Sophy, Lord Sanditon knows a lady who operates a very progressive academy for young ladies in Tunbridge Wells. He would like to introduce me to her, with your permission."

"Oh—let me think about it, Caroline. Talk to me tomorrow."

Joel, who was sitting beside Sophia on the forward facing seat of the town carriage, murmured, "Are you feeling quite the thing, Sophia? Do you have the headache? You don't seem yourself."

She grasped at the excuse. "I do have the headache. Do you

mind if I close my eyes and don't talk?" Then she was free to wallow in the anger that had been building up inside her since Joel had left their box to visit his inamorata.

Why was she so angry, she asked herself. It wasn't that she condemned him for having a mistress, or a dozen, if he chose. She and Joel had contracted for a marriage of convenience, and that contract had included no mention of outside romantic interests. She had no right to be jealous of him—which she wasn't, of course.

No, what she resented was the public humiliation she'd experienced. The audience at the Italian Opera House—more than three thousand people, at a guess, and a goodly percentage of them were acquainted with Joel—had witnessed Fannie Price's shameless posturing to him from the stage. A fair number must have noticed the delivery of notes to the box and Joel's subsequent absence, and drawn their own conclusion.

Was she being entirely too thin-skinned? No, she didn't think so. Lady Winwood had once remarked to her that it was easy enough to avoid scandal. One had only to be discreet in one's romantic affairs. Joel hadn't been discreet.

As he walked with her into the hall after their arrival in Brook Street from the opera, Joel said with an air of concern, "I think you tried to do too much, so soon after your experience in Battersea Fields. I hope you'll be free of the headache after a good night's sleep. Don't forget. Tomorrow night is our engagement ball. I guarantee you won't get much sleep on that occasion!"

Sophia smiled, saying pleasantly, "Oh, I'm sure the headache won't persist. I have every intention of enjoying our engagement ball."

"I, too. Until tomorrow evening, then." He lifted her hand to his lips, brushing a light kiss against her fingers.

The contact startled her. Since the beginning of their engagement he hadn't made any physical overtures to her, except the brief kissing of her wrist the day they had agreed to a marriage of convenience. Why had he done so now? Because he felt guilty about Fannie Price? She had to resist the impulse to snatch her hand away, thereby betraying her feelings. Instead, she allowed her fingers to linger in his grasp for a moment before gently withdrawing them. "Goodnight, Joel. Until tomorrow."

On the following night, Sophia and her sisters drove with Joel to Winwood House in Hanover Square. Georgina had asked them to arrive slightly earlier than the other guests, so the roadway around the railed central garden was not yet crowded with carriages. Number 24, however, was brilliantly lit from the ground floor through its first three storeys, and footmen in liveries and powdered wigs lined the red-carpeted steps.

As they began the walk up the long flight of stairs leading to the ballroom, Joel said to Sophia in a low voice, "You're not nervous about tonight, are you? It's just another ball, you know, even if it is in our honor."

Sophia smiled at him. "No, not nervous at all."

No, she wasn't nervous. In fact, she was quite at peace with herself, and with Joel. In the hours since she'd last seen him, she'd been doing a considerable amount of soul-searching about the incident at the opera. She'd concluded that she'd made far too much of it. Joel hadn't intended to humiliate her by leaving their box to visit Fannie Price. Most probably, he'd merely been trying to ensure that a third embarrassing summons from the actress wouldn't arrive, making an awkward situation even worse.

As to the fact that Joel had a mistress, well, most men did, although Bartholomew—staid, old-fashioned Bartholomew—certainly hadn't, at least none that she'd ever heard of. In any case, the liaison had begun before Joel ever met Sophia, and she had no way of knowing how deeply his affections were engaged. All in all, she had determined her best course was to simply ignore the incident.

Lord and Lady Winwood were standing at the head of the staircase. Georgina said approvingly to Sophia and her sisters, "You look lovely, all three of you. Caroline, Edwina, please take seats at the side of the room. Sophia of course, must remain in the receiving line until most of the guests have arrived."

As she walked away, Edwina said saucily, "All the more dances for Caroline and me, Sophy, while you're busy greeting your guests and well-wishers."

Joel chuckled. "I can't imagine a situation anywhere, at anytime, where Edwina would be without dancing partners!"

The guests started arriving then, and Sophia had to concentrate on faces and names. Fortunately, she'd acquired a social manner in her few brief weeks among the London ton. The receiving line wasn't the ordeal it would have been earlier, nevertheless, she sighed with relief when Lady Winwood said, "We've stood here long enough. I've ordered the orchestra to strike up. Late arrivals can seek us out."

Georgina drew Sophia aside. Her forehead puckered in a frown, she said in a low voice, "I've been wanting to talk to you about what, er happened at the opera last night."

"You mean Fannie Price?"

Georgina looked uncomfortable. "Yes, Fannie Price. That dreadful creature! I never dreamed she could be so vulgar playing to Joel like that from the stage, making it so obvious that he and she were . . . Well, that's neither here nor there. She put Joel in an impossible situation."

Before she could stop herself, Sophia blurted, "Perhaps she felt justified. She is Joel's mistress?"

Georgina looked even more uncomfortable. "Yes," she said reluctantly. "That is, I presume she is. Nephews don't confide too many details of their romantic entanglements to their aunts you know. But the relationship began long before he met you, Sophia. And in any case . . ."

"In any case, gentlemen do take mistresses, and their well-bred wives are supposed to pretend ignorance of the arrangements. I understand perfectly."

The worried expression faded from Lady Winwood's face. She beamed. "You have such good sense, Sophia. And I can assure you that you'll never be subjected to such embarrassment again. Joel won't allow it." After a moment she added, "My dear, we females must be practical about these situations. I'm sure the Price creature was never any more to Joel than a—a pleasant diversion."

Sophia smiled. "I'm sure you're right. I certainly don't intend to lose any sleep over the matter." And she meant what she said.

At a mid-point in the ball, before the supper interval, Lady Winwood exclaimed to Sophia, who was standing next to her at the side of the ballroom, "I don't believe it. I felt obliged to send him an invitation, but I never dreamed he would come!"

"Who?" Sophia stared at the tall gentleman who was slowly advancing toward them.

"Kennington. My brother. Joel's father," Lady Winwood said under her breath, as the gentleman stopped in front of them.

He bowed. "Georgina. You seem surprised to see me."

The Marquess of Kennington was not a young man. His still-thick hair was completely gray and there were lines in his lean face. However, his trim figure was erect and graceful and there was something about the cool, direct glance of his gray eyes that reminded her rather uncomfortably of his son.

"Well, Philip, I certainly didn't expect you to come all the way from Yorkshire for a ball," Lady Winwood retorted. "To my knowledge you haven't been to London for five years and more. You've always said you hated the place."

The marquess raised an eyebrow. "But this is a special occasion, is it not? My son's engagement ball. I felt I must make the effort." He gave Sophia a politely inquiring look.

Sounding somewhat less self-assured than she normally did, Lady Winwood said, "Lord Kennington, may I present Mrs. Ashley?"

Sophia curtsied.

The marquess's gray glance sharpened. "Sophia Ashley? My son's intended?" He turned to Lady Winwood. "I've come a long distance to make the acquaintance of my son's future wife, Georgina. I should like to have a private chat with her."

"Well, of course, Philip." Did Sophia only imagine a faint

note of apprehension in Lady Winwood's voice? "Why don't you and Sophia go to the morning room? There'll be nobody there. We've put the card players in the library."

"Mrs. Ashley?" The marquess extended his arm. Sophia walked with him down the stairs. He opened the door of the morning room and stood aside politely to allow her to precede him. He closed the door after them. Motioning for her to sit down, he took a chair opposite her. He looked at her closely for several long, unnerving moments. Sophia felt as if the brilliant gray eyes, so like Joel's, were piercing her soul.

"Well, Mrs. Ashley," he said at last, "this has been a rather sudden betrothal, has it not?"

"More sudden than most, I daresay," Sophia replied composedly. "Lord Leyburn—Joel—and I decided we wished to be married and saw no reason to wait."

"Indeed. I saw the announcement in the *Times*. I believe your father, Horace Dalton, was a clergyman?"

"Yes. He was the vicar of St. Bede's in Woodbridge."

"And his family? I'm not familiar with the name of Dalton."

Conscious of a slowly increasing feeling of resentment, Sophia eyed the marquess defiantly. "There's no reason why you should be familiar with the Dalton family," she said. "From your point of view I'm sure we're not distinguished. Let me give you the details. My paternal grandfather was a county squire in Cheshire. Papa was a younger son. Penniless, of course. In case you're interested in my mother, I should tell you that she was the daughter of Sir George Weare, a very minor baronet. As you've probably gathered, I'm a widow. My late husband was Bartholomew Ashley. He came from yeoman stock. Fortunately, he was able to turn his inheritance of a small farm into the ownership of a large cotton spinning mill."

As he listened, Lord Kennington's expression had grown steadily colder. "Permit me to tell you something of our family, Mrs. Ashley. The first Baron Hilliard came over with the Conqueror. The eighth baron was created Earl of Leyburn. King Charles II bestowed the title of Marquess of Kennington on the ninth earl, in recognition of some slight service rendered His Majesty's martyred father at the Battle of Naseby."

"A very distinguished ancestry, Lord Kennington. I congratulate you."

"I have no need of your congratulations. My family situation is self-evident," the marquess retorted. His eyes narrowed, becoming even colder. "With such an ancestry, I find it hard to understand why my son proposes to marry a young woman who is—pray forgive my bluntness—a social nobody. Perhaps you're about to tell me that the explanation is romantic, if rather vulgar? You and Joel fell madly in love with each other, as the saying goes?"

"I'm not about to tell you anything," Sophia snapped. "Your son and I have agreed to marry. That should be enough for you. We are both adults of independent means."

"Oh, but it's not enough. I refuse to consent to the marriage of my son and heir to a woman who is so far beneath him."

Sophia rose, blinking back angry tears. "Please communicate your views to your son and heir, Lord Kennington. I refuse to listen to any more of them." She marched to the door, pulled it open and hurried into the hall.

"Sophia—what's the matter?"

She looked up into Joel's concerned face. "Your father has just informed me that I'm not good enough to marry into the Hilliard family. I gather he's prepared to forbid the banns."

His face darkened. "Don't pay any attention to what my father said. He has nothing to say about my plans, marital or otherwise. Where is he, in the morning room? I'll speak to him immediately and put him straight." Placing his hand briefly on her shoulder in a reassuring gesture, he wrenched open the door of the morning room and stalked inside.

More agitated than she would have cared to admit, Sophia stood in the hallway for several moments, trying for calm. Then, fearful that someone might observe her distress, she retreated toward the rear of the hall to the library and slipped inside. The handful of card players, most of them elderly, glanced up briefly and indifferently at her entrance and immediately returned to their games.

Sitting down, Sophia took several deep breaths as she composed herself. The Marquess of Kennington's carelessly demeaning remarks had affected her like a knife wound to the heart. His opinion of her was even more chilling because it had been so impersonal. He didn't care a fig for her character, her appearance, her accomplishments. All that mattered to him was his conviction that she was an inferior human being who could not be allowed to join his family.

Sophia's spirits lifted as she recalled Joel's instant repudiation of his father's remarks. She felt both gratitude and admiration for him, because, though he and the marquess were estranged, it must surely be painful for him to go against his father's wishes.

Several minutes later, more relaxed, and confident she could face her fellow guests without a tell-tale revelation of her feelings, Sophia left the library. Passing the morning room door, which she noticed was slightly ajar, she paused instinctively as she heard her name.

"I forbid you to marry the Ashley woman," came the marquess's venomous voice. "I forbid you to desecrate the blood line of the Hilliards."

"Oh, for God's sake, Father, don't talk fustian. I won't be the first Hilliard to desecrate the sacred blood lines, not by a long shot. During the Civil Wars one of our ancestors married a farmer's daughter who sheltered him from the Roundheads, and your own grandfather married a banker's heiress to preserve the family fortunes during the South Sea Bubble. Tell me—if I had applied to you, would you have advanced me the fifty thousand pounds I needed to keep myself out of debtors' prison?"

There was a brief pause. Then the marquess said, "Not unless you had been willing to abandon this Tory nonsense and return to your family traditions."

"Exactly. You'd have let me rot in prison until I came around to your views. No, Father. I was more than willing to marry

Sophia Ashley in order to save my hide. It's true, she's far from the wife I would have chosen. She has no background, and no pretensions to gentility, but she's a handsome girl and she's learned to conduct herself like a lady. I don't think she'll disgrace me. And don't forget, she has money. A great deal of it."

While Joel was speaking, Sophia had stood listening, rooted to the floor unable to move a muscle to get away from the sound of his wounding voice. As he finished, however, several people appeared in the hallway, coming toward her in the direction of the library. Their presence roused her from her temporary paralysis. She hurried off before Joel or his father could emerge from the morning room and discover she had been eavesdropping.

Nine

On the following afternoon Edwina poked her head around the door of the morning room, saying, "Still working, Sophy? It's almost time for our visit to Somerset House. Joel will be here at any moment."

Sophia put down her pen, her lips forming the refusal she had been about to make. *No I don't care to visit Somerset House Today.* Instead, she said, "Thank you, Edwina. I'd lost track of the time. I'll go up and put on my bonnet and pelisse."

In her bedchamber Sophia buttoned her muslin pelisse and jammed a straw bonnet over her hair, steeling herself for a meeting with Joel. She hadn't wanted to see him, at least not so soon, not today, but at the same time she realized it would be a tactical error to avoid him.

She'd spent a miserable night, and an equally miserable morning, after overhearing Joel Leyburn's talk with his father.

She felt betrayed and humiliated and incredibly naive. She'd really believed in the pleasant, hypocritical facade Joel Leyburn had worn for the public. She'd really believed that he'd become reconciled to their marriage, not merely out of necessity, but because he'd begun to have some genuine liking and respect for her and her family.

Sophia had resentfully recalled all the instances of Joel's falsely friendly behavior. His good nature, almost affectionate, bantering with Tristan. His teasing, big brotherly attitude toward Caroline and Edwina. The numerous graceful little compliments he'd thrown her way. The crowning gift of his mother's necklace.

Everything he'd said and done had been a lie, designed to lull her into being a docile bride who would not disturb his comfortable way of life. He hadn't changed his mind about her, or her suitability to be his wife. He still regarded her as deeply beneath him, as someone he was prepared to marry only because imprisonment and disgrace were an infinitely worse fate.

During the long hours of the night Sophia had more than once decided to break off the engagement. How could she tolerate the prospect of marriage to a man who despised her origins, a man who thought of her, not as a person, but as a bank account? But if she didn't marry Joel wouldn't she be depriving Caroline, Edwina and Tristan of their only opportunities to escape from their narrow lives in Lancashire?

There was her own self-esteem to consider, too. Did she want to be branded a jilt, someone who had cried off from the match of the Season on the Marriage Mart? Or, worse still, did she want to face the innuendoes, the gossip, that it was Joel, perhaps, who had ended the engagement because in the end, he hadn't been able to stomach the idea of marriage to a Lancashire mill owner's widow?

In the end, Sophia had decided to let the engagement stand, with the promise to herself that she would never allow Joel to learn that she'd overheard his denigrating remarks to his father, or how much his words had hurt her. It went without saying that she would never be deceived by him again.

She pasted a pleasant expression on her face as she came

down the stairs and walked to the drawing room. Joel was waiting for her with Caroline and Edwina.

"There you are, Sophia," Joel remarked with one of his familiar engaging smiles that she now resented as a part of his practiced facade. "I came here today half expecting to hear that you'd quite worn yourself out with all that dancing last night and wouldn't care to visit the Royal Academy as we'd planned."

With what she hoped was an easy composure, Sophia replied, "Oh, I think you'll find, when you know me better, Joel, that I don't tire easily."

"I'm happy to hear it. I hope to enjoy many more balls with you in the future, that is, if I can manage to tear you away from your many eager partners!"

The pretty little compliment only irritated Sophia. She turned her head away to hide her feelings.

Passing by in the hallway with Mark Ingram, Tristan spotted Joel in the drawing room and came in. "Hallo, Lord Leyburn, you're just the man Mr. Ingram and I would like to see."

"At your service, Tristan." Joel cocked his eyebrow. "Are you returning from yet another of your famous excursions?"

"Well, er, yes, after a manner of speaking." Tristan slanted a sideways glance at his tutor.

Sophia exclaimed, "Mark! You didn't take Tristan back to Battersea Fields?"

"Indeed not, Mrs. Ashley," Mark replied grimly. "You have my word. Battersea Fields is out of bounds forever. Besides, their fair is held only on Sundays." He paused, looking acutely embarrassed. "Actually, Tristan and I went to Bond Street today to see Oliver Cromwell's head."

"It's a gruesome sight, Joel," Tristan said with relish. "The head's embalmed, you know."

Joel laughed. "Lord, don't I know. I had no idea the thing was still being exhibited. What else did you do today?"

"We tried to find somebody called the Irish Giant, who's supposed to be nine feet high, but no one seemed to know where he was," Tristan said. "I say, Joel, Mr. Ingram and I would like awfully to attend a sitting of the House of Commons. We were told we could attend only by a written order from a Member. Could you arrange a visit for us?"

"Certainly. I'll be happy to write you an order of admission. With your sister's permission, of course. Some of the sessions run very late in the evening."

"Oh, I'm sure Sophy wouldn't mind, just this once." Tristan grinned at his sister. "It will be sleep well lost, I'm sure you'll agree. Thanks, Joel."

Joel's lips curled in amusement as he watched Tristan scamper away. "I hope the lad won't be bored with our performance in the Commons," he remarked to Sophia. "We can be very long-winded! Well, then shall we go?"

Joel caught Sophia's arm to delay her after Caroline and Edwina preceded them into the hallway. "I wanted to show you something," he said, taking a piece of paper out of an inner pocket of his coat.

Her eyes widening, Sophia examined the I.O.U. for fifty thousand pounds. It was marked, *Paid-in-full.*

Giving a quizzical smile, Joel said, "Don't you feel relieved to know that your husband-to-be is no longer in danger of going to debtors' prison, thanks to your largess?"

"Oh, indeed, very relieved." A thought struck Sophia. "Strictly speaking you're no longer in danger of being forced into a marriage of convenience, either."

"What?" Joel looked dumbstruck.

Sophia shrugged. "You've paid your debt. You could change your mind about our marriage without incurring any penalty. What could I do to force you to keep to our bargain, legally or otherwise?"

"Sophia! What do you take me for? Force me to keep to our—our—bargain?" Joel expostulated. His outraged expression, which appeared to be quite genuine, faded as he looked more closely at her. Rather uncertainly he added, "I see what it is. You're funning, aren't you? You don't really believe I'd be so dishonorable as to break my word? Or that I would want to?"

"No, of course not," Sophia said lightly. "You were right, I was funning. Perhaps you should remember in future, however, that I do have a sense of humor. Shall we join my sisters?"

She felt a little smug as he helped her into the landau waiting in front of the house. For one of the few times in their acquaintance, she had thrown him off balance. She hoped to keep him there as much as possible. Her gratified feeling lasted through a rather dull afternoon of viewing the latest pictures to be hung at the Royal Academy.

Several evenings later, Joel and Sophia drove along Bond Street in the direction of St. James's Street and Pall Mall on their way to the premier event of the Season, the Regent's fete in honor of the French royal family at Carlton House.

Joel remarked, "Did I tell you how much I like your gown? That shade of blue-green is very becoming."

"Thank you." Sophia forced herself to sound appreciative. He was still playing the attentive groom-to-be, and she had no choice but to accept his posturing with what grace she could muster.

He cleared his throat. "We've had very little opportunity to talk privately of late."

With a slight feeling of surprise she realized that he was right. Since their engagement they had been constantly together, but invariably in the company of her family and his friends.

"I've been wondering—" he cleared his throat again, "are you annoyed with me, Sophia? You've seemed a little, well, distant, recently. Have I said something, done something, that has offended you without being aware of it?"

She gazed at his profile, etched against the darkening twilight sky outside. "Offended? Of course not. What could I possibly be offended about?"

"I'm glad to hear it," he replied, sounding relieved. "Sophia, as I said, we've had little occasion to speak privately since our engagement, and it occurred to me today that we haven't set a definite date for our wedding."

"Yes, that's true." Sophia frowned. "Actually, I was assuming there was no hurry to set a date, because we'd agreed tentatively that the wedding should be at the end of the Season, and that seemed such a long time in the future. But of course time has passed, and the Season will end in only six weeks. Yes, we should set a date. Some time in the last week of July, perhaps?"

"Much sooner, I think. Look, you came to London to establish your sisters. Wouldn't it be socially more impressive, in the event either or both of them found a suitable *parti,* if you and I, as Earl and Countess of Leyburn, graciously gave our joint consent to the marriages?"

"Why, very possibly, yes."

"Well, then. Shall we say the wedding will be Saturday week?"

Sophia suppressed a gasp. "Saturday week? What about the banns?"

"Oh, I'm told only the unfashionables post the banns these days. We'll have a special license. Fortunately, I know the Archbishop of Canterbury personally, though I daresay there wouldn't be a problem in any case. And what do you think about St. George's Church? I know Aunt Georgina leans toward St. George's, so close to her house and the elaborate wedding breakfast she and Uncle Horace intend to hold."

Joel paused, gazing at Sophia expectantly.

For one of the few times in her life, Sophia was speechless. Why was Joel insisting that they get married earlier than they had planned? He certainly wasn't motivated by any romantic urge to make her his wife as soon as possible.

Suddenly she clenched her hands together. Of course. He'd wearied of the necessity of spending his days and nights playing the role of attentive, dutiful fiancé. Once safely married, he need only escort her to the more important events and act as host when they entertained. The rest of his time would be his

own. Essentially he would be free to enjoy his bachelor pursuits
as he always had.

"Sophia?"

Recovering her poise, she replied, "I have no objection to
Saturday week." She could say it truthfully. She'd made up her
mind to go through with her agreement to marry Joel, so why
should the date matter? Possibly, as he'd suggested, Edwina and
Caroline might appear to be greater matrimonial catches if they
were already the sisters-in-law of the Earl of Leyburn.

"Capital. That's settled, then," Joel said, reaching over to
touch her hand briefly. He glanced out the window of the carriage. "I'm afraid the fete will be a dreadful squeeze. We were
invited for nine o'clock—along with two thousand other people,
so I hear—and already, at just past eight o'clock, a solid line
of carriages extends from the top of St. James's Street to Carlton
House."

Having virtually inched their way down St. James's and into
Pall Mall, Sophia and Joel finally left their carriage and entered
the courtyard of Carlton House, where a full band of the Guards
in State uniform was playing. Members of the Prince's Household received them in the hall to take their cards of invitation
and direct them to a suite of rooms on the ground floor.

"My dears, what a crush," Georgina murmured, who, with
Lord Winwood, joined them as they entered a large hall hung
with what Georgina described as the Regent's choice collection
of Dutch paintings.

Taking Sophia's arm, Lady Winwood said, gazing around her
with intense interest, "I'm utterly fascinated to see the interior
of this place at last. Few people have ever been inside Carlton
House, you know. The Prince has rarely entertained here. Well,
he really couldn't entertain, because then he'd have been obliged
to allow his dreadful wife to act as his hostess." Georgina shud-
dered.

Putting her problems with Joel out of her mind, Sophia found
herself equally fascinated with the Regent's home. She duly
admired the Gothic library, the golden drawing room with its

heavily gilded Corinthian pillars and the dining room, the ceiling of which was painted to resemble a summer sky.

The Gothic conservatory was the crowning glory of Carlton House, designed like a cathedral, with a nave and two aisles, and with stained glass windows containing the arms of all the kings of England and their heirs as Princes of Wales. Supper for the more important guests at the fete would be served in the conservatory.

"I can't believe my eyes," Sophia said in a low voice to Georgina as she gazed at the dining table, two hundred feet long, that extended the length of the conservatory and into the dining room. The table was already set with an elaborate silver service, and down its center flowed a stream of water, with mosses and flowers growing along its banks. Tiny bridges crossed the stream at intervals, and gold and silver fish darted in its depths.

"I've never seen the like," Lady Winwood agreed. "I don't say that I'd choose to decorate my table in such a way myself, but—" She paused, giggling, "Promise me that you and Joel will never preside over a dining table with a river flowing through it!"

Sophia laughed. "Oh, I think I can safely promise that."

Joel joined them, saying in a low voice, "The Regent is making his entrance."

Sophia had never seen the prince in person. She stared, mesmerized, at the man who was almost a legend to her, a stout figure in an ornate uniform, lavishly embroidered even on the seams, with the Garter star blazing on his chest. Still handsome in a high-colored, overblown way, the Regent nodded and smiled benignly as he walked through the room.

"He's wearing a field marshal's uniform," Joel murmured, a quiver of amusement in his voice. "One of his first acts as Regent was to appoint himself a field marshal."

In a few minutes the guests of honor, the exiled French royal family, arrived. Sophia studied them intently. She knew that Caroline, the scholar of the family and would-be schoolmistress, would be eager to know every detail about them. Sophia was only sorry she would have to report that the man who would be France's next king, after Napoleon was defeated, of course, was so fat he could scarcely walk, and that his daughter-in-law, the only surviving child of the dazzling Queen Marie Antoinette, was hopelessly dowdy.

Ever a good host, the Regent circulated among his guests. At one point, he came up to Joel's party. "Ah, there you are, Leyburn. And Lord and Lady Winwood." He gazed questioningly at Sophia.

Joel bowed. "Your Royal Highness, may I present Mrs. Ashley?"

The prince eyed Sophia with distinct approval, and graciously acknowledged her curtsy. Up close, she discovered that his famous charm, despite the ravages of time and dissipation, was still very real. As was his eye, apparently, for the ladies.

"I say, Leyburn, I do keep *au courant* about my friends' doings," he remarked jovially. "I'd heard you were to become a Benedict at last. When is the wedding?"

"Saturday week, sir."

"Splendid. Tell my equerry the time and place. I'll be there to see you leg-shackled. I love weddings."

"But Joel," Sophia muttered in a panic after the prince, with another affable smile, moved away, "It will be a small wedding, we agreed. Family and friends only."

Joel grinned. "Face it, Sophia, we'll have one extra guest. Divine right of kings, and all that."

Georgina gave him a reproachful look. "Don't be frivolous, Joel. I hadn't planned on entertaining royalty. And I must say," she added with increasing indignation, "I hardly expected to receive the news of the exact date of my nephew's wedding from the Prince Regent!"

The ton's notion of a small wedding, confined to family and friends, was different from the modest event such an occasion would have been in Lancashire, reflected Sophia. She was in a minor state of shock as she glimpsed the crowded interior of St. George's, Hanover Square, and began the walk down the aisle on Tristan's arm on the morning of her wedding.

The pews in the tunnel-shaped nave were filled—the Regent occupied the first pew with several members of his household—and a number of guests were sitting in the galleries. Small wedding, indeed. Joel's friends must have included most of the members of the House of Commons, as well as every prominent member of the ton.

Dismissing her errant thoughts, she concentrated on following Caroline and Edwina down the aisle to the chancel railing, where Joel and Lord Winwood waited with the priest.

She knew she looked well, in her gown of gossamer silk gauze in her favorite shade of deep blue, with a circlet of white rosebuds twined in her hair, but she felt curiously light-headed, and her hands were like lumps of ice. One part of her mind accepted that she was indeed getting married. Another part insisted she was living in a dream from which she'd soon awaken.

Stealing a sideways glance at Joel, she thought he appeared paler than usual. However, his hand, when he placed the ring on her finger, was quite warm and vital. His voice, too, was calm as he made the responses, and his eyes, when he looked down at her after the priest had pronounced them man and wife, were their usual cool, incisive gray. Apparently his heart wasn't pounding, and his nerves weren't skittering wildly on the surface of his skin.

Then it was over. She walked down the aisle on Joel's arm, past a blur of faces, signed the registry with leaden fingers and climbed into the carriage for the short drive to Winwood House in Hanover Square.

"Well, we've actually done it," Joel commented as the carriage swung out of George Street into the square. "Do you think you'll find it difficult to adjust to being a married lady, Sophia?"

She looked into his composed, faintly amused face and took a deep breath, willing her treacherous feelings under control.

She would not let him know that the ground felt like shifting quicksands beneath her feet. "Why should I find it difficult?" she asked, looking straight into his eyes. "Recall, I've been married before."

An indefinable expression crossed his face. Chagrin? Uncertainty? She couldn't tell.

"In one respect, I will be obliged to adjust, however," Sophia went on in a matter-of-fact tone. "Never in my wildest dreams did I ever suspect that folks would one day be calling me Lady Something-or-other."

If she had momentarily disturbed Joel's poise, it wasn't apparent as he replied with an easy smile, "It's Lady Leyburn, Sophia. You must begin getting accustomed to your new name."

If the London version of a small wedding differed from a similar event in Lancashire, so, too, did the wedding breakfast hosted by the Winwoods. The wedding had taken place close to noon, at the latest allowable legal hour, and the breakfast was really a lavish afternoon banquet, served at small tables set up in the large ballroom. Sophia and Joel and the Winwoods sat at the table with the Regent and several of his equerries.

The prince ate copiously and appreciatively. "My dear Lady Winwood, allow me to congratulate you on setting a most excellent table," he told Georgina. "I quite fancy this materlote in Bordeaux sauce. You must give the recipe to my chef."

A little later he cocked his head at Sophia, saying, "I shouldn't be surprised if you're our next great political hostess, Lady Leyburn. You must assist this husband of yours as much as possible. I value him, you know. He's one of my mainstays in the Commons."

Nor did the prince's affability end with Sophia and Joel. A wide-eyed Edwina reported, "Sophy, His Royal Highness told me he admired my gown, and said he hoped to be invited to my wedding!"

On the whole, contact with royalty filled Sophia's family with awe. Caroline murmured, "Sophy, who could have imagined that the prime minister of England and the Prince Regent would both be guests at your wedding?"

For once Tristan, in the tow of Mark Ingram, was largely speechless, finding little more to say than that he understood the design of the Regent's new mews in Brighton was all the crack, and he'd like to see the building. He didn't quite like to mention the subject to the prince himself, although the Regent seemed a very good sort, so could Sophy wangle him an invitation, did he think?

"Tristan!" Mark said in a strangled voice.

"Now, what is it?" Tristan inquired innocently.

Sophia sighed. "Never mind, Mark. Tristan, I am not going to discuss the Regent's stables with him on my wedding day."

At last the interminable afternoon was over, and it was time to go. Sophia went upstairs to change into a carriage dress and pelisse and bonnet. Her sisters accompanied her.

Her eyes brimming with tears, Edwina sniffled, "I hate to see you go, Sophy."

Turning from the wardrobe, where she was hanging Sophia's wedding dress, Caroline exclaimed, "Don't be such a peagoose, Edwina. Sophy isn't going to the Antipodes. She and Joel will be back in Brook Street on Monday."

Edwina wiped her eyes. "I know, but things won't be the same, will they? Sophy's a married woman now."

Forbearing to remind Edwina that, until Bartholomew's death, she had also been a married woman, Sophia patted her sister's shoulder, saying, "Caroline is right. I'll be back before you know I'm gone. And I'm sure you'll be very comfortable with Lady Winwood. It was kind of her to invite you and Caroline to stay with her during the next few days."

Sophia hugged her sisters and bade them a cheeful goodbye. As she went downstairs to join Joel in the waiting carriage, however, she knew exactly how Edwina was feeling, and shared her misgivings. Things wouldn't be the same, especially for her family, now that she was Lady Leyburn.

Ordinarily Sophia would have been charmed by an afternoon drive on a smiling June day, through Knightsbridge, Kensington, Hammersmith, Kew and Chiswick along the great bend of the Thames to Richmond. Today, though, she had to ignore the scenery and concentrate all her attention on conducting a prosaic, friendly conversation with a man she'd thought she knew very well, but who had suddenly become her stranger-husband. A totally different person, somehow, from the agreeable, attentive companion of their engagement. A man with whom tonight she would be . . .

She made in involuntary movement.

"What is it, Sophia? Aren't you comfortable?"

"Oh, yes. Perfectly." She managed a smile. "I was quite impressed by the compliment the Regent paid you at the breakfast. Apparently you're one of his greatest supporters in the Commons."

Joel laughed. "A royal exaggeration. Prinny likes to think that he's single-handedly leading the assault against Napoleon, you see, and he values me because I'm one of his Tory warhawks." After a moment Joel said, "I hope you'll like the Emperor's House. It was generous of Dick Saintsbury to offer it to us for the weekend, expecially since Richmond is only ten miles from London."

"The Emperor's House?"

"It's a villa just off the Richmond Green, facing the river. Built on the site of the Middle Gate of the old palace, I'm told. Saintsbury's family calls it the Emperor's House because of the statues of Roman emperors in the niches on either side of the portico."

"It sounds very grand."

"Not at all. As I recall, it's simply a very comfortable Palladian-style villa. Actually, I wouldn't mind owning a similar property, as a refuge from the city during the summers. Perhaps we should consider the idea."

The imagery conjured up by Joel's remark threw Sophia into a momentary panic. When she'd agreed to marry him, her thoughts on the subject had somehow stopped short with the wedding ceremony. Now here he was, broaching plans for a joint future she hadn't begun to contemplate.

Apparently he didn't notice her discomfiture. "We're passing through Kew," he said, glancing out the window of the carriage. "We'll soon be in Richmond."

The Emperor's House, as Joel had intimated, was a charming, extremely comfortable dwelling, with extensive grounds planted with fine elms, acadias and Turkey oaks, fronting on the Thames. Attentive servants showed Sophia up to a well-appointed bedchamber, connected by a dressing room with another large bedroom which she assumed belonged to Joel.

Removing her bonnet, Sophia was repairing her coiffure when a knock sounded on the dressing room door. Joel said, "Sophia? It will be an hour before dinner is served. Shall we go for a stroll? I don't think you've been in Richmond previously, and it's a place well worth visiting."

"I'd enjoy a stroll," Sophia called through the door. Anything, she thought with relief, except spending a solitary few hours with Joel, pent-up in their honeymoon refuge. She'd exhausted all her conversational skills during the drive from London.

Joel extended his arm to Sophia as they left the house to enter an area on the west side of the Green flanked by a rude stone arch and a single red brick building. "This is the Old Palace Yard," he explained. "All that's left of the old royal palace. I believe the premises were demolished when King Charles II returned after the Restoration."

Normally, Sophia would have enjoyed the leisurely stroll around the Green, seeing the Theatre Royal, the Old Court House and the lovely Queen Anne houses in Maids of Honour Row. Now, however, she was far too conscious of the firm muscle beneath her fingers as they rested on Joel's broadcloth sleeve, and the faint odor of shaving soap and perfectly laundered linen as he leaned toward her to point out another Richmond landmark, to pay undivided attention to the scenery.

She chided herself. Why was she so distracted by his physical presence? She'd certainly been in close proximity to Joel many times before, in carriages, at the dinner table, in the figures of the country dance and the cotillion. She answered her own question. Joel was her husband now. That was the difference.

"You're very quiet, Sophia," Joel observed as they left the Old Palace Terrace and returned to the Green. "Perhaps you're tired of sightseeing."

"Oh, no not at all," she gabbled, and realized she was gabbling. "Actually, I was thinking how Caroline would love to see all this. She's the scholar of our family, you know. I wish we'd brought her with us."

Joel raised his eyebrow. "Oh, come now, Sophia, I know it isn't unusual for newly married couples to be accompanied by relatives on their wedding journeys, but I heartily disapprove of that notion."

She promptly felt like a fool and was unable to think of a single coherent remark as they walked back to the Emperor's House.

Dick Saintsbury had left his villa fully staffed. His French chef had prepared an exquisite wedding supper. The dining room was a modest size, and, though she and Joel sat at opposite ends of the polished mahogany table, Sophia wasn't conscious of a vast distance between them.

"This chicken is uncommonly good," Joel observed. "What does the chef, Monsieur Nicholas, call the dish? Oh, yes *Les filets de volaille de la marechale*. Now, what do you suppose that means? Which of the wives of Napoleon's marshals is he honoring? No matter, it's delicious."

So were the desserts. *Les gateaux de feuilletages pralin. La gele ce citrons moule*. But the taste of the dinner, including the desserts, was like sawdust in Sophia's mouth. She pushed aside her plate abruptly and rose from the table.

"Joel, I don't care for coffee. I'm very tired. It's been—a—a momentous day. Will you excuse me?"

"Certainly." Joel caught her hand as she passed him. Brushing her fingers against his lips, he murmured, "I'll be with you shortly. A bottle of port is a poor companion on a wedding night!"

In her bedchamber, Sophia tried to calm her errant nerves. Her abigail was of no help. Rose, her eyes agleam with lascivious imaginings, helped her into the silken blue nightdress and the matching peignoir, saying, "You're a beautiful bride, ma'am—I mean, my lady. Just as Lord Leyburn is such a handsome bridegroom."

"Yes, he is. Rosie, I won't need you any more tonight."

After the abigail left, Sophia walked to the window, gazing out over the Richmond Green in the lengthening twilight. She knew she'd been deliberately closing her eyes to the reality of her marital relations with Joel. Obviously, he planned to consummate their marriage. It was, after all, expected of a bridegroom. She knew, with a sudden burst of bitterness, that he would exhibit a suitable passion—*noblesse oblige*—whether or not he actually had any desire to be with his plebeian, unwanted wife.

A soft knock sounded at the door of the dressing room. In a moment, Joel appeared in the doorway. He was wearing a dressing gown and pointed Turkish slippers, and he carried a wine bottle in one hand a pair of glasses in the other.

"It occurred to me that we replied to all the toasts our guests offered us at the wedding breakfast," he said with an easy smile. "But we never toasted each other."

He set the glasses on a table and poured the champagne. Handing a glass to Sophia he said, lifting his own glass, "To my bride."

Her mouth dry, Sophia murmured, "To my bridegroom."

"Dick Saintsbury did well by us," he said, draining his glass and pouring another. "This is a very fine vintage. Brought into the country from France by our very efficient corps of smugglers, no doubt," he added, grimacing. "As a Member of Parliament I should be properly outraged."

He drained his glass and set it down. Gazing at her appreciatively, he said, "I like your nightdress and robe. Blue is your best color. But I expect you know that."

"Thank you. Yes, I like blue." She noted the glimpse of bare skin at his throat and wondered if he was wearing anything beneath his robe.

He walked slowly toward her. Placing his hands on her silken shoulders, he bent his head to kiss her. The touch of his lips, gentle but firm, searching out the sweetness of her mouth, sent fiery arrows of longing coursing through her body. But the memory of his wounding remarks about her to his father, and his cavalier disregard of her feelings at the opera when Fannie Price summoned him to her side, came between her and her sudden desire for her husband. She would not—she could not, for the sake of her fragile self-esteem—allow this man to know how powerfully his physical magnetism affected her. With a supreme effort of her will she kept her lips unresponsive to his kiss.

Lifting his head, he gazed at her questioningly. Then, slipping his arms around her, he drew her close to him. He buried his face in her hair and murmured, "Did I ever tell you what beautiful hair you have? It smells like roses." His lips brushed her throat and went even lower to the swell of her breasts beneath the fragile silk of her peignoir. In a panic she felt the hardness of his arousal and stiffened, refusing to relax against him.

Abruptly Joel released her and stepped back. His face an expressionless mask, he said, "We are married, Sophia. Married couples usually make love on their wedding night. Do I gather you don't wish to consummate our vows?"

Between stiff lips, Sophia said, "We agreed, when we became engaged, that our marriage was primarily a business arrangement. Nevertheless, I'm aware that other factors are involved in our situation. You will be the next Marquess of Kennington, and eventually you will require an heir! I'm quite prepared to do my duty."

"Duty!" The word escaped Joel like an expletive. "I don't make love according to duty. I've never forced myself on an unwilling female, and I don't propose to start now."

Joel drew a quick breath, obviously battening down his anger. "Sophia, I realize now—how it escaped me previously I don't know—that you have no interest in engaging in relations with me. I respect your wishes. You're correct—eventually I will need an heir. This isn't an overwhelming problem, however. I hope my father lives for many years in the future. Shall we say this? Perhaps, as we grow to know each other better in the course of our marriage, you may find yourself more amenable to—er—physical love."

"That might be best. We're virtual strangers to each other. I find it difficult to . . ."

"I understand perfectly, Sophia. Don't concern yourself with regrets of any kind. Goodnight."

After Joel had closed the door of the dressing room behind him, Sophia collapsed on the bed in a fit of weeping. She'd have felt used, soiled, if she'd allowed her husband to make love to her out of a mechanical sense of duty, when he despised her and everything she stood for. And yet . . .

Sophia buried her face in her hands. Her flesh ached from the denial of the hotly sensual impulses that Joel's caresses had aroused in her.

Ten

True to his word, Caroline's new admirer, Lord Sanditon, had arranged a visit to the Tunbridge Wells Female Seminary, and Sophia had accompanied the pair as chaperon.

Miss Tredgold, the headmistress of the seminary, reminded

Sophia a good deal of her masterful-minded old headmistress, Miss Beaton, at the academy in Chester. However, Miss Tredgold seemed even more authoritarian than Miss Beaton.

As Sophia, with Caroline and Lord Sanditon, sat before Miss Tredgold's desk in her office, the schoolmistress expounded on her theories of female education at great length, never pausing long enough to admit of a comment or a question from her listeners. "And I can't emphasize enough," she finished her monologue, "that we must make more room for serious instruction in our female academies by discontinuing the teaching to young females of such useless skills as painting on fans, netting, shell-work, lace-making and wax-work."

Sophia, who as a former schoolmistress herself had been listening with growing impatience, saw her chance. "What about dancing, music, water-coloring, the fine points of etiquette? Aren't they important, too, in the education of young girls?"

Miss Tredgold looked displeased. "My dear Lady Leyburn, those are mere social accomplishments, to be acquired as needed, outside the formal educational experience. "Females, above all, must use their minds, by dint of studying history, mathematics and literature."

Sophia gave it up. On the drive back to London from Tunbridge Wells, she kept largely silent as Caroline and Lord Sanditon spoke enthusiastically about Miss Tredgold and her seminary.

"Oh, I'd like so much to have a part in a school like Miss Tredgold's, where girls could obtain an education equal to that of their brothers," Caroline sighed.

"Indeed," Lord Sanditon seconded earnestly. "Then we might produce more women of the caliber of Hannah More and Mary Wollstonecraft."

Privately, Sophia considered that most parents of young girls would not care to have their daughters resemble either of these two ladies, estimable as both were, but she forebore comment. She believed that Caroline would lose her enthusiasm for advanced female education once she was safely married, and Lord

Sanditon appeared to be an ideal suitor for her. He was attractive, well-born, financially independent and he shared her serious views of life and society. More important, he seemed genuinely smitten with her.

They arrived back in Brook Street in late afternoon. As Sophia entered the hall she saw Mark Ingram emerging from the library. "Back so soon, Mark?" she inquired. "Where did you and Tristan go today?"

"Nowhere, in point of fact. Lord Leyburn took Tristan down to Epsom to visit the stables belonging to a friend. There was no room for me in the curricle, so I stayed behind, catching up on my reading." Mark smiled. "Actually, I was a little relieved. It's becoming more difficult to think of fresh places to take Tristan."

Sophia laughed. "I daresay he wouldn't object to revisiting some of the places where he's already been. Hyde Park, for a balloon ascension, for example?"

As she went up the stairs to her bedchamber, Sophia thought approvingly of Tristan's jaunt to Epsom with Joel. The visit to a gentleman's country home and stables would be a good example for Tristan, a glimpse of the kind of life she wanted him to enjoy when he became an adult and owned his own estate.

How had Joel come to think of inviting Tristan to accompany him to Epsom? It was true, Joel had often been amused by Tristan's brash curiosity, which originally led into the Battersea Fields episode. On the other hand, most men-about-town would certainly have no interest in squiring a stripling about. Was it possible that Joel had begun to like Tristan for himself, whatever were his feelings for Sophia?

As she entered her bedchamber her abigail rose from a chair beside the hearth. "Ye're a mite late, my lady. I've laid out the primrose silk fer yer dinner party tonight, if ye agree."

"Yes, thank you, Rosie. The primrose gown will do very well."

Sophia's reply to the abigail was absent-minded. She was thinking about Joel, trying to untangle her impression of his behavior since their return from their abbreviated wedding trip to Richmond a week ago. After the disaster of their wedding night she'd half-expected him to be hostile, resentful, at the very least coolly aloof. He hadn't exhibited any of those traits. In fact, he'd been his usual pleasant, courteous self. The only difference in their relationship was that he was now living under her roof, in a bedchamber two doors down the corridor from hers.

Well, perhaps there was one slight difference. She'd sensed a faint, almost indefinable distance in his manner. And not once in the past week had he touched her in any way, except to put out a hand to help her in or out of a carriage and then the contact was so fleeting that he might have been snatching his hand from a burning brand.

Rosie was arranging her hair as she sat in front of the dressing table when Tristan's voice sounded in the corridor. "Sophy? Are you decent?"

"Yes. Come, Tristan."

Her brother bounced into the room saying, "Sophy, what a great gun Joel is! He took me to Evasham—that's an estate near Epsom—where his friend Sir Edward Rokesby has a stud farm. You've never seen so many beautiful horses in your life. One of them was last year's Derby winner. How I'd love to own a horse like that. But Joel says it would cost a fortune to buy him."

Sophia said, smiling, "What an interesting excursion. Did it give you ideas for the future?"

"How do you mean?"

"Oh, I thought you might be planning to have your own stud when you grow up."

Shaking his head, Tristan said, "Oh, no. Operating a stud is a business in itself. When I'm managing our mill I won't have the time to devote to a stud. Well, then, I'll leave you to your primping. Joel says you and he are going to a political dinner tonight."

Sophia frowned as Tristan scampered out of the room. Several months of assiduous intellectual pursuits in London had apparently not dampened Tristan's desire to operate a cotton spinning mill. Well, enrollment at Oxford might turn the trick. Providing that she and Mark Ingram could persuade her young brother to attend.

"Will you wear the sapphire necklace, my lady?"

Sophia gazed at the beautiful, glittering thing in the jewelry case the abigail was holding out to her. She remembered so well when Joel had given it to her, before their marriage, and how touched she'd been to learn that the necklace had belonged to his mother. According to Lady Winwood, Joel's father had in his possession a fabulous collection of jewelry, the property of his late wife, and which he had always intended would one day belong to the next Marchioness of Kennington.

Sophia shrugged. She doubted very much that she would ever wear any of the pieces. Joel's father had departed to his estate in Yorkshire immediately after his acrimonious encounters with Sophia and his son, and he'd given no sign that he recognized the marriage. Perhaps, she thought wryly, she might afford the marquess a vindictive pleasure by informing him that his son's marriage was a total sham.

"No, the sapphires wouldn't go well with the primrose gown, Rose," she told the abigail. "I'll wear the pearls tonight." She responded to the light tap at the door, calling, "Come."

A footman entered. "His lordship says to tell ye he will be waiting in the drawing room, my lady, and ye'll be pleased to come down whenever ye're ready."

"Yes. Thank you, Jebson."

When Sophia walked into the drawing room a little later the room was empty. She sat down in a chair near the door to wait for Joel. Soon, she heard footsteps in the hall, and stood about to join him, only to pause, immobile, at the sound of a shrill voice wailing, "But m'lord, I cain't go back ter the mistress wif'out wot she sent me 'ere fer. She'll 'ave me 'ide, that she will!"

Noiselessly, Sophia moved to the drawing room entrance and

peered cautiously around it. Joel was standing at the front door
of the house with a soberly dressed young woman, obviously
of the serving class. The young woman was wringing her hands,
looking up anxiously into Joel's face.

"Take her this," he said coldly. "She'll be perfectly satisfied,
I assure you."

The woman gasped, looking at the banknotes Joel had handed
her. "Lor! Ain't never seen this much rhino all ter once, so ter
speak."

"Go along with you, then. Goodnight."

Sophia heard the front door opening and quickly moved into
the center of the drawing room. Joel entered a few moments
later. He seemed perfectly calm.

"Oh, you're here, Sophia. Did I keep you waiting long? A
business matter came up."

"That's all right. I've only been here a few minutes."

"Shall we go, then?"

During the drive to Dick Saintsbury's house in Golden
Square, Joel was more silent than usual. Sophia knew better
than to ask him questions he most certainly wouldn't answer.
She did wonder, though, who the mysterious woman was, and
why she had visited Joel on what appeared to be a matter of
some urgency. He'd given the woman a large sum of money.
Was he being blackmailed? If so, why? The image of Fannie
Price passed before Sophia's mental eye. But no, the thought
was ridiculous. Why would Fannie Price feel impelled to blackmail Joel? She was already very much in possession of his
heart. Perhaps he had more than one mistress.

She broke what was becoming an uncomfortable silence.
"Tristan really enjoyed his visit to the stud. Thank you for inviting him."

Arousing himself from his thoughts, Joel said, "It was my
pleasure." He smiled. "There's never a dull moment when that
young brother of yours is around." He went on, "I hope you
won't be bored tonight. Dick Saintsbury and his friends have
no interests except politics."

Joel was quite right. After Dick Saintsbury's initial polite greetings—"I hope you enoyed your stay at the Emperor's House in Richmond, Lady Leyburn," and, "all his friends are delighted that Joel has abandoned his bachelor ways"—Saintsbury and his guests, predominantly younger Members of Commons from the Midlands and the North, plunged into an impassioned discussion of politics. They debated interminably the conduct of the war in the Peninsula, the depressed state of the economy, the possibility of the Whigs returning to power when the Regent completed his probationary first year in power.

Paradoxically, Sophia found herself enjoying the evening more than she would have anticipated. For one thing, Saintsbury and his friends were talking about the real problems of a real world, rather than the superficial gossip of the ton, with which she had never really been comfortable. Also, she felt a kinship with these enthusiastic young Tories from her own area of the country.

And on the return drive to Brook Street, she was flabber-gasted to receive a compliment from Joel. "Dick and his friends were very impressed with you," he began.

"Really? Why?"

"They thought you were very knowledgeable about the situation in the Nottingham hosiery districts. They're concerned about the outbreaks of violence in those areas. In the month of March alone, for instance, more than one hundred hosiery frames were destroyed in Nottinghamshire and Derbyshire."

"Oh, that. Yes, Mr. Saintsbury did seem intensely interested in the subject." Sophia shook her head. "I deplore the destruction of property, which should be inviolate, but I'm inclined to sympathize with the hosiers. If it were only a question of opposition to the introduction of new manufacturing methods, in this case the substitution of wide frames for the narrow frames formerly used, that would be one thing. Workers shouldn't be allowed to impede progress. As it happens, however, the use of these wide frames results in a cheaper, inferior product, stockings that fall apart after a few wearings. Even more important to the hosiers, their hours of work and wages have been sharply reduced."

There was a tremor of amusement in Joel's voice as he said, "There you see what I mean? Saintsbury says you're the most intelligent woman he's ever met."

Sophia felt completely taken aback. "Mr. Saintsbury gives me too much credit," she mumbled. She cleared her throat. "Fortunately, we needn't fear the outbreak of such violence in Lancashire, not in my cotton spinning mill in Woodbridge, at any event. My workers are reasonably content. Oh, I've had to cut some of their hours, in order to distribute the available work among more of the workers, but they understand the problem is temporary. Once Napoleon is defeated the cotton spinning business will be prosperous again."

"Perhaps you're being too sanguine, Sophia," Joel said quietly. "Lancashire is just as depressed economically, because of the war and the blockade, as either Yorkshire or Nottinghamshire."

"I trust my workers," Sophia said firmly. "Many of them worked for Bartholomew when he began his spinning operations on the family farm. They're very loyal."

He shrugged and dropped the subject.

When they reached the house in Brook Street they walked side by side down the second floor corridor, pausing outside Sophia's door. Joel looked down at her, smiling faintly. "I enjoyed the evening, Sophia. I hope you did."

"Oh, yes. Very much."

Sophia felt a slow heat rising in her lower abdomen. He was so close. She could smell the distinctive, crisply clean masculine fragrance she'd grown to associate with him. His eyes slowly lightened to a gray flame. Groping, he raised his right hand, brushing her cheek like the faint fluttering of a moth's wing. Abruptly he lowered his hand.

"Goodnight, Sophia."

"Goodnight."

She opened her door and closed it behind her, leaning against the cool wood to support her trembling body.

Her abigail rushed to her. "My lady? Are you feeling poorish?"

"No Rosie, only a trifle fatigued," she lied. She was perfectly aware that if Joel had continued his caress she would have melted into his arms. She hoped he hadn't noticed the effect his nearness had had upon her. It was only a physical reflex, after all. It had nothing to do with the core of their relationship. But the incident caused her to speculate once again about why Joel was so carefully refraining from any show of resentment about the debacle of their wedding night.

On a morning several days later a considerable crowd had already gathered at the landing stairs of Westminster Bridge when Sophia and Joel arrived with Caroline and Edwina. Several large barges, equipped with rows of chairs, brightly colored awnings and a bank of seats for the rowers, were moored at the stairs.

As they left the carriage Joel remarked, raising an eyebrow, "This is quite an elaborate affair."

"Oh, yes," Edwina said eagerly. "Lady Middleton told me she wanted our riverside picnic to be one of the memorable events of the Season. Oh, there's Nevil. May I sit with him, Sophia?"

"Why not?" Sophia returned dryly. The irony was lost on Edwina, who hastened to join Captain Royce. Sophia had no doubt at all that this picnic had been organized by Lady Middleton solely to afford her son Nevil an opportunity to impress Edwina.

The barges soon filled, and the rowers began navigating the vessels upstream. It was a beautiful July day, sunny, not too warm. Sophia relaxed in her chair, listening dreamily to the musicians playing in one of the forward barges, as the boats skimmed the water past Hammersmith and Kew and glided along the great bend of the Thames at Chiswick.

"You seem very thoughtful, Sophia," Joel said from his chair beside hers.

"Oh, no. Lazy is a better word."

She stole a sideways glance at Joel. He was his usual urbane self, superbly dressed in his impeccably tailored coat, tightly fitting pantaloons and shining Hessians. She'd been surprised when he decided to be a part of the picnic excursion. It wasn't an occasion a polished man like him should have felt any obligation to attend. Lady Middleton obviously intended the picnic—aside from her desire to allow Nevil to be with Edwina—as an opportunity for unmarried couples to learn to know each other better, suitably chaperoned by dignified matrons like herself.

"Oh, I doubt that you're ever lazy, Sophia," Joel drawled. "You're much too efficient, managing your family and your business and Lord knows what else."

Sophia darted another look at him. Was he being facetious? Or was there an acid edge to his remark?

The barges glided past Richmond—Sophia felt an odd pang as she glimpsed the grounds of the Emperor's House, the place where she and Joel had stayed during their brief honeymoon—and pulled into an anchorage on a sloping beach leading to the extensive gardens of a large Italianate house. Near the beach a number of small tables were grouped on the smooth grass, set with linen and gleaming china and crystal. Attentive servants in livery hovered behind the tables.

"Wardour House, I believe," Sophia said as Joel helped her out of the barge.

"Yes. Haven't been here in years. I'd forgotten that Lady Middleton's sister is married to the Earl of Wardour. I understand Lady Wardour is very fond of her nephew, Nevil."

Sophia felt a pang as she realized how her lack of knowledge of the relationships among the prominent families of the ton prevented her from understanding fully the small points of the social gatherings she attended. So their hostess today was Captain Royce's aunt. He was even more exclusively the focus of this excursion than she had imagined. She wondered how many other well-placed relatives he had.

The attentive, soft-footed footmen served a delicious lunch. The sommeliers poured fragrant French wines. The musicians played soothing airs. Sophia relaxed again, until she spotted Edwina walking with Nevil Royce along a curve of the bank away from the picnic area. She said abruptly, "Joel, please go after Edwina and Captain Royce and tell them not to stray away from the rest of us."

Not moving, Joel said, "Why should I do that, Sophia? Surely you don't suspect Nevil of any design to molest your sister?"

Sophia flushed scarlet. "Certainly not. I simply want to avoid any damage to Edwina's reputation."

Joel frowned. "I doubt that anyone would raise an eyebrow at the sight of Nevil walking with Edwina. The on dit is that he's smitten with your sister and is on the verge of a proposal. Matter of fact, the betting book at White's is taking odds on the event."

"That's obscene," Sophia retorted angrily. "My sister's name being bandied about the clubs? Why don't you do something about it?"

"No need. There's no disrespect intended, I assure you. Club members will bet on anything, including how long it takes a fly to climb a windowpane."

"And I assure you that your gamblers at White's will never profit from betting on Edwina's activities!" Sophia snapped. "I won't allow Nevil Royce to even propose to my sister."

Joel gazed at her, his expression thoughtful. "Why do you dislike Nevil so much, Sophia?"

"Because he tried to seduce my sister, that's why!" Sophia glared at Joel. "When he first met her, in the Park, and later at Vauxhall Gardens, he assumed she was a lightskirt, ripe for the plucking."

Joel shook his head. "That's not true. I've known Nevil for

many years. From the first moment he laid eyes on Edwina, he was besotted with her. His intentions have always been honorable."

"That's what you say. I don't believe you," she said bitterly. "Oh, doubtless he realized he had to drop his scheme to seduce Edwina, once she became the prospective sister-in-law of an earl! However, even if his intentions are now honorable, I still don't consider him an eligible suitor for my sister. He's a younger son, without prospects—in fact, his wounded arm may never recover enough for him to rejoin his regiment—and I think Edwina could make a much more advantageous marriage."

Joel gave her an oddly considering look. "Do you know what I think, Sophia?" he said softly. "I think you're a snob. Also a very illogical chaperon."

"What?" Sophia couldn't believe what she was hearing.

He nodded. "I don't think you'll meet many young men who can claim a lineage as distinguished as Nevil's. Granted, his pockets are pretty much to let. On the other hand, if you're interested in highly connected marriages for your sisters, I might remind you that Nevil's ancestry far outranks that of young Sanditon."

Joel motioned to Caroline, walking with Lord Sanditon in a direction opposite to that taken by Edwina and Nevil. "I notice you haven't asked me to request Caroline and her swain to stay in sight."

"That's different!"

"Why?"

"Oh—because. Lord Sanditon is a peer in his own right, well-to-do, a Member of Parliament. He would never try to take advantage of Caroline. He's too much of a gentleman."

"I rest my case. I think you are a snob, Sophia."

Sophia turned her head away, too angry to reply. How dare Joel accuse her of snobbery, merely because she preferred an eminently suitable man like Lord Sanditon as a husband for one of her sisters rather than Joel's old comrade, the rakehell Captain

Royce? Her resentment continued during the remainder of the picnic festivities and the barge ride back to Westminster. She didn't address a word to Joel during the return river journey, and barely replied to his remarks with civility.

On an afternoon several days later, Joel came into the morning room, where Sophia was working on her accounts.

"I just received a message from Nevil Royce," he said, glancing at the note in his hand. "He proposes to call on us—both of us—at four o'clock, on an important personal matter."

Sophia put down her pen. "Do you know the nature of this personal matter?" Her voice was cool. In fact, their relations for the past few days, since their return from the barge picnic, had been cool to the point of frigidity.

"No. I can guess, however."

"As can I. I presume we must receive him?"

"Yes. I needn't remind you that Nevil is one of my oldest friends."

"I hadn't forgotten," Sophia said grimly. "I needn't remind you that I would never be guilty of incivility to one of your friends."

At four o'clock, promptly, Nevil Royce strode into the drawing room, where Joel and Sophia rose to greet him. He was impeccably dressed and groomed, though he displayed a definite nervousness. His arm was still supported by a sling.

He bowed. "Joel, Lady Leyburn."

Sophia inclined her head. "Pray sit down, Captain Royce."

Joel remarked, "You said in your note that you had an important matter to discuss with us, Nevil."

"Yes, well, er, the fact is, I've come to request Edwina's hand in marriage," Nevil blurted.

"I can't say I'm surprised," Joel responded dryly.

Smiling weakly, the captain continued, "No, I daresay my intentions have been plain to everyone in the ton for weeks now." He looked directly at Sophia. "Lady Leyburn, I've been madly in love with Edwina since the first moment I laid eyes on her. She tells me she returns my affections. We wish to be married."

Having made his declaration, the captain seemed to lose some of his apprehension. He gazed expectantly at Sophia.

"I believe it's customary in such circumstances to ask a prospective suitor what he plans to bring to his marriage," she said coolly.

"Oh, of course." Nevil sounded rattled. "Well, as I think you already know, Lady Leyburn, I'm not a wealthy man. I have an allowance from my family, sufficient to support a modest establishment. My godfather, who I'm happy to say is still in good health, has told me he plans to leave me a substantial legacy in his will. Then there's my army pay, rather miniscule, actually. And I understand from Edwina that you've promised her a generous dowry. I think, provided we watch our expenses carefully, that we could live quite comfortably on our joint incomes."

"What about your physical health, Captain Royce? You're still wearing a sling."

Nevil flushed. "My wound is still touch and go. The surgeons can't guarantee that my arm will ever be strong enough to enable me to resume my career in the Guards."

Sophia gave him a direct, uncompromising look. "So the situation is this, Captain Royce, you wish to marry my sister, even though your finances are quite modest, largely dependent, in fact, on Edwina's dowry, and despite the fact that your health is seriously in question. I regret to say that I can't consider you a proper suitor for Edwina's hand."

Nevil paled. He rose, saying stiffly, "I must, of course, accept your decision. Good-day, Joel, Lady Leyburn."

After Nevil left the room, Joel turned on Sophia. "How could you be so cruel and unfeeling?"

She faced him down. "I'm surprised at you. I thought you understood, when we married, that I expect my sisters to make advantageous marriages as a result of our business arrangement. And you certainly should have realized by this time that I don't consider Captain Royce to be an advantageous match for Edwina. I think she can do much better."

Taking a deep breath, Joel said, "Edwina and Nevil are deeply in love with each other. Doesn't that count for something?"

"Very little. Actually, I'm surprised you would ask such a question. This much I've gathered since arriving in London and talking to your Aunt Georgina and her fashionable friends; romantic love is the last requirement for a successful marriage match to the ton. One lady, in fact, informed me that she considered a love-match a trifle vulgar."

Joel stared at her, frustration written deeply on his face. "Sophia, I'm going to tell you something that I would guess no one has dared to tell you since your father and your husband died and you became the head of your family. Perhaps no one has spoken to you in this way in your entire life."

"Yes?" Sophia responded icily.

"It's this—you're a domestic tyrant. You mean nothing but good for your family, but your idea of what's best for them is always inflexible. You never consider what they want. You pay no attention to their wishes. You always know best. But do you?"

"How dare you say such things? Since my father died, the welfare of my sisters and my brother has been my sole concern."

Sighing, Joel said, "Sophia, I'll say it again. From the best of motives, you've become a dictator. Once you've made up your mind about a proper course of action, you won't permit anyone to gainsay you. Take Edwina. If she wanted to marry a ne'er-do-well, someone with no standing in society, I'd be the first to agree that you should forbid the match. However, she happens to love a fine young man, who, though he'll never be wealthy, is eminently respectable. Edwina and Nevil could have a full and satisfying life together. They would be received by everyone."

"Oh, I daresay being received by the ton is the highest happiness a young couple could enjoy!"

Ignoring the interruption, Joel went on. "Then there's Caroline.

You've apparently already decided that she and Sanditon are perfectly matched. It's very obvious that he's attracted to her, and I shouldn't be surprised if he made her an offer, but supposing she's not fond enough of him to marry him? Caroline has always seemed to me to be an independent young lady. What then? Would you attempt to force her to accept Sanditon?"

Before Sophia could reply, Joel continued. "And Tristan. Just the other day, on our trip to Epson, he told me he didn't want to attend Oxford. He was afraid, though, that you would be very hurt if he didn't matriculate. I'd like to offer you some advice—Tristan is still very young. Why don't you wait a few years until he's older to decide on a university career?"

Jumping to her feet, Sophia exclaimed, "I don't need any advice from you about my family. Edwina and Caroline and Tristan are my concern only, nothing to do with you!"

Rising, Joel said quietly, "I was under the impression that I'd become a member of your family, or vice versa, if you prefer."

"In name only. Ours was always a business proposition. When I married you I didn't give up the management of my business, my fortune or my family. You have nothing to say to any of them."

Joel's face paled. His eyes turned a glacial gray. "I called you a domestic tryant. I didn't mention still another aspect of your tyranny. You apparently believe you can manage me in the same fashion you manage your family. If you really believe that, Sophia, you've made one of the worst mistakes of your life!"

He gave her a cursory bow and left the room.

Eleven

Sophia knocked on the door, paused, and knocked again. "Edwina," she called, "please let me talk to you."

From behind the bedchamber door came a muffled voice. "I don't want to talk to you. I don't want to see you. I don't want to see anyone."

"Edwina, please. If we could just talk, I'm sure I could explain—"

"Go away, Sophy. There's nothing you could say that would explain what you did. You've ruined my life."

Baffled, Sophia turned away from the door and returned to her own bedchamber. Since yesterday afternoon, when she had informed Edwina of her decision not to allow her to marry Nevil Royce, her sister had barricaded herself behind her locked bedroom door, refusing to admit even Caroline. Sophia had tried repeatedly during the evening, and again this morning, to reason with Edwina, but with no success.

As Sophia sank dispiritedly into a chair in her bedchamber, Caroline knocked perfunctorily and entered the room. Perching on the bed, she said, "So Edwina still won't talk to you."

"No. I can't understand it. I knew she'd be indignant, hurt, angry, when I told her about Captain Royce, but I never dreamed she would refuse to talk to me at all."

"I don't know why you're surprised," Caroline said coolly. "What I can't understand is why you rejected Nevil's proposal of marriage. Be honest, Sophy; if, back in Lancashire, a gentleman like Nevil Royce had offered for Edwina, wouldn't you have given the match your blessing?"

"Why . . . possibly. Yes, I daresay I would have done so. But that was then and there, not here and now. When I brought you and Edwina to London I wanted you both to make brilliant marriages."

Caroline flushed. "Sophy—"

"Nevil Royce isn't a brilliant match," Sophia said firmly. "Edwina could do infinitely better. Haven't you noticed how the Earl of Chelford has been angling after her at all the parties lately? Georgina Winwood told me the other day that she thinks it very likely Lord Chelford will make an offer."

"So?"

"So wouldn't you rather see your sister the Countess of Chelford than plain Mrs. Nevil Royce?"

Throwing up her hands, Caroline exclaimed angrily, "Sophy, will you never learn? You're such an intelligent woman, but sometimes I think you don't even try to understand. Look, when it comes to Edwina's marriage, it's not what I want that counts. Or what you want. It's what Edwina wants." She paused, biting her lip. "I'm sorry. I shouldn't have lost my temper." After a moment she continued on a softer note. "Do you remember that day in Chester last spring, when you had to retrieve Edwina and me from the academy after Miss Beaton expelled us? I accused you then of managing our lives, of never listening to our opinions. I actually called you a—"

"Domestic tyrant," Sophia finished. She fell silent, remembering bleakly that Joel had used the same expression to her yesterday.

"Yes, well—I was much too harsh," she continued. "I know how well-meaning you are, how much you love us. But Sophy, I think eventually you must realize that, although you can guide Edwina, Tristan and me, cherish us, provide for us, you can't live our lives for us. We're human beings, not puppets that you can manipulate as you will."

Caroline rose from the bed. Walking over to Sophia, she patted her gently on the shoulder, saying, "Please reconsider. Let Edwina marry Nevil." Then she left the room.

Settling back into her chair, Sophia allowed herself to wallow in hurt feelings. To be called a domestic tyrant, by both her sister and her husband seemed so grossly unfair. Young people needed guidance and authority. That's what elders were for, to keep the young from making mistakes they would regret for the rest of their lives.

She'd honestly thought she was doing what was best for Edwina. Her sister was very young, and for the past several years she'd been falling in and out of love with a great regularity with any attractive man who came into her orbit. Music instructors, sons of neighboring cotton spinning mill owners, rakish Guards captains. Sophia had considered Captain Royce to be simply another in the passing parade of young men, and that Edwina would forget all about him once a more engaging suitor appeared on the horizon.

Supposing Sophia was wrong? Supposing Edwina genuinely loved Nevil? It wasn't a brilliant match, certainly, only a respectable one, although Caroline was quite correct—a few short months ago in Lancashire Sophia would have considered Nevil a genuine catch. However, if the match wasn't a brilliant one, it was undeniably, perfectly respectable. So if Edwina sincerely loved Nevil . . .

Sophia shook her head. She was still convinced that she had a right—no, a duty—to guide her sisters and her brother. She still thought Edwina was throwing herself away on Nevil Royce. No matter. Was she prepared to make Edwina bitterly unhappy? Was she prepared to be estranged from her sister, perhaps permanently.

Slowly Sophia rose from her chair, went to the door of the bedchamber and walked down the hallway to Edwina's room. At the door, she lifted her hand to knock and paused, listening to the sound of hopeless weeping coming from inside the bedchamber.

Sophia's heart turned over. Edwina, elfin and mercurial, had never nursed a misfortune for very long. Her tears had always been like a spring shower, brief and quickly forgotten.

"Edwina," Sophia called through the door. "I've changed my mind. You can marry Nevil Royce."

The weeping continued for several seconds. Then Sophia heard the sound of running feet. Edwina threw open the door. Her clothes disheveled, her hair a messy tangle of curls, her eyes red and swollen from crying, she stared at her sister.

"Sophy? You really mean it?"

"I do. I only want you to be happy. And if Nevil will make you happy, I'm content. I promise to do my best to love him like a brother."

Edwina smiled a watery smile. "Nevil will never believe that when I tell him. Tell him yourself, and then prove it to him!" Her face transfigured by joy and relief she threw her arms around Sophia.

"Come."

Sophia looked up from her dressing table as Joel entered her bedchamber. He was formally dressed in a dark blue coat, waistcoat and breeches, and his cravat was a masterfully tied creation.

"Good evening, Sophia."

"Good evening, Joel," Sophia said coolly. "I really didn't expect you."

"Oh? Why not? Tonight is the Albritton ball, isn't it?"

"Yes. On the other hand, last night was Mrs. Forbes' soiree and the night before that was the opera. So, when you didn't come home for either event, I naturally assumed you wouldn't be escorting me to this ball, either."

Joel picked up a gilt chair, turned it around and sat down facing Sophia, his arms resting on the back of the chair. "We had a flaming row two nights ago, you'll remember. I thought it unlikely you would want to see me for a spell. Frankly, I wasn't particularly eager to see you either! So I went to my old lodgings. My lease hasn't expired yet."

I don't believe you, Sophia thought. I'd lay odds you were with Fannie Price, who was scheduled to sing at the opera two nights ago, and whose role was sung by a substitute instead. Aloud, she said, "And what brought you to Brook Street this evening?"

Settling himself more comfortably, Joel replied, "I saw Nevil at White's this afternoon. He told me you had withdrawn your objections to his suit. I wanted to congratulate you. Your decision was both generous and wise."

Sophia did her best to keep calm. She still rankled from his tongue-lashing of several nights before. He had no right to call her a domestic tyrant, to criticize her care of her family. Well, yes, Caroline had called her a tyrant, too. But Caroline had admitted she'd been too harsh. And Caroline loved her.

Clearing his throat, Joel said, "By any chance, did anything I said cause you to change your mind about Nevil and Edwina?"

So that was it. With his usual bland arrogance, Joel had assumed it was his intervention with Sophia—that infamous tongue-lashing—that was responsible for her decision to allow Edwina to marry Nevil. Joel wanted credit for resolving his dear friend's romantic problems.

"I'm sorry to disappoint you," she said, giving Joel a level look. "Actually, it was Caroline who was responsible for my change of mind. She asked me to reconsider my decision and I did. All I've ever wanted is for Edwina to be happy."

For a moment Joel's lips tightened. "We all want Edwina to be happy."

"Yes. However, I'm still not sure she will be. Edwina has a penchant for falling in and out of love. I refrained from telling her that romantic love seldom lasts, that none of her romantic loves had lasted before. Star-crossed lovers over the centuries have refused to believe in such heresy! But I very much hope that Edwina doesn't awaken one day and realize she should never have married Nevil."

Rising, Joel replaced the chair in its usual place. "I don't think you need worry about that," he said, his face expressionless. "I'm positive Nevil will make Edwina very happy. Are you ready to leave for the ball? Incidentally, you look very handsome tonight. You always know what colors become you."

Sophia walked into the drawing room several mornings later to greet Lord Sanditon.

"I apologize for calling at such an hour, Lady Leyburn. I knew you would have a throng of visitors in the afternoon, and I wanted to speak to you privately." The viscount cleared his throat. He appeared mildly uncomfortable. "I'm sorry Lord Leyburn isn't at home. I'd hoped to speak to both of you."

"If you'd prefer to wait until my husband is present . . . ?"

"No, not at all. You, I understand, are Miss Dalton's guardian."

"Pray sit down, Lord Sanditon," Sophia said, feeling a twinge of excitement. "You wished to speak to me about Caroline?"

"As you must have observed, Lady Leyburn, I was tremendously impressed with your sister from the first moment I met her," the viscount said earnestly. "Her beauty, her deportment, her character—especially her character. I have never met a young woman with such seriousness of purpose, such a desire to benefit humanity. In short, I find myself very much in love with Caroline, that is, with Miss Dalton. I've come here to request your permission to pay my addresses to her."

Suppressing an urge to smile at the elaborately formal, almost stilted, declaration, Sophia said, "You have my permission, Lord Sanditon. I think you and Caroline are excellently suited. I should be most pleased to welcome you to our family." She rose, saying, "Shall I send Caroline down to you?"

His face suffused with relief and joy, the viscount said, "Yes, thank you. I—er—I should like to know my fate as soon as possible."

"Oh, I hardly think you need worry about your fate," Sophia said, smiling. She rang the bell, telling the footman who answered to inform Miss Caroline that Lord Sanditon had called and was waiting for her in the drawing room. Then she retreated to the morning room to wait in pleasurable anticipation for Caroline's announcement that she was about to become the Viscountess Sanditon.

She waited for fifteen minutes, and then checking the clock at five-minute intervals, she waited another fifteen, impatiently tapping her foot. Finally, she rang the bell for a footman.

"Is Lord Sanditon still in the house?"

"No, my lady. He took his leave—oh, nigh on half an hour ago, as best I recall."

"Thank you, Jepson. Oh—another thing. Did Miss Caroline accompany Lord Sanditon?"

"No, my lady. I believe Miss Caroline is in her bedchamber."

Sophia went up the stairs and tapped at Caroline's door. "Caroline? Can I talk to you?"

"Come in, Sophy."

Caroline rose from her chair as Sophia entered the room. Her back ramrod-straight, she said composedly, "I've been waiting for you, Sophy. The answer is no. I didn't accept Lord Sanditon's proposal."

Suppressing a pang of angry disappointment, Sophia said, "I see. May I ask why you saw fit to reject such an advantageous offer? I thought you liked Lord Sanditon."

"I do. Very much."

"And you certainly can't fault his ancestry, or his position in society."

"Not at all. Lord Sanditon is a most distinguished man."

"Well, then?"

"Sophy, I know Lord Sanditon is a great catch on the Marriage Mart. He has intelligence and character, wealth and social position as well as a promising political career. Most people would say I'd taken leave of my senses if I rejected his proposal. But you see, I don't love him. I don't want to spend the rest of my life in a loveless marriage."

"Caroline, for heaven's sake!" Sophia cried impatiently. "You may be only seventeen, but you're a level-headed girl. You must know as well as I do that romantic love is vastly overrated. Talk to Georgina Winwood. She knows more about the domestic arrangements of the ton than any woman alive. She'll tell you that the best marriages are based on mutual respect and liking and interests, which you and Lord Sanditon share in abundance. And I can corroborate her opinion from my own experience."

Her attention caught, Caroline gave Sophia a curious look. "Your experience? You mean your marriage to Bartholomew? You never talked to us about it—well, we were all so young at the time, Tristan was only ten or so—but we always assumed it wasn't a love match, that you married Bartholomew to give us a home after Papa died. But what about Joel? Didn't you marry him for love?"

Caroline paused, her eyes narrowing before she continued, "Wait. I remember now. Nevil once told Edwina and me that Joel was in some kind of frightful financial difficulty about the time that you and he became engaged. Sophy! Did you pay Joel to marry you so that you could become a countess? I never thought you could be so mercenary!"

Embarrassed and angry, a hot color flooding her cheeks, Sophia blurted, "Don't you dare accuse me of being mercenary. If you must have it, I married Joel for his position so that you and Edwina could meet elgibile marriage partners. He married me to escape debtors' prison!"

She broke off, appalled. How could she have revealed information so intensely personal? She, who had always guarded her privacy so fiercely? She flinched at the look of shocked comprehension that had appeared on her sister's face. After a moment she said, with a kind of brittle composure, "We're discussing your affairs, Caroline, not mine. I think you've acted too hastily. I suggest you write a note to Lord Sanditon, asking him to wait for a few days while you reconsider your answer."

"No." Caroline's lips clamped together.

Like a mule, Sophia thought resentfully. "Don't be so foolishly stubborn, Caroline," she urged. "If you throw away this opportunity, you may never get another like it. Oh, I realize that you have had several young men angling for you of late but supposing none of them come up to scratch? Are you prepared to return to Lancashire without a proposal of marriage?"

"I certainly am," Caroline flashed. "It was entirely your own idea, Sophy, to bring Edwina and me to London to find us husbands. I never asked you to do so. I'm not sure I wish to be married at all! In any event, I'm not ready to compromise my principles as you have done. I refuse to enter into a loveless marriage just to satisfy your ambitions for our family. And I resent your interference—again!—in my life!"

Sophia gasped. "Interference! Caroline, how can you say

such things to me? I only want you to be happy. You know very well that I would never force you to marry Lord Sanditon, or anyone, against your will."

"Good," Caroline snapped. "We understand each other, then." Turning on her heel, she went to her wardrobe, from which she snatched a pelisse and bonnet. "I don't want to talk any more, Sophy," she said, marching to the door. "I'm going for a walk, to clear my mind, and to have a little privacy!"

Staring helplessly at her sister's departing figure, Sophia found herself fumbling for an explanation for this latest family crisis. How could Caroline throw away an opportunity that so many girls would have killed for? She liked Lord Sanditon, she'd admitted that. She admired him, she shared so many of his principles. Then why . . . ?

Sighing, Sophia walked slowly out of the room into the corridor, nearly colliding with Joel.

"Is something wrong?" he inquired. "Caroline just rushed past me in the hall downstairs, dragging on her pelisse as she went, declaring that she was going for a walk. Shouldn't you have sent her abigail with her? She seemed quite overset."

It was the last straw. "If you wish Caroline to take her abigail with her when she leaves the house, you tell her. She won't listen to me," Sophia said crossly. She swept past him, walking down the hall to her bedchamber. Joel followed her into the room.

"You may as well tell me about it," he said, closing the door behind him. "Why is Caroline overset?"

Sophia flared, "If you must know, she refused Lord Sanditon's offer of marriage this morning, and then, when I suggested—merely suggested—that she reconsider her decision, she flew into a rage and accused me of interference."

"Interference?" Joel raised an eyebrow. "You? Perish the thought."

Losing her temper completely, Sophia exclaimed, "I don't need your sarcasm, thank you. And if you're thinking of telling me again that I'm a domestic tryant, don't bother. You were explicit enough the first time."

Joel's expression changed. "I'm sorry. I was sarcastic." He paused. "About Caroline. Try not to resent her decision. In your heart of hearts you know you wouldn't want her to marry against her wishes."

Turning her back on him, Sophia sat down at her dressing table. "Thank you for your opinion—unasked, of course," she said coldly. "Would you leave now, please? I should like to prepare for lunch."

Several days later, seated at her desk, Sophia stared down unseeingly at a pile of bills and invitations. She felt drained and stale and put upon.

She'd made her peace with Caroline, after a fashion, but the atmosphere in the household had remained uncomfortable, because Caroline, characteristically pricklish, had merely retreated into a wary truce. "It's all very well to say you want me to be happy, Sophy," she declared. "But you want me to be happy on your terms. You'd try again in a shot to persuade me to marry Lord Sanditon if you thought you had any chance of succeeding."

With Joel, Sophia had settled again into their familiar polite, bloodless relationship. She regretted her outburst on the day that Caroline had rejected Lord Sanditon's proposal. She would have preferred to conceal from Joel how much she still resented his criticism of the way she conducted her affairs with her family, and she certainly didn't want him to think that his opinions carried any weight with her.

A footman tapped at the door and brought in a note on a tray.

Sophia broke the seal and quickly scanned the note. She stiffened and read the note again, this time more slowly.

"My dear Lady Leyburn: We have never met, but we have seen each other on several occasions, and I think you know quite well who I am. It is essential that we talk, and as soon as possible. I am sure you would not wish to contemplate the possibility of an unpleasant scandal. I will expect you to call on me at my lodgings at Number 21 Queen Anne Street no later than two o'clock this afternoon. Respectfully, Fannie Price."

Her face burning with anger, Sophia crumpled the note and tossed it to the floor. A moment later she picked up the crumpled paper, smoothed it out and reread it. Polite and guarded though her letter was, Fannie Price was undoubtedly hinting at blackmail. If Sophia ignored the note, could the woman really be capable of spreading harmful scandal? Could Sophia afford to take the risk?

She rang the bell. "Tell the coachman that I wish to use the carriage immediately," she told the footman.

Number 21 Queen Anne Street, on the Portland Estate near Cavendish Square, was a charming eighteenth century house, in which Fannie Price appparently occupied the upper floor. A trimly dressed maidservant led her up the stairs. With a slight shock Sophia recognized the girl as the young female who had called on Joel some days before with a tearful message from her mistress.

The maidservant ushered Sophia, not into a drawing room or parlor, but into a bedchamber. Sophia paused on the threshold, staring at the Titian-haired beauty propped up against the pillows of the elaborately draped canopy bed. The bed hangings and the window treatments, the upholstery of the fragile gilt furniture, were all of heavy, pale-gold satin. The thick-piled Aubusson carpet glowed in jewel-like pastel colors. It was an expensively furnished room, and its mistress presided over it from her bed with a queenly self-possession.

"Miss Price?" Sophia said stiffly. "I'm Lady Leyburn. You wished to see me?"

Fannie Price's perfect teeth parted in an angelic smile. Her red-gold hair was arranged in a cascade of tumbling curls, and she wore a clinging chiffon peignoir in a luminous shade of pale green that enhanced the faint rose of her apple blossom complexion. Looking at her, Sophia felt gauche and unattractive.

"Thank you for coming, Lady Leyburn. I travel as little as possible these days, because of my health. You see, I'm increasing."

A cold lump settled in Sophia's stomach. She could see now the slight swell in Fannie Price's opulent figure beneath the delicate chiffon of her robe.

"Won't you sit down, Lady Leyburn?"

"Thank you, I would rather stand."

Shrugging, Fannie said, "As you please. I thought we should meet as soon as possible, in view of my—er—condition."

"Oh? And why should your, er, condition concern me, Miss Price?"

"You can't be serious! Good God, Lady Leyburn, I'm carrying your husband's child!"

Sophia looked at the singer coldly. "So I gathered. I repeat, I fail to understand why I should be concerned. Unless, that is you're considering some sort of blackmail, in which case I would remind you that the fathering of by-blows is a fairly common occurrence among the ton. I doubt very much that the revelation that my husband had fathered a child out of wedlock would cause a scandal serious enough to warrant the payment of hush money."

To Sophia's utter astonishment, Fannie's eyes filled with tears. "You think I brought you here to blackmail you? How cruel, how unfeeling of you."

Taken aback, Sophia demanded, "Well, then, why did you ask me to come here?"

Wiping her eyes with a lace-trimmed handkerchief, Fannie said, "Why, to spare Joel's sensibilities, of course. You see, he desperately wants his child to be properly provided for, and at this time he doesn't have sufficient funds to do so. Under the circumstances, he's too embarrassed to apply to you. So, I decided to go to you myself."

"I don't understand," Sophia said blankly. "Joel has an independent income, large enough to enable him to provide adequately and generously for your child, and I'm sure he will do the honorable thing. However, this baby, after all, won't occupy the same social position as Joel's future, er, legitimate issue, or require the same level of support. As for his feeling embarrassed . . ."

Fannie disclaimed angrily, "You certainly don't understand! Joel doesn't regard my child as just another aristocratic byblow. My baby will be the child of the woman whom Joel passionately loves and would have married, if it hadn't been for you, Lady Leyburn!"

"Are you saying that Joel proposed marriage to you?" Sophia blurted.

Her eyes blazing, Fannie said, "You find it hard to believe that Joel would take a wife from the stage? Oh, we knew we'd meet with social disapproval, but we loved each other so much. We decided to brave it out, hoping that, in the end, people would come around. But before we could set a date, Joel got into serious financial trouble. He wouldn't tell me the details. All he said was that he had to marry money or go to debtors' prison. Then you came along."

Fannie paused, gazing resentfully at Sophia. "He swore he didn't care for you," she went on in a gratified tone. "He told me I was the only woman he had ever loved, or could love, and that our child would always be first in his heart, no matter how many other children he had. But he couldn't bring himself to ask you for a large enough sum to support our child properly. For one thing, he was afraid you'd become so angry that you might refuse to go through with the marriage. Later, after you and Joel were actually married, I assumed he could use as much of your fortune as he saw fit, but now he insists you have retained control of your money. So . . ."

"So you decided to go to the source," Sophia said in a choked voice. "Very well, Miss Price. You do have a claim of sorts. I will send you a draft of five thousand pounds. That, wisely invested, should ensure the future of your child. Good-day."

In the carriage, riding back to Brook Street, Sophia had to fight back the scalding, angry tears. So Joel had been—still was—madly in love with his actress-singer mistress, and Sophia was merely the unwanted wife who had interfered with his plans to marry Fannie. And what about his pledge to keep secret the details of his marriage of convenience, to pretend to the world that he and Sophia had married for love? Instead, he had talked freely to his mistress about the details of his loveless marriage. And the woman had probably talked as freely to her own friends and acquaintances. Was London society—or at least a part of it—laughing at Sophia behind her back?

How would he react when he learned that his wife had contributed five thousand pounds for the support of his illegitimate child? No. Sophia clenched her fists. She didn't want him to know about it. It would be too humiliating. She breathed a little easier. Most likely he would never find out about that transaction. Fannie Price would be reluctant to admit to Joel that she'd gone behind his back to ask his wife to provide for their child. As for Sophia . . . She couldn't tell Joel about the money without also telling him about her visit to Fannie Price and revealing to him how deeply she had been hurt by the singer's confidences.

By the time she reached her house Sophia had recovered her composure enough to talk to Edwina and Nevil Royce, who greeted her as she passed the door of the drawing room.

"Sophy, could we talk to you?"

Entering the room, Sophia said, smiling, "Is there a problem? I must say, you don't look troubled."

In fact, thought Sophia, there was a glow of almost unearthly happiness about Edwina and Nevil these days. As they stood side by side in front of her they weren't physically touching each other, naturally. Edwina had been far too well-trained by Sophia and the schoolmistresses at Miss Beaton's academy to indulge in that kind of unseemly deportment in public. But one had the distinct impression that, if they were alone, the pair would be locked in an ardent embrace.

"Troubled, Lady Leyburn? Perish the thought," Nevil said, beaming. "Now that Edwina and I are betrothed, I don't expect to have a troubled moment as long as I live!"

"I trust your optimism isn't misplaced," Sophia said dryly. "Now, then, you wanted to talk to me?"

"Well, as you know, Sophy, the Season is almost over, and most folk will be leaving London," Edwina said. "Nevil and I were wondering about your plans. Where will you and Joel be staying? And will Caroline, Tristan and I be with you?"

"Why . . . I don't know. I hadn't really thought about it."

"Well, please do think about it, Sophy. Nevil needs to know where he can visit me during the next few months while we make the arrangements for our wedding!"

As she went down the hallway to her morning room office, Sophia frowned, reflecting once again on her ignorance of the customs of the ton. Had she been born to her present position, she would have been prepared for the close of the Season. She would have realized that London emptied at the end of July or as soon during the month as Parliament rose. People left their homes in Town for their country estates, or the country estates of their friends, to participate in leisurely house parties and hunting and fishing excursions.

Well, she thought glumly, as she sat down at her desk, she and Joel would have to come to some decision about where they would be living after the Season ended. Certainly she had no country estate to which to retreat. And since Joel had quarreled with his father, the Kennington estate in Yorkshire wasn't available, either. Sighing, she reached for her pen. She'd promised to send Fannie Price five thousand pounds, and she saw little point in postponing the disagreeable task.

"Sophia? Do you have a minute?"

Sophia looked up as Joel entered the morning room, several opened letters in his hand.

Glancing at the topmost of the letters, he said, "It's just occurred to me that we haven't made any plans for the after the Season. Here's an invitation from my old friend Jock Driscoll for the grouse shooting in Scotland. And another from Dick Saintsbury to stay at his family estate in Dorset. I've also received a number of verbal invitations, including one from Aunt Georgina and Uncle Horace to join them at their home in Derbyshire. Do any of the invitations appeal to you?"

Recalling her interview with Fannie Price that afternoon, Sophia's emotions surfaced like bitter gall. Suddenly, she couldn't bear the look of his handsome, self-assured face. Words came unbidden, but sounding as if she'd been considering the subject for some time. Coolly, she said, "As a matter of fact, I've decided to return to Lancashire as soon as the Season ends. My mill manager accuses me of neglecting the business shamefully."

Obviously taken aback at her announcement, Joel said, "Somehow I assumed you were taking care of your duties satisfactorily via the mails. Well, how long would it be necessary for you to remain in Lancashire while you settled any problems with the cotton spinning mill? Of course, the partridge shooting doesn't start until the first of September and the cubbing some time after that—"

"Actually, I hadn't planned to leave Woodbridge until after Christmas, when I presume you will want me to go to London for the reopening of Parliament."

Joel folded his letters and sat down opposite her. "Well, if that's what you prefer. Of course, I've never spent any period of time in a cotton-milling town, and I don't know if—"

"In fact, you've never visited in a milling town at all, I fancy," Sophia cut in dryly. "I daresay the experience would be boring in the extreme for you. Fortunately, there's no need to put yourself to the test. I suggest you accept the invitation that most appeals to you and enjoy yourself with your friends."

Joel stared at her fixedly for several moments. "Let me understand you. Are you saying that you prefer that I don't join you, your sisters and your brother in Lancashire after the Season?"

Shrugging, Sophia said, "It's entirely up to you. However, I can't believe you would have much in common with the inhabitants of Woodbridge. As for myself, I won't have any need to impress folk with my brilliant marriage in the wilds of the provinces. So . . ."

His face turning into a cold mask, Joel rose, saying, "So, in your opinion, it would be quite profitless for either of us if we were to spend time together in Lancashire. I agree with you, my dear. I'll make my plans accordingly."

Twelve

Sophia stood by the window in her office at Woodbridge House. She stared down at the rows and rows of windows of the cotton-spinning mill and watched smoke belch into the air, a gritty coal smoke that had long-since changed the texture of the trees and grass, ponds and streams. She wanted to be glad to be back in Lancashire, but ever since her arrival yesterday, she had known an uneasiness she couldn't explain.

The trip had been uneventful along the northwesterly roads and the summery landscape provided many pretty sights to exclaim over with Caroline and Edwina, Tristan and Mark Ingram. During the journey, she had kept her mind focused purposefully on Woodbridge and her duties at the mill. She told herself that once she resumed her position as mistress of Bartholomew's house as well as her activities in her office, she would be happy.

But looking out at the mill and hearing the rumblings of the factory, happiness still seemed to be out of reach. She was having difficulty concentrating for one thing. Her thoughts seemed to reach back to London and to her townhouse in Brook Street. When she thought of Joel, she couldn't help but remember her talk with Fannie Price. What would he say if he discovered she had paid his mistress five thousand pounds? Should she even have done so? Maybe she should have discussed the matter with him.

But then there never seemed to be any discussion with Joel. He had his own ideas about how things should be—with Edwina, Caroline and Tristan. His complaints still rankled—he considered her to be a domestic tyrant.

Her thoughts turned to Edwina and Nevil. The truth was she had never seen her sister so happy, wearing the glow of a young lady very much in love. Though she tried to deny that Joel had in any way persuaded her to change her mind—after all, it was Caroline who had prompted her to evaluate her position—she had to admit that his strident opinions had left a mark of doubt on her abilities to properly shepherd her siblings into adulthood.

In the valley below, beside the river Weirton, the factory hummed and hammered just as she had left it. The sounds rising up the hill were in an odd way comforting yet couldn't seem to dispel the worrying, nagging feelings which had dogged her heels since leaving London. She had an unhappy sensation that she had not conducted herself entirely well, especially in her cold farewells to her husband.

Her husband. Whatever was to become of him, she wondered.

"Lady Leyburn?"

Sophia turned around and saw that her manager was peeking his head around the door. "I knocked several times, m'lady, but there was no answer. I do be sorry if I am disturbing ye."

"No, no, not at all," Sophia answered quickly realizing that her thoughts had prevented her from hearing his knock. "Come in, Mr. Walcot. You are looking well."

"Thank you, my lady, and may I congratulate ye on yer marriage."

Sophia smiled thinly. "Thank you." During the trip north, she had nearly forgotten her title and rank until she arrived at Bartholomew's house and noticed how oddly nervous the familiar servants had become in her presence. Being referred to as my lady in London was one thing, but hearing her title and courtesy addresses in Lancashire was quite another.

Mr. Walcot shifted on his feet.

Sophia waved him to a chair opposite her desk then took up her seat at her desk. "We've much to discuss though I must tell you that your correspondence with me during the Season was very helpful." She saw a grateful light in his eye which quickly became replaced with a spark of concern. She continued, "You mentioned in your last letter that progress on the new steam mill had been hindered, but you didn't say why."

Sophia watched Ned Walcot's expression grow grim. "There were a fire, m'lady."

Sophia blinked at her manager several times. "A fire?" she asked, startled.

Mr. Walcot nodded. "Yes, 'twere contained easily enough, but it set back construction on t'mill by several weeks, as I'm sure ye can imagine. I didn't want t'worry ye while ye were enjoying yer honeymoon, but now that ye're back, 'tis best we discuss the situation."

Sophia leaned back in her chair and clamped her hands tightly together on her lap. She had never seen such a dispirited look on her manager's face before as he began to speak of the attitudes in the village of Woodbridge, at the mill and in the surrounding mills as well. A machine-smashing north, in Manchester, was his first topic. Afterward, he introduced a matter which took her by surprise. There were talks locally of a revival of Luddism in which groups of men joined together to form secret societies with equally secretive handshakes and other signals for the purpose of destroying progressive machinery. Ostensibly, these groups held secret meetings on the moors. "And not jest those that wish fer violence no matter wat t'occasion, but men that ye know, especially young hot heads, like Dick Frawley—"

"Tristan's friend from the village school?" Sophia broke in, stunned.

Mr. Walcot nodded.

"I had no idea!" Sophia exclaimed. "I knew that there have been problems elsewhere, in Nottinghamshire, but I can't believe that our mill, our village has been affected."

Mr. Walcot stared hard at her, his lips set in a grim line.

"What is it?" she asked. "What is it you wish to say to me?"

"You've been a good mistress, but I wouldn't be doing me duty if I didna warn ye, and explain how hard hit the folk be, with work and wage cuts—"

"But surely you've explained our predicament—the embargos, the selling price of cambric alone has dropped from twenty-five shillings for each twenty-four square yards to ten shillings. The steam looms are the only way we can compete—"

"Which takes away more jobs, more hours and 'tworst of it 'tis that the folk are living on little more than potatoes. The land as ye know is not fit fer gardens like the southern counties. Many are starving and the new looms—

"Are beginning to seem like an enemy." Sophia looked away from Mr. Walcot and thought that her own problems seemed somehow insignificant to the difficulties facing her mill and the villagers who worked at the mill. "So you think that arson may have been involved in the fire?"

Ned Walcot nodded. "But we've made progress and I still think the new looms will be ready by November or December."

"It's the only way we'll be able to compete."

"I know," he responded. "I tell the workers again and again, but times be hard."

"You must make them understand, Mr. Walcot and to help them see that once Napoleon has been defeated, the industry as a whole will enjoy better profits. The war can't last forever."

As Mr. Walcot left her office, Sophia knew Ned would do all he could to ease the worries of his workers. He was a good man and well-respected among the cotton-spinners. She was convinced they would listen to his reasonings.

Whether they would or not, Sophia decided she would do all she could to review the accounts and see if it would be possible to adjust the workers' wages, even a mite, in order to relieve some of the distress of the situation, particularly since summer would soon be dwindling away and the onset of the harsh northern winters would begin taking their toll.

After she had been laboring over the ledger books for two hours, a welcome knock sounded on her door and a moment later, Edwina bounded into the room waving a letter in the air. "I hope I am not disturbing you," she cried, her green eyes sparkling and her face lit with joy. She wore a pale green silk gown in pretty contrast to her creamy complexion and her curling red-gold hair. "Nevil is coming!" she breathed at last, clasping the letter to her chest and twirling in a circle.

Sophia couldn't help but laugh outright. "I've never seen you happier, Edwina."

In proof of this statement, Edwina twirled over to her elder sister and leaned down to place an affectionate kiss on her cheek. "And I have you to thank for it."

Again, Sophia laughed.

"Oh, but I almost forgot to tell you! Nevil had a letter from Joel. He said to tell you that your husband is enjoying grouse shooting in Scotland, but of course you would know that—" Her sister broke off suddenly and eyed Sophia curiously. "I just realized that you've not had a letter from Joel yet."

Sophia felt a heat rise on her cheeks. "No, I have not, but then we've only just arrived home and you know what men are once they have their guns in hand."

"I suppose so," Edwina responded. "I know Nevil likes to hunt. Oh, but I miss him so much just like you miss Joel."

These words, so innocently spoken, caused another wave of warmth to suffuse Sophia's cheeks only this time from a different source. As Edwina expounded on the virtues of her husband-to-be, Sophia realized with a start that she did miss her husband.

But that was impossible. How could she miss Joel when theirs was merely a marriage of convenience and when he made it clear in his words and actions that he held little respect for her.

She recalled with biting humiliation the words he had exchanged with his father the night of their engagement ball.

A sense of bitterness soon replaced any fondness she might have been feeling. When Edwina bounded from the room, she again set herself at the ledgers knowing that in becoming deeply involved in the management of the mill, she would soon forget the dull ache in her heart.

A week later, Nevil arrived which seemed to lighten the spirit of the whole house. His love for Edwina grew with each day of his visit and plans for a December wedding made the evening discussions lively and welcome, especially for Sophia, who desperately needed the diversion.

The stress of the factory was taking a toll on her. She had been able to increase the wages of her numerous employees but only by a fraction of what was really needed to help alleviate the situation and the number of those on poor relief increased weekly. The debt she had paid off for Joel and the money given to his mistress had diminished her ability to do more and the remainder of her fortune was committed to the new steam-based factory and to her own family.

As summer drew to a close with the onset of a chilly September, another factor added to her distress. In all these weeks, she had received only two letters from her husband. Of course neither her sisters nor Tristan said anything to her, but Joel's name was carefully avoided in the face of his absence and his indifferent correspondence. Even her siblings had begun to sense something was amiss.

In mid-September, Sophia left her office after a grueling day of once-again reviewing the long, black ledger books. She entered the corridor which separated her office from the hall and heard familiar voices. Her heart lurched at the sound and without retreating to her office to await a formal announcement, she walked quickly into the foyer and embraced Georgina Winwood.

"I know it was terribly impolite of us not to have written beforehand, but the truth is, Horace and I have just come from

Scotland—grouse-hunting of course with Jock Driscoll—and we couldn't pass south without seeing you. You are greatly missed, my dear." Lady Winwood embraced her and placed a kiss on her cheek.

Sophia again felt her heart jump. Was she *greatly missed?* Joel was still in Scotland. Had he sent his aunt purposefully to Lancashire to relay such a message? Sophia gave herself a mental shake. What fanciful musings were these? Greatly missed, indeed.

"You know you must never stand on ceremony with me," Sophia responded. "You will always be welcome in my house. Horace, how do you do? May I offer you a glass of sherry?"

Horace slipped off his greatcoat which slid into the hands of a waiting maid. She felt suddenly embarrassed that she didn't have a proper butler to wait on personages of rank. Certainly were Joel living at Woodbridge House, she would have to hire— She cut her useless musings short as Lord Winwood responded to her offer of refreshment. "I would greatly appreciate it, Sophia. Thank you so much. It must be my age, but once a chill gets into the air, my bones ache."

Georgina turned toward her husband and pinched his cheek. "You are very brave to be traveling about the countryside with me, and I am deeply grateful."

With her guests' outer traveling garb placed in the hands of the maid and orders for accommodations delivered, Sophia led the Winwood's to her drawing room. Bartholomew had been a man of simple, though elegant tastes and the large, though not lofty chamber of mahogany paneling and royal blue velvet window and furniture dressings could not help but please.

"What a lovely receiving room," Lady Winwood said sincerely, seating herself on the sofa near the stone fireplace. Coal was piled up in the grate, ready for the evening's fire. She directed her gaze to the window opposite the fireplace. "And what an, er, interesting view."

Sophia couldn't help but smile. "Our Lancashire landscape

has certainly changed. The lovely green rolling hills and moor-lands are shrouded by coal-dust and smoke."

Lady Winwood, drawing off her gloves, observed, "I daresay you find you must set your housemaids to dusting more than once a day."

Sophia smiled. "I certainly do!"

"There seem to be factories everywhere," Horace said. "Why, on passing through Manchester, I saw chimney smoke from some of these mills rising three hundred feet in the air—time and again."

Sophia nodded. "The effect on the land is not pleasing, but I'm sure in time that will change."

Horace frowned. "We crossed a river coming up here. I daresay not much lives in that stream."

"The trout have been gone for some time. It's the waste from the dye vats."

Both Lord and Lady Winwood shook their heads in wonder. Sophia, still wondering at their sudden, unexpected arrival, inquired about their summer activities, where they had been and how they had enjoyed their stay in Scotland. Georgina, ever the gossip, told her every scrap of news she had acquired during her tour of five different homes since mid-July. Horace made himself at home in what used to be Bartholomew's favorite winged chair, placing his feet on a footstool and sipping with obvious delight his glass of sherry. His enjoyment soon over-took his fatigue of traveling and after a few minutes, he was snoring gently in the chair.

Georgina looked at him fondly, then placed all her attention on Sophia. "So tell me how you are. You look well, though I must say a little fagged, perhaps?"

Sophia, who was finding Georgina's company to be a kind of comfort that surprised her, found herself relaxing a little. She shared with her the trials which had met her on her return from London, the general unrest of the weavers, the drop in prices for finished fabrics, the poor food-stuffs available for her work-ers.

Lady Winwood eyed her curiously. "Now that I recall, Joel mentioned something like that to me, that you had written to him on more than one occasion indicating your mill was experiencing difficulties. You aren't in any kind of danger of reprisal—some sort of machine-smashing as I've heard happens occasionally?"

"No, of course not," Sophia assured her. "My workers know I've done all I can to help them. I have an excellent manager who keeps in touch with the spinners and weavers, letting them know what is happening in the economy generally."

"This is all so strange to me," Lady Winwood said. "I've never known anyone in Trade."

Sophia knew that the viscountess's remark was not meant to be hurtful, but she felt the color on her cheeks rise anyway. "I suppose when I was a girl learning my letters, I never supposed I would be balancing ledgers, either."

"Do you think you will always manage the mill?"

"I can't imagine doing anything else," Sophia replied honestly.

"But what of one day being mistress of the Kennington properties?"

Lady Winwood's words startled Sophia into the awareness yet again that she was no longer mere Mrs. Ashley, but Lady Leyburn whose husband would one day be the Marquess of Kennington.

She would have answered Georgina's question, but at that moment Tristan entered the room on his usual bouyant step with Mark Ingram in tow. "I say," he cried. "It is you! We were told at the stables that you'd come, but I wouldn't believe it! How are you, Lady Winwood?"

"Tristan," Sophia called to her brother gently. "Your best bow, if you please."

"Almost forgot!" he returned. To her ladyship, who was smiling affectionately at him, he made a bow ending with a silly flourish of his hand which caused Georgina to laugh.

"All right, young pup!" she called to him. "Enough of your antics. How are you, Mr. Ingram?"

"Very well, thank you, my lady."

Sophia could see that Mark would have continued the courtesies had not a violent snore suddenly erupted from Lord Winwood followed by his sitting abruptly up in his chair and exclaiming, "Huzza!"

Sophia bit her lip to keep from laughing and only kept from staring at Horace with the greatest effort. A glance toward the young men, told her they were also restraining their amusement.

"Oh, for heaven's sake, Horace," Lady Winwood cried. "You dozed off, awakened shouting and now you've given all of us a fright!"

He blinked at each one in turn, then explained. "By God, if I didn't dream Lord Wellesley had vanquished that rascal Bonaparte."

"That's a dream I should certainly toast!" Mark exclaimed.

"Me, too," Sophia said.

"Here, here," Tristan added. "We won't see a moment's peace in the countryside until the war's over, that's for sure."

All eyes became fixed on Tristan. Sophia lifted her brows, a little surprised by her brother's comprehension of their situation.

"What do you mean, boy?" Lord Winwood said. "Yes, do sit down. Joel tells us there's a bit of unrest brewing in the Midlands. Is that what you mean? And while you're at it, tell me about this factory you are so determined to manage when you grow up—yes, yes, I know all about it."

"Well, sir . . ."

Sophia watched her brother settle in comfortably next to Lord Winwood and begin expounding on his vast knowledge of the mill. She was stunned by what she saw and heard. Of course Tristan had professed several times his intention, his interest, in taking over the management of the mill, but she had never really listened to him before. He explained knowledgeably about how Bonaparte's Continental system had harmed the manufacturers, about the manner in which the cessation of trade with America had also affected the mills, and how there had even been talk of a resurgence of Luddism.

"Luddism!" Horace cried. "Good God—secret armies, machine-smashings, combinings. Sounds like a Jacobite uprising to me."

"No, no!" Tristan assured him. "It's nothing like that. The Luddites don't want a revolution—they just want decent wages and work, the common rights of any Englishman."

"Ho-ho!" Horace cried. "I can see a future for you in the Commons with such a passionate way of expressing yourself. Say, why don't you show me this factory of yours."

"Really!" Tristan cried. "I'd love to, that is, you don't mind do you, Sophy?"

She watched Tristan rise to his feet, his eyes alive with excitement. She had listened to him talk of the Luddites in such a knowledgeable way that a terrible suspicion crossed her mind—that he might know some of them personally. Remembering, too, that he had gone to school with a number of the mill workers' children when he was young, did not allay either her suspicions or her concerns that her brother might be too closely connected to the unrest in the village for her comfort.

Taking a deep breath, she responded to his original question. "No, of course I don't mind," she said, restraining the truth of her feelings. "But I'm wondering if Lord Winwood might prefer to rest from his travels before taking on a tour of the mill." She glanced toward Horace who had now gained his feet.

"Nonsense," he said. "I'm fit as a fiddle." Then with a chuckle, he added, "Besides, it would already seem as though I've had a bit of a rest." The wry, humorous expression on his face, caused everyone to laugh together.

When all three men departed, Lady Winwood opened a different subject entirely. "I'm glad they're gone," she admitted, leaning toward Sophia a little. "You see, I had something of a particular nature I wanted to say to you, to ask you, really."

Now why wasn't Sophia surprised? "Please, ask me anything."

Georgina settled back into the cushions of the royal blue velvet sofa and looked at Sophia piercingly for a long moment. "I don't mean to distress you, my dear, but I feel I ought to tell you that I was very much surprised when I learned that you had not accompanied Joel to Scotland or that he had not given up his own pleasures to keep you company here in Lancashire. To say the least, it presents a very odd appearance."

The meat of gossip, Sophia thought ruefully. "We—that is, Joel and I agreed that since my duties in Woodbridge were extensive, that he shouldn't have to be bound to my obligations. I wanted him to enjoy himself elsewhere. You can see that even if he were here our social life would be very limited. For that reason—"

"For that reason you would keep the man you love at arm's length?"

"What?" Sophia retorted, stunned. "I—I don't know what you mean, on any score. The man I love? You yourself know that ours is a marriage of convenience only."

Lady Winwood narrowed her eyes. "You're a goosecap, Sophia Leyburn. For all your intelligence, you haven't the perception of a sparrow."

"I'm not in love with him, if that is what you are driving at. I have never really agreed with such romantical nonsense and certainly at my age—"

"Your age?" Georgina queried, then burst out laughing. "That's right, you're in your dotage. Even a simpleton could see as much."

Sophia knew a kind of discomfiture she had never before experienced. "Really, Georgina, I don't know what you mean, but I wasn't referring to myself in terms of advanced years so much as not being a schoolroom chit all starry-eyed from having read Byron and thinking that one must be violently in love to be happy."

"What about a little in love, then?" she asked, giving the uncomfortable subject another turn.

"A little in love?"

"Yes, wouldn't you say, you're a little in love with Joel?"

"No," she responded firmly. "I am not."

"Ah," Lady Winwood responded irritatingly. "Then I am very much confused. I must be mistaken."

Sophia wanted to end the subject, but Lady Winwood had a look on her face that said she knew something. "Mistaken about what?" Sophia could not resist asking.

"Well, it is a mystery to me that if you are not in love with Joel, why you would have paid off his mistress?"

Sophia was shocked. Her mouth fell agape. "What do you know of that!"

"Then it is true?" she asked.

"How could you have learned of that?"

"Five thousand pounds, wasn't it?"

Sophia rose to her feet abruptly and began pacing the room. "I don't see—I don't understand—how can you know—how could anybody know—"

"Because she boasted to Joel of it, of course."

"He knows then," she cried, turning to stare at Lady Winwood.

The viscountess nodded. "He gave her an additional sum to leave England, which I understand she has. By the way, there was no, er, by-blow."

Sophia was feeling light-headed and returned to sit in a chair opposite Lady Winwood. "I suppose I behaved foolishly then."

"Perhaps a little," Lady Winwood said. "I don't know. I might have done the same in your shoes. Fanny Price was far too garrulous for my tastes. She could never keep her tongue about any of the men she drew to her—and she drew them all at one time or another."

Sophia was reeling from Lady Winwood's revelations. "Was—was Joel very angry?"

"Not when I spoke to him, in fact, I would say he was a little repentant. I think he feels he ought to have dealt more swiftly and firmly with the rapacious Cyprian. I couldn't agree more. So, tell me, why did you pay her the money?"

Sophia thought back to the interview with Fannie Price and the woman's insistence that Joel was madly in love with her. "To prevent a scandal," she replied quietly. "I sensed that she would not leave either Joel or myself alone until she'd gotten what she wanted—for her child."

"I assure you, there is no child."

"She lied to me then. She even must have put a pillow under her gown."

"She is an actress," Lady Winwood reminded Sophia.

"You may be right, after all. I don't have the perception of a sparrow."

"Not about Fannie, apparently, and not about Joel either, if I've missed my mark."

Sophia turned her gaze back to her friend. "You are mistaken. What do I know about love?" She had spoken the words before she could prevent them passing her lips.

"More than you know and more than Joel knows, as well. In fact, I am beginning to think I've never known a more stubborn pair than the two of you. But I won't dwell on any of this further. There is, however, one matter I will put before you. Your name is being bandied about the ton, and none too politely, because the pair of you are not together. You've not produced a first child, yet, and until you do, the kind of separation you are now undertaking will only be looked at with suspicion. Even though everyone is aware that yours is a Marriage of Convenience—"

"What do you mean?" Sophia broke in hastily. "I thought—Joel and I strove to keep our affairs private, to make certain no one knew of our arrangement—"

"You are being far too naive, Sophia. There are a dozen ways news like this becomes known. For one thing, by the time Joel had paid off his debt, the true nature of his friend's suicide had become known as well as the fact that Joel had co-signed a note to the moneylenders. Add to that his well-known estrangement with his father, then his betrothal to a complete unknown who happens to be the widow of a prosperous mill-owner, then the fact that Joel is not cast into prison, and the truth becomes known. The truth will out, as Shakespeare said, and it has."

Sophia was so completely dismayed by this revelation that for a long moment she couldn't speak. So the entire *beau monde* knew that she had bought a husband. She was only surprised that she hadn't been shunned for her part in the bargain. She said as much.

Lady Winwood smiled. "Because I don't think you've ever quite understood—you've made your way into polite society. Matches are made every day for reasons other than romantic interest, but not all persons who bring property only to a marriage are accepted."

Sophia was dumbfounded. "But I thought—"

"You were wrong," she finished. "Yes, yes, I know what you've thought, and more than once you've offended even me by holding to such opinions that many of us care only for birth and social position."

"I—I guess I've never thought of it this way. I always supposed that Joel's rank—"

"Women rule London society," Lady Winwood said firmly. "Why do you think there are five Patronesses for the Almack Assemblies. It is we who dictate who shall be acceptable among our ranks and who shall not—the men merely adhere to our judgments. From the first, when I saw how you conducted yourself in Hyde Park, not putting yourself forward as many do, and certainly not accepting the unwelcome attentions of any man, told volumes for your character and your high-mindedness, the very same qualities I am convinced prompted Joel to take my original proposition seriously in the first place."

Sophia had never looked at the situation in this way before. She could see as well that Lady Winwood was speaking a measure of the truth.

Lady Winwood continued, "However, aside from our differing opinions, I do wish you might consider inviting your husband back to Lancashire. It would seem he was distinctly under the impression that you did not want him around and he is far too proud to beg to come home. I will not argue with you further about whether you are in love with him or not, but I would urge you, at least in this first year of marriage, to follow the conventions as much as you can. Once you've conceived a child, then of course, what you choose to do afterward becomes a matter of personal perference."

There was something in Lady Winwood's manner which led Sophia to believe that her friend had some scheme afoot. Leading Lady Winwood to her bedchamber in order that she might dress before dinner, Sophia promised that she would consider taking her advice.

"You will not regret it," Lady Winwood promised.

That evening at dinner, Sophia felt happier than she had in a long time. Her sisters and brother were present, all content, along with Mark Ingram and Nevil Royce. But the addition of two such familiar and warm people as Lord and Lady Winwood, made the dinner seem almost festive. She grew aware that the Season in London had given her much more than just a husband, but friends she esteemed, and a love of society that surprised her. For so many years she had by necessity devoted herself to an aging husband, the operation of a mill and the care of her younger siblings, that friendships and lighthearted amusements were out of the question. To some extent, her return to Lancashire had forced her back into that earlier role. But the Winwoods' presence provided a relief to her labors and responsibilities and for that she was very grateful.

The subject of the mill took hold of the conversation early on as a fine dinner of thinly sliced Yorkshire ham, a variety of vegetables, jellies and sauces was served. Lord Winwood could not keep his own astonishment quiet as he expounded on the humidity of the air in which the spinners and weavers worked, on the particles of cotton which floated in the air, on the long rows of furnace fires, the rumbling of the wheels, the endless flashes of white proceeding from carding machines, then seized by the teeth of a myriad of whirls and cylinders and stretched into threads to be lost in a forest of spindles. He had never seen anything of the like and no longer professed even the smallest wonder that Tristan was so captivated with running such a miracle of modern invention.

"And to think I can hardly tie my cravat!" he exclaimed at last, a statement which sent nearly everyone into whoops.

The evening continued in such a light-hearted manner, with Edwina and Caroline entertaining everyone with ballads, duets and sonatas performed at the pianoforte. Only with some sadness, did Sophia watch the evening drawing to a close, knowing that in the morning her guests would be leaving.

On the following day, Sophia bid good-bye to her friends with both a sensation of loss as well as a spark of anticipation. The night had given her counsel and when the last turn of the wheels of Lord Winwood's traveling coach was heard on the gravel drive, Sophia turned back into the house to do as Lady Winwood had suggested—to invite her husband home to Lancashire.

Thirteen

A week later, with September on the wane, Sophia sat anxiously in the royal blue velvet drawing room awaiting the arrival of her husband. She had spent the morning pouring over her black ledgers, but the figures ran together again and again until finally she simply cast them all aside, rose from her desk and left the room not to return.

Instead, she had gone to her bedroom and changed from her somber gown of a small printed brown and beige calico into a simple, high-waisted gown of a soft, forest green velvet. The sleeves were long in response to the increasingly frosty autumn days and a thick bank of glowing coals kept the chill from the paneled room.

She was seated in Bartholomew's comfortable chair, her slippered feet on the footstool and trying to concentrate on a book of sermons she had pulled from the shelves of the library an hour earlier. The sky was drizzly and gray, a dull light illuminating the pages over her left shoulder.

She would read a word, then her gaze would drift to a piece of lint on her skirt. She would remove the lint, return her gaze to the page and to the word. She would read the word again, again her gaze drifted away—it was no use! Her mind was all for wondering when Joel would arrive. Her eyes could not be kept on the page and her ears were tuned toward any sounds which might come from the gravel drive. She knew she would be able to hear her husband's traveling chariot if she listened carefully and it would seem listening was all she could do.

This is ridiculous, she thought to herself, closing the book with a snap and tossing it on a table at her elbow. She rose to leave the drawing room intending to return to her office when suddenly she heard the sound she had been waiting for all morning.

Joel had arrived. She quickly sat down again.

Taking up her book, she opened it up on her lap and sat waiting tensely. She heard the butler's steps on the hall—the butler she had hired recently in anticipation of Joel's arrival. She heard the faint mumblings of pleasantries. She heard footsteps approaching. Her heart was in her throat. Really, she shouldn't be so nervous, so excited. Why was she?

Then he was standing there, in the wide doorway of the room, tall and handsome in his traveling gear, a smile in his gray eyes.

"Hallo," he called to her, a faint smile on his lips.

She knew the oddest impulse to run to him, to cast herself into his arms. Instead, she closed her book carefully and set it aside. "I was glad you were able to come," she responded, noticing that her fingers were trembling.

She rose from her seat and smiled at him. At the same time, he advanced into the room.

"I was surprised by your letter, Sophia," he said. He approached her and took her hand in his own, holding it gently within his clasp. "But deeply gratified, more than you can know."

She could hardly breathe, she realized with a start. He was too near for comfort. She felt almost dizzy. "I—I felt it was the right thing to do."

She looked into his gray eyes and had a curious sensation of being lost.

"Do you know how beautiful you are?" he whispered. How intense his eyes became.

She caught her breath. He was still holding her hand, he was leaning toward her, as if to kiss her. She wanted him to, yet was frightened by the idea of it. She lowered her gaze from his and drew back from him, at the same time withdrawing her hand from his clasp. "You have always paid me the nicest compliments. You haven't needed to."

"Haven't I?" he asked.

She laughed lightly, trying to recover her composure. "Well, no. Ours is a marriage of convenience. It certainly isn't necessary for you to do the pretty with me. I am after all, just your wife." She glanced up at him and saw that the light in his eyes had dimmed and her heart sank. She knew she had said the wrong thing but she was so inexperienced that she didn't know how to make it right.

"Yes, a marriage of convenience," he murmured, an edge to his words.

Sophia heard the bitter note in his voice. Then he wished himself well out of it, she thought. She turned away from him approaching the fireplace, feeling utterly blue-deviled. She bit back tears of disappointment.

"Why am I here, Sophia?" he asked at last.

Why, indeed, she wondered. With her back to him, she began, "Lady Winwood came to call about a week ago. She informed me that gossip is rampant among the *beau monde*." Turning back to him, she squared her shoulders. "Her advice to me—to us—was that to be separate as we were when we were so newly married, was causing tongues to wag and that until we produced a child together, we ought to be living under the same roof. I agreed with her."

"So that's it?" he asked. "That's all?"

"I thought you would want to preserve at least the appearances of our marriage."

"What?" he cried, then caught himself. She had ruffled his cool reserve but she didn't understand why.

"I didn't mean to distress you," she said. "I am trying, Joel, to make the best of our marriage—I just—" she broke off, tears now hotly in her eyes. She placed a hand to her lips and took a deep breath to staunch the strange emotions which were threatening to ruin her composure.

"What? What did you almost say?" he asked, taking a step toward her, his tone gentle.

She blinked back the tears and took another deep breath. "Nothing—that is, I don't know what it was I meant to say. You will have to forgive me. I've had a rough time of it since returning to Woodbridge House. The mill—"

"Yes, I know," he said softly.

She shook her head. "What do you mean?"

He smiled faintly. "Well, Tristan wrote me twice and in each of his letters—though I don't think he quite understood how much he was telling me—he informed me of the delays in getting the steam loom factory built, of the unrest among the villagers, he even hinted of talk of a secret society—King Lud, again, I suppose."

Sophia felt such an enormous relief at having the subject turned away from her marriage, that she didn't hesitate to enter into a discussion of the mill. She sat down in Bartholomew's chair, he took up a chair beside her and for the next half hour she poured her troubles into what she could see was his willing ear. He listened sympathetically, nodding frequently, and responding that her concerns and the mood of Woodbridge was similar in villages and towns all over the Midlands.

"I don't like to say it, but I think the factoried counties are on the verge of riot," he said at last.

"No," Sophia assured him. "I am persuaded it is not as bad as that. Once the war is over—"

"The war may not be over for years," he said soberly.

His statement, backed as it was by his experience in Parliament for so many years, struck a chord of fear in her heart. How long could the situation hold if there was no relief in sight?

"Then you think I ought to be concerned—that there might be trouble even here, in Woodbridge?"

"I don't know," he answered honestly. "But you might want to take precautions as many mill-owners are doing. Set guards at the doors day and night."

"I can't believe that my mill would be under attack," she said. "I've done so much—I even increased wages not long ago."

He lifted his brows. "You did?"

"Well, I won't let my workers starve and the cost of corn is so dear."

He looked at her with an odd light in his eye. "That was very generous of you. It is not commonly done."

"If a mill can't support those who labor, then it only makes sense that at some point the mill will fail—if only we can get through the winter."

He leaned forward in his chair and reached over to take her hand. "I'm here," he said. "And I mean to be of use to you, if you wish for it."

Sophia heard the sincere note in his voice and gave his hand a squeeze. "I do wish for it," she whispered, feeling as though a burden had been lifted from her shoulders. He smiled, and she returned his smile.

"Sophia," he said in a low voice. "I didn't just come because—"

But he got no further since at that moment, Caroline, oblivious to their presence, entered the room with Mark Ingram in tow. She did not at first perceive Sophia or Joel and her face was etched with worry. Mark was beside her, speaking with some urgency, "But I don't see how we can—" he then caught sight of Sophia. "Oh, I say," he cried astonished.

"Sophia!" Caroline exclaimed. "I didn't see you, that is—" Her gaze landed on Joel. "You've arrived! Why wasn't I told!" At once, the consternation left her face and she entered the drawing room on a quick tread, crossing the room to embrace her brother-in-law fondly. "How we've missed your conversation at the dinner table. You were the only one to keep Tristan in check when he would bore us to tears about gas-lighting or steam engines or the like."

Sophia was bowled over by Caroline's obvious affection for Joel, welcoming him like a brother who had been absent for years. The sight of her sister greeting her husband with such sincere feelings, made her very content. While Caroline was asking about his summer, Sophia ordered a glass of sherry for Joel which she knew he would enjoy. He thanked her warmly when the butler offered the glass to him. Before taking a first sip, he lifted the glass to her in a silent toast.

Since Mark had just asked him how many brace he shot each day, his attention was soon diverted away from her. Sophia took up her seat near him and contented herself with watching him and listening to him. She thought with a smile that she had missed hearing his richly timbred voice.

"Joel, you've come at last!"

Sophia looked up to see Tristan in the doorway of the drawing room, an expression of joy on his face.

"Hallo, Tris," Joel called to him. "Come, here. Let's have a look at you? Been at the books or have you buried yourself in cotton?"

Tris strode happily into the drawing room though Sophia could see that his color was heightened. "Can't make heads nor tails of Latin," he returned. "Never could."

"Wasn't much good at it, myself," Joel replied generously. "But the effort of study taught me a little of discipline."

"I know, I know," Tristan responded. "Mark has told me often enough."

Sophia could see he wasn't in the least offended and she turned again to marvel at Joel. How many times had she said nearly the same words to her brother in an effort to encourage his studies but always he flew into the boughs. She remembered recently telling him that working with a tutor at home was one thing, but once he was at Oxford, he would need a mind ready for dedicated concentration. For some reason, her words had put him instantly on his mettle, whereas right now, her brother was all but worshipping Joel.

"Well, if you like I can take you right now," he cried enthusiastically.

Sophia blinked. Having been lost in thought a little, she had missed part of their conversation. "Take him where?" she asked, startled.

"To see the mill, of course!" Tristan cried, turning to look at her as though she hadn't a brain in her head.

"No," Sophia responded promptly. "Don't be absurd."

"Just because you don't want him to see the mill, doesn't mean that *he* doesn't!" Tristan cried offended.

Sophia was taken aback by her brother's defensive reaction. "On the contrary, Tristan," she said giving her head a shake, "I know Joel will want to see the mill, and I don't mind at all that you're the one to give him a tour, but he's just arrived."

Tristan bit his lip. "Sorry, Sophy," he said repentantly. "Wasn't thinking." He turned back to Joel. "Another day, when you're rested."

"That would be best," Joel said. "And Sophia is right, I do want to see every last corner of it. I've been hearing about these mills for so long that I vow I am bursting with curiosity."

At that Tristan beamed. "What a rapper!" he cried. "I know you're not *bursting* with curiosity, but you will like the mill. It's a marvel, truly."

Joel chuckled and the tense moment passed. Sophia wondered again how it was that Joel had developed such an easy rapport with her brother.

When Nevil and Edwina arrived from an outing in his curricle, the family circle was complete and Sophia experienced a return of the joy she had known a week earlier when Lord and Lady Winwood had stayed in her home for the night.

During the next few days, Joel disappeared into the factory with Tristan which gave Sophia time to adjust to his new presence in her home and to the odd shift in their relationship which she couldn't quite explain. Somehow the separation of the summer had given them an appreciation of one another that had not been present before. Joel was more attentive to her than ever, making certain a screen was placed near her in the evenings against the encroaching chill of the fall nights, kissing her hand in the hall while bidding her goodnight, and always inquiring at the end of each workday how she fared.

From the time of their betrothal, he had been courteous and civil as he was now. But was she mistaken in thinking that he now looked at her with a warmth in his gray eyes that had not been there in the spring?

Such thoughts began to be common for her, somedays to the point of torture.

There was one thing for which she was very grateful—not once since his arrival at Woodbridge House had he mentioned Fannie Price. Not that she had expected him to, but she had supposed he would reprimand her for her conduct. The fact that he so kindly set aside the fact that she had paid off his mistress, was perhaps the reason she finally brought the subject forward.

Having been left alone quite thoughtfully by her siblings one evening that she might have some time alone with her husband, Sophia sat on the royal blue velvet sofa, opposite Bartholomew's chair in which Joel had taken up permanent residence. She liked seeing him there because she had respected her prior husband

and knew that he, in turn, would have approved of a future marquess behaving with such a lack of self-consequence in his home.

Tonight, she was nervous, however, knowing that for her own sake she needed to explain why she had visited Fannie Price.

"What is it?" Joel asked, startling her out of her reveries. "You've seemed a little on edge since dinner. Is something amiss at the mill?"

Sophia smiled faintly. "No, not at all. Well, at least nothing out of the ordinary." She looked away from him, then met his gaze squarely. "I wish to apologize to you for—for Fannie Price." She gulped, waiting to see his reaction which turned out to be a mere lifting of his brows in faint surprise.

"Miss Price?" he queried.

"Georgina told me—"

"My dear aunt talks too much—"

"In this case, I have been grateful she told me of your discussion with her about, about what happened. She is gone then?"

Joel nodded. "Very much so. My man saw her on a ship heading for the Colonies. You needn't have given her the money."

Sophia felt the color rise on her cheeks. "I didn't know what to do or even what to believe. She sent me a note and I already knew by her harassment of you at the opera that she was unlikely to leave either of us alone, that I needed to see her." Sophia looked at him and quite innocently blurted, "She was so very beautiful and she convinced me so easily about her, er, condition. It is no wonder, I mean, I can see why you, that is—oh, dear!"

She broke off, knowing that her cheeks were now flaming. Joel laughed and rose from his chair. He came to sit beside her on the sofa, something he had never done before, and took quick possession of her hand. He placed a soft kiss on her fingers. "She was a gifted actress, nothing more."

"Uncommonly so, I begin to think. She will certainly enjoy a successful career in America."

At that, Joel chuckled. "I think what I like best about you is your practical approach to just about everything."

Sophia wasn't certain what he meant, but she needed to address the hardest part of all. "I was convinced you were in love with her," she said, looking at his profile, wanting to hear his response.

Again, he kissed her fingers, letting his lips linger against her skin. Sophia drew in her breath at the seductive softness of his lips.

"No, I wasn't in love with her."

"Never?" she asked, as again he assaulted her fingers, causing her to feel dizzy.

"Never," he murmured. He then laid her hand gently on her lap and released her fingers only to take her chin in his hand. His lips were very close to her. "Sophia, from the first, I have wanted to—"

But he got no further because from the foyer a shouting suddenly rose to the rafters. The butler's voice hurtled into the drawing room, "Good God, 'tis Master Tristan! Lady Leyburn. Lord Leyburn, come quickly! He's been shot!"

Within a matter of seconds, Sophia was in the hall standing over her brother refusing to believe what she was seeing. Tristan's eyes were closed, his complexion white and a pool of blood could be seen forming on the planked wood floor beneath his head.

Joel scooped him up in his arms and snapped a series of orders to the butler which Sophia did not quite hear though she understood enough to know that a doctor was to be summoned immediately. He carried Tristan up the stairs to his bedchamber. Sophia threw back the bedcovers and Joel gently laid him down. She retrieved a towel from beside the basin in his room and gave it to Joel who, kneeling beside the bed, began to dab at the pitiful wound on the side of Tristan's head.

Sophia stood just behind Joel, her hands clenched painfully together. "Well?" she asked, fearing the worst. Her knees were shaking badly. "Is he going to die?"

"I don't think so. It seems, that is, the pistol ball must have just grazed his head. I can't find anything."

Tristan began to writhe beneath Joel's touch. Sophia instinctively rounded Joel and took hold of Tristan's hand, gripping it tightly which seemed to calm him. "It hurts," she heard him murmur, words which caused relief to flood her.

"Do stop!" Tristan cried. "You're hurting me!"

He came to his senses with a start, his far hand now clutching Joel's sleeve in an effort to prevent him from cleaning the wound.

"Easy, lad!" Joel cried.

"Joel," Tristan murmured, wild-eyed. "I shouldn't have gone—but I had to." He winced then slumped into his pillow.

"He's fainted again," Joel said. "I think he's lost a bit of blood."

Edwina and Caroline entered the room, both crying out at the sight of their brother. Edwina immediately began weeping. Sophia released Tristan's hand and took both Caroline and Edwina in tow, ushering them out of the chamber.

"Stop crying, Edwina, please," Sophia said. "Tell me where Nevil is. I think he might be of some assistance to us. He must know a great deal about wounds of this sort."

"What do you mean?" Caroline asked. "Has Tristan been shot?"

Sophia nodded. "But by whom? Who would want to hurt Tristan? Tristan, of all people?"

"I don't know."

"Nevil just arrived," Edwina said, stifling her tears. "He's stabling his horse."

At that moment, Mark appeared at the top of the stairs and came walking briskly down the long hall, his face creased with worry. "I had gone to meet Nevil at the stables, but a servant came running and told me. Is he—?"

Sophia understood his question at once. "He is badly hurt and has swooned twice. A pistol-ball grazed his head but Joel thinks that's all it is—just a graze."

"Thank God," Mark breathed.

He seemed inordinately distressed and a suspicion crossed Sophia's mind. Sending Caroline and Edwina to intercept Nevil, she drew Mark into the library across from the top of the stairs and closed the door behind her. Turning to face her brother's tutor, she said, "Is there something I should know?"

He looked at her and blinked, his brown eyes pinched and fretful. He gestured hopelessly with one hand. "I'm not sure— that is, I've suspected something was afoot for a week or more. Tristan, who does not always attend to my lessons, has been particularly inattentive of late, much more so than usual. In the mornings, he would be almost blear-eyed and yawning with each tick of the clock."

"What is it then that he's been doing? I don't understand."

Mark's complexion paled. "I think he's been to some of the meetings on the moors."

Sophia gasped. "You mean, they're not just the rumors I've believed them to be and that Tristan has—you're saying he's become a member of King Lud's army?"

"As to the latter, I can't say, but I do believe that the societies we've heard about are more than rumors. Whether he's joined one of them or got caught in the wrong place at the wrong time I can't say. I just feel so responsible, like I should have told you or Joel—"

He broke off and Sophia could not find words to comfort him because she agreed with his opinion. "Yes, Mark, you should have. Even if you suspected something of an entirely different nature. For one thing, Tristan shouldn't be out in the cold damp night air any more than the rest of us. For another he's only a boy—barely fifteen—and doesn't have the sense you have or I or Joel to recognize mischief if he saw it. I'm deeply disappointed. He could have died and might still if his wound doesn't heal properly."

"Do you think I haven't thought of that!" Mark cried. "I anything happens to him, I don't know what I'll do."

Sophia heard sounds on the stairs and knew that Nevil had

arrived. She left Mark to consider the folly of his restraint and met Nevil just as he arrived on the landing.

"I can't believe it," he said, his expression stunned. "I thought I'd left the war in the Peninsula."

"I know," Sophia said. "Only do come look at him. I'm sure you've seen more of this than the rest of us."

Nevil nodded. "I'll do anything I can."

After Sophia showed Nevil to Tristan's room the butler arrived with a message that Ned Walcot needed to speak with her, that he was waiting for her in her office.

Sophia hurried down the stairs and joined her manager. He had his black hat in his hand and a grim expression on his face. "The guards ye posted outside the new steam-loom factory fired at some men approaching the building not a half-hour past," he said. He couldn't look at her as he finished, "Master Tristan were wi' 'em—the guards fired in fear of t'mob. I can't say as I blame 'em—but—"

Sophia felt her knees weaken. "Are you saying Tristan was *with* them? You must be mistaken."

He shook his head. "Tristan weren't wearing a mask. After he fell t'others scattered and the guards recognized him. Is he—?"

"No, at least—no. He's been injured on the left side of his head, but he's still very much alive. We've of course sent for the surgeon."

"I dunna know what t'say, m'lady."

Sophia sank down in the chair by her desk and shaded her face with her hand. She struggled to bite back the tears which were hot on her lids. She had to compose herself, to think. Tristan—taking part in a raid on a mill? Unthinkable. A Luddite? Impossible. Why would he be when he loved the mill as he did? She thought back to all the discussions her family had had about all the issues involved and now that she thought about it, it was always Tristan who took the side of the weavers, complaining that they should enjoy better living and working conditions, that their artisanship should be honored, that the steam-loom factory ought to wait for a year or two.

But why would he have found it necessary to join in a violent protest by attacking the factory? Why couldn't he have come to her?

She lowered her hand, the reality of her relationship with her brother crashing down on her just as it had with her sisters. Both her sisters and Tristan saw her as the enemy, an autocratic parent-figure who they felt obliged to contest at every turn. Was she so terribly unsympathetic? She remembered how defensive Tristan became when she so much as mentioned Oxford or an alternative to his becoming a mill-manager.

In the end, she had to admit to herself that her own reign as a domestic tryant, as Joel had so harshly put it, was in part responsible for tonight's debacle.

She lifted her gaze to Mr. Walcot's face. "Please do what you can to keep tonight's events quiet. Ask the guards to forget that Tristan was present and to come to me tomorrow to discuss what happened. I don't quite understand how he came about to be at what seems to have been a raid on my mill, but I will see what I can do to find out the truth. You may return home now, and, thank you, Mr. Walcot. You've proven your friendship over and over and no less so than tonight."

Mr. Walcot nodded. "I just be that sorry I am fer t'young master."

"I know." She rose and took her leave of him then slowly mounted the stairs. When she reached Tristan's bedroom door Joel emerged quietly, closing the door behind him.

"Nevil is with him," he whispered. "The boy will do, don't worry." He opened his arms to her, a gesture which caused Sophia to readily accept his embrace and let the tears fall where they would.

After a few minutes, she was able to compose herself and to accept his kerchief with which to dry her cheeks. She then re-layed all that Mr. Walcot had told her of the attempted raid and that she had been right to take his advice about posting guards. She then told him the awful truth that Tristan had been among the rioters and that one of the guards had shot him.

"Good God," he murmured, supporting her with an arm about her shoulder.

Some time later, the doctor arrived and after examining Tristan and dressing the wound, he indicated that he thought the boy had been deuced lucky but would undoubtedly survive the incident to give his sister a great deal more tremblings and palpitations. These words delivered with a joviality and optimism intended to comfort her brought more tears flowing freely down her cheeks. She remained with her brother all that night and had her vigilance relieved in the early hours of the morning by Joel who said he would stay with Tristan so that she could get some rest.

The next day, by noon, Tristan was sitting up in bed and sipping a thin gruel as Joel fed him. Her husband had clearly not left his side, evidenced by his sadly-wilted shirtpoints, by his stubbly face and by the dark circles beneath his eyes. But never, Sophia thought, had he looked quite as handsome as he did now.

"You've not seen your bed," she said quietly. "Why don't you go now and I'll take care of Tristan."

Tristan, his voice weak, said, "Yes, do go Joel and, er, take this gruel with you."

Sophia looked at her brother, who had a faint smile on his lips, and was ready to box his ears for funning at a time like this. Joel however, with his lighter hand, merely laughed and told him to do as he was bid or he would hire a second tutor to teach him his Latin and Greek lessons in the evenings. "To keep you out of mischief, if nothing more," Joel added. He smiled wryly, winked at Sophia, then disappeared into the hallway.

Tristan looked at Sophia, then looked quickly away. "I suppose you've come to read me the riot act," he grumbled.

At his choice of words, Sophia started to giggle then stopped herself. For some reason, her anger was gone. "No," she drawled trying to restrain a chuckle. "I shan't read you the riot act but I think the village constable will want to."

Tristan jerked his head toward her, his eyes wide with surprise. "Oh, you mean, because last night—sort of a riot—oh—" Sophia bit her lip, Tristan smiled, and the pair of them fell into whoops, though not for long. Tristan suddenly laid his head back on the numerous pillows propped up behind him. "I don't think I should be laughing, at least not for a day or so. My head hurts dreadfully!"

"So your head is paining you, eh?" Sophia asked, lifting a spoonful of a cold, watery gruel to his lips.

"Yes, very much so," he said, grimacing.

"Well, I think it is the very least you deserve for giving me such a fright."

Tristan opened his eyes to look at her and then opened his mouth to sip the gruel. When she had dabbed at his lips with a napkin, he smiled faintly. "I like you much better this way, Sophy," he said quietly. "I remember you laughing more when mama was alive. Joel has made you happy, hasn't he?"

Sophia was thunderstruck by Tristan's observation. "Well, yes, I suppose he has," she answered quietly.

She fed him more of the gruel and after he had finished most of it, he said, "It wasn't what you must be thinking, Sophia. I was trying to stop them and I got caught in the middle."

"One of the secret societies on the moors?"

He nodded. "But don't ask me to tell you anything else. I can't—I just can't. Many of them are my friends."

Later, she turned Tristan over to the capable hands of the housekeeper. In the quiet of her bedchamber, she reflected on everything her brother had told her.

So there had been secret meetings after all. She had been hoping it was all hum, but now she knew for a fact trouble was brewing even in Woodbridge. She wasn't certain what she ought to do about Tristan's refusal to open his budget about who had been involved in the attack on her mill, but for the present she didn't want to press him, certainly not while he was recovering from a head injury.

Settling as much in her own mind, her thoughts turned to

what her brother had said to her about not laughing so much since her mother died. She realized what he had said was true. For a very long time, she had not had a great deal to smile or laugh about, not until now.

And for the first time she had to admit the truth, Joel had made her happy. He was very subtly changing the way she saw her world and in the kindness of what she was beginning to believe was his nature, he was helping her to feel that she was not quite so alone.

Fourteen

Two weeks later, as October began to dwindle away, Tristan emerged from his bedchamber for the first time since the incident at the mill. He was sick to death of coddling, he proclaimed as he greeted each of his three sisters in turn, kissing their cheeks and thanking them for their attentiveness. Sophia watched him with a quiet gratefulness that he had been spared. An inch only had made the difference between life and death for her brother, such a narrow increment by which to measure sadness and happiness.

Later, when Joel and Nevil had gone out for a ride, when Mark was preparing for another lesson for his student and the twins were busily planning Edwina's wedding breakfast, she had a chance to speak with Tristan. Previously, she had not wanted to broach the subject of the dissension at the mill because he grew fatigued so quickly when engaged in conversation. But his complexion had taken on a rosy hue and he seemed as fit as ever.

"I don't want you to take part in any more of these meetings," she said carefully. "I'm sure you understand now how dangerous they are."

To her surprise, she watched a certain mulish expression

overtake Tristan's face. He set his jaw, ground his teeth slightly and each cheek became dotted with a red spot.

"Now whatever have I said," she countered, "that you could possibly take amiss?"

"You wouldn't understand," he murmured. They were sitting in the blue drawing room. Sophia had a sampler on her lap she was embroidering. She was sitting in Bartholomew's chair near the hearth and Tristan sat opposite her, well-forward on the velvet sofa. He lowered his head, clasping his hands between his knees and sighed.

"Try me," she said, lacing her needle into the sampler of yellow daffodils.

He looked up at her quickly, an earnest expression in his green eyes. "You don't go about the countryside enough, Sophy," he said. "You don't know how it is. The suffering—good God, bread or potatoes for breakfast and dinner. I know you gave your workers a bit of a raise, but the cost of flour is exorbitant because of the Corn Laws—the children are so thin, many of them are taking ill. I'm worried that some won't survive the winter."

Sophia sat heavily back in the tall chair. "I can't do more than I'm doing—"

"You could do a lot more," he said, shaking his head. "You've enough wealth at your command—"

"But it's not my wealth," she said. "I inherited it from Bartholomew but the responsibility I have is to protect as much of it as possible, to insure that you and your sisters will always be provided for. You are too young to understand that these responsibilities must always supersede the sufferings of the poor. If I were to give everything away, what would become of you or your sisters?"

He looked at her with a degree of hostility that shocked her. "Then will you at least consider postponing the completion of the steam-loom mill? At least for a year or two?"

"I can't do that!" she cried. "We've discussed this enough for you to comprehend that I won't be able to compete if I don't upgrade our manufacturing process. Already, the mills to the south are out-producing us. Where do you think we will be if we can't sell our cloth at any price because it's too late to market and too expensive."

He seemed thoughtful for a moment. "Then at least wait until the spring, or better yet, the summer. Winter will be setting in soon."

"There's something else you need to consider," she added quietly. "If I were to give another raise, then what sort of message would I be sending to the rioters? Have you thought of that?"

"Of course I've thought of that, but you are misjudging the situation, Sophy, and you won't believe me because you think I'm still a child."

Sophia bit her tongue to keep from speaking her thoughts. Of course she still thought of him as a child. What else besides a child would have been joining in outlawed meetings on the moors? "I shan't argue with you on that head," she said. "For you would no doubt come the crab. Why don't we forget about all this for a while. I'll speak with Mr. Walcot and see what he thinks can be done." Trying to change the subject, she smiled and asked how his lessons were going and whether or not he thought he would soon be ready to enter Oxford. "For I'm certain once you are there, and can discuss theories of government and business with more knowledgeable young men, you'll gain a better understanding of—"

"Bartholomew didn't go to Oxford," Tristan cut in. "In fact, he went to the very same school I attended here in Woodbridge, and he did all right."

Sophia lifted her chin slightly. She was fatigued with his arguments. "You are not Bartholomew," she responded crisply.

He rose suddenly to his feet, his complexion high. "I may not be, but there isn't a day that goes by but what I wish he was still alive. He knew I had a feel for the mill, he even encouraged me to spend as much time there as I wished for. And never once did he make me feel that I needed to be something I'm not!"

"Tristan!" Sophia cried, as he stalked from the chamber. She was angry that he had raised his voice to her and equally distressed that he had so misunderstood her. She didn't want him to be something he was not, she just wanted him to make the most of his opportunities. Why couldn't he understand that?

She sat for a long time in the chair, her gaze pinned to the doorway where she had watched him vanish. She didn't say as much to him, but after his accident, she had determined more than ever to get him away from Woodbridge as soon as possible. She couldn't do anything for the present because Edwina and Nevil were to be married sometime in December, the invitations for the wedding awaiting only a selection of the date of the wedding. But after that, even if it meant spending Christmas in some other part of the kingdom, she meant to leave Lancashire.

Just as she picked up her embroidery again, Caroline swept into the room, her blue eyes blazing. "I have just been speaking with Tristan, Sophy, and he tells me you are still intent on Oxford. Can't you see what a mistake that is for our brother?"

By this time, Sophia had had quite enough arguing with her siblings. "Tristan's future is my concern, not yours. Yours is to find a good husband and raise a family."

Caroline moved to stand over her, a vision in a high-waisted gown of deep brown velvet, a lovely reflection of her dark brown hair. She placed her hands firmly on her hips and stated, "You speak like you are a dowager a hundred and fifty years old. So, Tristan and I are to do as we are bid—he must go to Oxford and become just the sort of gentleman you think he ought to be and I am to find a husband. Well, you have a great many surprises in store for you, if you are not careful."

"Sophy, I'm very disappointed. When you changed your mind about Nevil and Edwina, I truly believed you had finally gotten some sense into your head. But now, I see I was mistaken."

Sophia was livid. "Indeed," she responded frostily, meeting Caroline's hard gaze squarely.

Caroline laughed. "Yes, utterly mistaken. You are as stubborn and cold as you ever were. I suppose this means you haven't spoke to Joel about any of this."

"Joel isn't the one responsible."

"Well, if you think he would agree with you that you're doing the right thing by Tristan, you're wrong."

"Why do you fight me?" she asked, shifting the subject slightly. "I'm only thinking of what's best for Tristan. He nearly got himself killed recently, in case you haven't noticed, and all because he decided it would be very wise to get involved with a few secret, and quite illegal, meetings."

"If you recall, he was trying to stop the raid on your mill."

"He's just a boy. He should have told me or Ned Walcot or even Joel what was going forward instead of trying to have an effect all by himself."

"He felt a loyalty to his friends from childhood that apparently you can't begin to comprehend. What would you have had him do? Turn traitor?"

"Turn traitor!" Sophia cried, dumbfounded. She jumped to her feet, her embroidery sliding off her lap to the floor, and met Caroline face to face. "Of all the absurdity you have spoken for the past few minutes, this is the most ridiculous. You can't possibly use the word traitor unless you mean to speak of all of Tristan's so-called friends. They are the ones breaking the king's law."

"What is all the shouting?" Joel called from the doorway. "I found several servants clustered near the stairs when I came in from riding."

Sophia found her cheeks growing hot with embarrassment. "We—that is—Caroline and I were just discussing Tristan's education."

Caroline moved away from Sophia and approached Joel.

"She's speaking of sending Tristan off to Oxford again. You must speak to her, show her how silly such a notion would be."

Sophia opened her eyes wide. It was clear to her that Caroline and Joel had already broached the subject and further clear that they were in agreement. She might have felt embarrassed at his arrival since she had been caught in a quite unladylike demeanor—goodness, even the servants had been listening to their squabbles!—but the reality that Joel had taken up sides against her brought her former anger returning to her.

She watched Joel say a few quiet words to Caroline then bid her sister to leave the room. To her amazement, Caroline did so without a single word of protest. By the time Joel reached her, she was bristling with resentment. "I see you have sorted everything out with my sister. I suppose now you mean to tell me all that I'm doing wrong—again—and how I would benefit from your worldy-wise guidance."

"Stubble it, Sophy," he said, wearing a half-smile. "I'm not the enemy any more than Caroline or Tristan is. Sit down and tell me what the fuss is all about."

For some reason, his calm almost light-hearted attitude laid her feathers and she resumed her seat. He drew an Empire chair forward from near the window and sat down next to her.

"We were arguing about Tristan's future, of course. Caroline has strident opinions about his career at University. I suppose you don't think he should attend Oxford, either."

She leveled her gaze at him, daring him to agree with Caroline.

He smiled more broadly still. "A term or two at Oxford would certainly do the boy no harm, but—just in case you haven't noticed—he is no scholar."

Sophia took a deep breath. "Unless I much mistake the matter, many of the young men who attend Oxford or Cambridge are not scholars."

Joel chuckled. "Touché," he replied simply. "The fact is, the boy is set on his own future. You would do well to help him achieve that future instead of hindering him at every turn."

She was silent apace. "I don't want him killed because he enjoys being at the mill."

"Your concern is not without merit. Tensions in the country-side are mounting daily it would seem. Nevil and I stopped at the alehouse for a tankard only to be regarded with open hostility."

Sophia jerked her gaze toward Joel. "You can't be serious. I can't believe anyone would dare—"

He smiled faintly. "What? To defy us because we represent the government? We're all Englishmen when all is said and done. Still, I'm not comfortable about the unrest I see. Word has it that there have been machine-smashings in Nottingham."

"Well, it won't happen here," Sophy said firmly.

He reached over and took her hand, patting it gently. "It almost did, if you'll recall."

Sophia was comforted by Joel's touch. She thought over all that Tristan had told her. "Tristan is deeply concerned," she said. "He also feels I have not been into the countryside enough, that I have not seen the suffering as he has."

"That might be true," Joel responded with a slight frown, "but more important for the present, you might remember that Tristan is a young man, very near to adulthood, and like the rest of us, he won't readily accept a woman's interference in his affairs, and especially not his sister's."

Sophia fell silent. She knew he was speaking the truth, but she didn't know how to do anything else than what she had been doing for the past five years. "He just doesn't seem to understand that I've been responsible since mother and father died, responsible for him and for our sisters."

Joel rose to his feet and, still holding her hand, bid her come to him. When she gained her feet as well, he took her into a warm embrace and held her fast. "My poor Sophy," he murmured, his breath warm on her ear.

There was nothing of sarcasm in his voice, only a kind compassion which melted her heart. *My poor Sophy.* Tears rimmed her eyes suddenly. She couldn't remember the last time she had been so sweetly comforted. The burdens of trying to direct her siblings all these years, as well as her own life, had taken a toll on her, she knew as much, but she never complained. She loved Tristan, Edwina and Caroline. They were her family. But she had so long played the part of mother and father all rolled into one that for this brief moment, as Joel held her and stroked her hair, she knew a fatigue that surprised her.

He drew back from her slightly, though still holding her close, that he might look down into her face. "You've borne it all, haven't you?" He stroked her cheek lightly with his finger.

She nodded, looking into his eyes. She saw that he understood a little of her trials and a wave of affection poured over her. Without thinking, she leaned toward him and placed a kiss on his lips. When she drew back, he smiled down at her and without asking for permission kissed her hard in return.

Sophia gasped at the quick dart of pleasure his kiss gave her. She slipped her arms about his neck and leaned fully into him. She heard him groan, a sound which caused shivers to race down her spine, and for a long moment she forgot all her troubles in the sweetness of his embrace.

What would it be like to love Joel, she wondered, to be held in his arms for hours on end, to share secrets with him, to enjoy his body close to hers.

"Sophy," he whispered. "I've wanted you from the beginning. You know I have, only say that you want me, as well. I know ours is a marriage of convenience, but we could make it more, couldn't we?"

Sophia felt some of her pleasure drain away from her at his words. A marriage of convenience. He would never have *chosen* her. His debts had forced their union. She started to pull away from him.

"Now what have I said?" he asked, unwilling to let her go completely. "Sophy, you must talk to me. Faith, but you're the most *silent* female I've ever known. Most ladies gabble and gabble until you want to stuff cotton in your ears. But you! It's as though you've taken a vow of silence. Tell me! what are you thinking?"

Sophy swallowed hard, a kind of fear roiling within her. "You—" she began, stumbling over her words. "You spoke the truth once, to your father. You wouldn't have married me, ever, except for your need of my fortune. At one time, I thought our marriage reasonable, but I just can't seem to accustom myself to it."

"Why do you struggle so? I don't. I am content in having married you. I have no regrets. Do you?"

Sophia shook her head. "No," she drawled. "Not precisely."

"Have I not been patient with you? I've waited a long time." Suddenly, he blurted out, "I want my husbandly rights."

At that, Sophy drew back sharply from him. "Your husbandly rights?" she cried, stepping away from him.

He ran a hasty hand through his hair. "I didn't mean it that way. I mean, yes, I suppose I did. But you're a deuced pretty woman and when I have to look at you every day, to hear the sweet sound of your voice, to watch the way you sway when you move—it's a bit more than flesh and bone can bear."

Sophy opened her mouth to speak but wasn't sure what to say. She didn't know whether to be offended, amused, or astonished. For one thing, she did not like to think of any love-making they might engage in as his *husbandly right*. On the other hand, he had set his hair to flying every which way because of his obvious wish to take her to bed. Lastly she hadn't realized he took pleasure in her voice, or in the way she walked or in what little beauty God had given her.

Fortunately, she didn't have to say a word for at that moment Edwina and Nevil, arms linked tightly together, entered the room on a spritely tread. "We've decided to marry on the first Saturday in December even if it is Nevil's birthday. We don't want to wait any longer than that."

Nevil turned to eye his bride-to-be with a hungry look that

caused Joel to draw close to Sophia and whisper, "I know just how they feel."

That night, Sophia waited anxiously in her bedchamber for Joel to come to her. They had not spoken of the kiss they had shared earlier in the day, nor had Joel indicated he intended to visit her. But she was convinced somehow he would. She had dressed herself therefore in a pretty gown of fine cambric trimmed with pink ribbons, she had left off her habitual mob cap and brushed her long dark brown curls to a silken sheen, and a refurbished fire cast the room in fiery glow.

But Joel didn't come to her, a fact which both relieved her yet distressed her. No words of real love had been exchanged between them and though she knew Joel longed for her, she sensed that he was as much trapped by their marriage of convenience as she was. She didn't love him, or did she? Was love merely an excitement one felt or a result of trust built up over a hundred daily exchanges?

Joel had proven his character to her a dozen times, but what did that mean, merely that he was a good man, not a man who saw her as anything but the lady he married to get himself out of a fix. Yet he wanted her, he wanted her badly. But what did that mean? She felt dreadfully confused.

She fell asleep to such musings and awoke the next morning with a dull headache. When she saw Joel, she greeted his friendly smile with something of a cool nod of her head. He responded by staring at her for a hard moment before responding. "Is this how it is to be?" he asked, cryptically.

Sophia's head thrummed steadily. "I don't know what you mean?"

"I kissed you yesterday," he whispered, as they walked along the hall toward the landing.

"Yes," she murmured. She wanted to add that he also failed to come to her bedchamber, but she couldn't speak the words. Rubbing her neck slightly, she continued, "I've a lot I must do today. I have an appointment with Ned Walcot to review the situation at the mill. I expect to be engaged the entire day."

He caught her at the elbow and forced her to stop and face him. "Will you always be running away from me by hiding yourself in that curst mill?"

His gray eyes had a fiery hue that caused her to take a step backward. "But I'm doing no such thing," she responded quickly. "I have responsibilities—a dozen of them. Would you have me turn my back on them?"

"I would wish them to the devil if it meant you wouldn't turn your back on me."

"But I'm not—it's you, Joel—or perhaps our situation. I don't know—I don't know what to think. I don't know how to—"

"M'lord!" the butler called from the top of the stairs. "A footman's just arrived from Yorkshire with urgent news! He traveled all night!"

"Good God!" Joel cried, immediately setting off toward the landing. Sophia was not far behind him.

A few minutes later, Sophia watched Joel reading a letter from his father, his face dark and inscrutible except for the twitching of a nerve in his cheek. He had covered his mouth with one hand. When he finished reading the letter, he folded it up carefully and turned to her.

"Father is ill," he said quietly, tears just rimming his eyes. "He is not—" he paused, obviously stricken. Taking a deep breath, he continued, "He is not expected to live."

"Joel," Sophia breathed, taking a quick step toward him and placing her hand on his arm. "Not when you've wanted so very much to be reconciled with him."

She was in his arms and he was holding her fast before another word was spoken. She felt his pain, a tangible thing as he crushed her in a grief-stricken embrace.

"I must go to him," he murmured.

"Yes, of course," Sophia said.

After a long moment, he drew back from her, and taking her

hands in his, he looked deeply into her eyes. "Will you come with me?" he asked.

"I want to," she said. "Truly. But what of Tristan and the mill, not to mention my sisters?"

He lowered his gaze from hers and nodded. He did not seem angry as he responded, "I understand." He released her hands, bid her not be concerned about him, and ascended the stairs.

Sophia watched him go, her heart torn as to what she ought to do. She knew her duty was first to her siblings and it was clear to her that though Joel might complain of her style of management, he understood her sense of obligation. But when he reached the landing and glanced down at her, an expression of anguish in his eyes, she found herself utterly torn for the first time in her marriage.

She wanted to be with him, to support him in a time which she knew to be of crushing importance to him. For many years he had wanted to be reconciled with his father, only Lord Kennington would not permit his son to enjoy a relationship with him unless he left off his Tory associations and returned to the Whig fold, which of course Joel could not do.

Sophia moved to her office and tried to ignore the growing sense of distress which was overtaking her with each tick of the clock. Ned would be with her in half an hour at which time she would take a tour of the mill herself and see what, if anything, could be done about a situation that was becoming increasingly rife with difficulties.

But as she reviewed one ledger after another, she finally realized that the numbers were all blurred together, that she had absorbed nothing of the information contained in the records and that her thoughts were fixed exclusively on her husband's need of her. She closed the last ledger with a snap and covered her face with her hands. She wanted desperately to go with Joel but how could she just pick up and leave?

She heard the door open, thinking Joel had come to beg her to accompany him but instead Caroline entered the chamber, looking a little stiff-jawed which instantly put Sophia on her guard.

"What is it, Caroline?" she asked, leaning back in her chair and folding her hands on her lap.

"While you are gone to Yorkshire," she said, "I wonder if you will consider something. I've been meaning to ask you for some time, but because of all the trouble with Tristan and of course, Edwina's marriage, I knew you were frightfully busy. I hope you won't say no."

Caroline's assumption that she would be traveling with Joel to Yorkshire, surprised Sophia. "In the first place," she began, "I've already told Joel that I must remain here. I've far too many responsibilities to simply leave on a whim."

The look of stunned disbelief on Caroline's face made Sophia squirm. "On a whim?" Caroline asked, dumbfounded. "Your father-in-law is dying, your husband is in agony, and you call that a whim?"

"A poor choice of words only. It's just that I have my duties here."

"You have a duty to Joel," Caroline responded sharply. "Or have you not noticed as much? And even if you could deny such a duty simply because your marriage was not based on a deep romantic love, what of Joel's sacrifices? Or do you truly think he wants to be here in Lancashire with nothing to engage him except Tristan's constant exclamations about spinning looms, cogs and gears and the marvels of steam-power?"

Sophia's mouth had fallen agape. "His sacrifices," she stated quietly. "Why have I not seen as much? I should go, shouldn't I?"

"Of course you should go. Though I don't like to mention it at such an unseemly moment, you are going to be the next Marchioness of Kennington and the staff at his lordship's house will want to meet their new mistress."

Sophia felt the blood drain from her face. She felt dizzy, not with the wonder of what her future was, but of the truth of her forthcoming obligations. She leaned forward, placing her elbow on the desk and dropping her head onto her hand. "What a fool I've been. I never once thought a whit about any of it, only that I wanted all of you to benefit from Joel's rank and connections."

"Do you know what I think?" Caroline said with a soft chuckle. Sophia looked up at her sister and blinked. Caroline continued, "For a lady who manages a mill you are woefully birdwitted when it comes to everything else."

Sophia smiled crookedly. "I guess I am."

"Which leads me to my point," Caroline rushed on. "While you are gone to Yorkshire, will you consider lending me a thousand pounds that I might open my school? I am hoping to form a select seminary in Chester. Miss Beaton's school was insufferable beyond words and I have a dozen ideas—about how—I . . ."

"A school!" Sophia cried, rising from her chair. "You are not opening a seminary, you are going to find yourself an acceptable husband, with a reasonable competence upon which the pair of you might live and you are going to raise your own children. I had thought you had finally come to your senses and left off this ridiculous notion of opening a school."

At that, a strange expression came over Caroline's face. "Mark was right," she murmured.

"What?" Sophia asked, tilting her head. "What did you say? What does Mark have to do with this?"

Caroline smiled resignedly. "Nothing, except that he recommended I not broach the subject with you, that he was certain you would find the notion a silly one and you did."

"Well, Mark is right. You should listen to him. He is a man of great good sense."

For some reason, this made Caroline smile. "I should listen to him, shouldn't I?" she responded. "Maybe like you, I haven't a great deal of sense, either."

Sophia relaxed and smiled. She moved around the side of the

desk and gave her sister a quick hug. "I knew you'd be sensible about all of this."

"I'm sorry to have distressed you, Sophy. Don't give my idea another thought. As for Joel, I think I heard him in the hall. The carriage has already been brought round."

Sophia needed no further encouragement to whisk past her sister and fly down the hall and into the foyer. She found Joel, his expression grim, pulling on his gloves at the bottom of the stairs.

"I wish to come with you," she stated. "Will you wait for me? I didn't know what I was thinking earlier. My place is with you. And I can manage the mill through my correspondence."

An expression of relief flooded his face. Sophia smiled. "I won't be but a moment or two. Will you see that my maid is sent to my bedchamber? Oh, and when Ned arrives, tell him of my decision and that I know he will handle every eventuality with his usual swift hand." She darted up five steps then hurried back down. "What of Tristan?" she asked anxiously.

He seemed inordinately pleased that she had turned to him for advice. "He'll do—at least for the present. Mark has promised to keep a close eye on him. Besides, I don't expect us to be gone much above a week. We'll return as quickly as possible."

Sophia released a sigh of relief. "All right then. I'll hurry."

It was only when Joel's carriage finally reached the King's Highway and began traveling northeast toward Yorkshire, that Sophia felt her first qualms about her conversation with Caroline. Her sister's assurances that she had misjudged the direction of her life now seemed so unlike Caroline that she began to wonder what it was her sister had really said to her and what she meant to do next. Besides, now that she thought on it, she had made no such assurances.

But as the wheels of the carriage pressed on toward Yorkshire, as Joel began expressing in a greater detail than ever his distress over his estrangement from his father, her concern about Caroline disappeared.

Fifteen

"Get her out of here." Lord Kennington lifted a shaking hand and pointed at Sophia.

"She's my wife, Father. She'll stay."

A fit of coughing overtook the marquess and his valet carefully lifted the ailing man to a sitting position to make him more comfortable. When the fit had passed, Sophia noticed the flecks of blood on the white sheet in front of the marquess. Her heart was deeply saddened by all that she saw, not less so by the venom in Lord Kennington's manner, voice and stare.

She felt Joel's arm about her shoulders and glancing up at her husband, she saw that tears had filled his eyes. She slipped an arm about his waist and hugged him.

When the marquess recovered from his spell, he spoke in a raspy voice. "If she chooses to stay, then she'll hear things she won't want to here."

"I intend to stay, my lord," Sophia said calmly. "Speak your mind, if it pleases you."

He glared at her. "Well at least you show a little spirit but don't think I don't know what you are—a handle-grabbing adventuress. My son could have had any of a dozen better-mannered, better-dressed, better-birthed females than you. You're passable enough but there's not a servant in my house who won't always treat you as you deserve to be treated so don't think when I'm gone you can act as mistress with even the smallest effect. Hah!" Several coughs followed his mean-spirited speech.

"As for you—" He shifted to glare at his son. "If you think you've come to my bed to gloat, you are fair and far off the mark. I'm not dead yet and by the time I've finished with my solicitor there won't be anything left to you except the barest bones of all the entailed portions. And now leave—I don't need ghouls hovering over my bed."

"As you wish, Father," Joel said stiffly. "Come, Sophy." He guided Sophia to the door, pausing only at the sound of another fit of coughing before passing into the darkened hallway beyond.

Sophia wanted to tell him his father was only speaking out of his illness, but before she could open her mouth, Joel stopped dead in his tracks and suppressed a deep sob. She looked up at him and saw that tears were flowing freely down his cheeks. Never, had she seen him in such an unhappy state.

"Joel," she whispered. "He didn't mean a word of it, I promise you. It's just that he's so ill."

Joel wiped his eyes hastily with quick sweeps of his hands. "Oh, he meant it all right. You see, I killed my mother and he never forgave me for it."

Sophia, still standing close to him, searched his face. Had she heard him correctly? "Whatever do you mean?" she asked.

He began to walk, heading toward their bedchambers. A long carpet runner of blacks and burgundies quieted their steps as they moved along. "Father waited for years to get married, then fell violently in love with my mother. He worshipped her. Then the doctors told him my birth had so weakened her that she probably should never try to have more children. She began to sicken and fade and within a year she was dead."

Sophia slipped her arm about his. "But that's not fair," she murmured.

He chuckled sadly. "He's thrown it up to me a score of times over the years. Maybe that's why I joined the Tories. I couldn't bear being around him, knowing that when he looked at me he saw only my mother and what he had lost in her death."

When they arrived at Sophia's bedchamber, he said, "You will want to rest before dinner. We've had a trying journey and a terrible welcome-home."

Sophia smiled. "I'm not tired. Won't you come in and we can talk a little more?"

Joel hesitated. Sophia opened the door and taking his hand drew him into her bedchamber. "Good God it's cold in here," he remarked.

For some reason this made Sophia laugh. "I suppose your father is practicing economies."

At that Joel laughed since Lord Kennington was known to be as rich as Croesus. He moved to the fireplace and piled up the coals on the hearth. Before many more minutes, the coals were blazing and turning to a fine glowing pink. Beside the gray stone fireplace was a small settee. He bid Sophia sit beside him and he slipped his arm about her shoulders.

"Thank you for coming with me, Sophy," he said, looking down at her affectionately. "I don't know what I would have done without you." He lifted his hand and lightly stroked her cheek. "I've never felt free enough to tell anyone about my mother. Do you know how safe I feel with you?"

Sophia was both surprised and pleased. "You do?" she queried. "Then I ought to return the compliment. Do you know how appreciative I am of the sacrifices you have made for me and for my sisters and brother? You didn't have to stay in so uninteresting a place as Woodbridge, but you did and you've lightened my load by keeping everyone in cheerful spirits. Thank you, Joel."

Sophia could feel the warmth of the fire through the blue velvet skirts of her gown and on her hands and her face. She felt every breath Joel was taking. She saw the light in his extraordinary gray eyes, as he looked down at her. His hand was gently caressing her face. A moment later, his lips were on hers, asking the question which had only one answer.

The cozy, four-poster bed of mahogany was richly carved and hung with a flowery chintz of blue, yellow and pink. When he carried her from the settee to the bed she felt as though she had entered a spring garden, so odd to think of spring as the frosty autumn wind battered the diamond-paned windows. His kisses became fevered as he began struggling with the buttons of her gown and afterward with the knot of his neckcloth.

Sophia couldn't help but laugh, a sound which caused him to catch her up in his arms and kiss her harder still. "You've brought great joy to my life," he said. "I'm so glad I married you, Sophy."

"You are?" she whispered. "I didn't know. I thought—"

"You've had foolish thoughts," he said. "Many of them." Words were lost in the embraces which followed and in the wrestling with unwanted clothing.

Before long his hands were speaking a rhapsody to her body, his fingers gentle on her skin, touching her and bringing delicate rivulets of desire floating through her. She became lost in his kisses and in the joining which followed. Her thoughts became liquid and free. She had no care in the world that Joel's presence couldn't allay, she had no fear for the future that the touch of his lips couldn't dispel.

The rhythms of life began to move in her. She knew that in this joining her life was changing, forever. She was giving herself to her husband in the best way, as a token of her admiration and value for him.

She disappeared into another world full of mist and pleasure and sublimity beyond anything she had known before. Each pulse of his body over hers seemed to ease a strange loneliness in her heart. She wrapped her arms tightly about his neck. She heard him groan with pleasure. She kissed him hard in return when he sought her lips. Together they rose to the heights of love to gently float away into a place of calm and peace.

Afterward he remained beside her for hours, holding her, caressing her, loving her. Sophia knew the moment was precious and reveled in each kiss, each touch of his hands, each embrace. Only when hunger overtook them both, did Sophia have the smallest comfort in watching him leave her bed.

When he did, one truth surfaced above all the others, something she had been unwilling to see while he had been beside her—not once in all their lovemaking had he told her, he loved her. Perhaps she was being silly, but without this endearment she felt that in his heart he still saw their marriage as one of convenience and not one that could bring him love.

On the following day, she felt vulnerable with him, afraid of all that she was beginning to feel for him. She knew she was not being warm and openhearted toward him and when he first tried to kiss her and she turned her head away, he drew back appearing as though she had slapped him across the face.

"What is it?" he cried. "What have I done now?"

She heard his words and wondered at them. More than once she had quickly put him on the defensive. "N—nothing!" she cried.

"Then why did you turn away just now."

Sophia shrugged. "I don't know. Last night was wonderful. I—I just can't help but be afraid that now you would feel you must do the pretty, speak sonnets to me, and the like." She looked up at him hopefully.

He smiled then laughed. He took her in his arms. "I know my husbandly duty," he said, holding her tightly to him.

Sophia sighed. His embrace comforted her but the last thing she wanted to hear was that he was willing to be a good husband to her. What she wanted to hear was that he loved her. Was she hoping for too much?

The Marquess of Kennington refused to see either of them again, even though they remained four days in Yorkshire. On the fifth day, Joel consulted with the physician and learned that though Lord Kennington was gravely ill, he would undoubtedly survive to see the New Year. Joel wanted Sophia to return to her family and after forcing his presence on his father, bid the old man good-bye, promising to return following Edwina's marriage in early December.

When Sophia asked how his father had taken his assurance that he would return, Joel smiled. "He was not as venomous as I expected him to be which gives me hope."

Sophia smiled and patted his arm. She knew he was making light of the situation in order not to feel over-despondent. For herself, the mansion was too cold to be comfortable and without sufficient staff to do more than overwork all the servants, especially given the distances involved in traveling from the kitchen to the bedchambers to the attics and to the drawing rooms. The house clearly had felt the want of a mistress for years, a fact pressed upon her by the housekeeper, Mrs. Diehl, who with nervously jingled keys, stated her hope that the great house might know a kinder hand in the future.

Sophia thought she looked frightened when she offered her hints, a fact which did not surprise her given Lord Kennington's disposition. She was grateful Caroline had enlightened her about her future role in her husband's house and so she was able to assure Mrs. Diehl that she knew she had been doing an excellent job and that she would undoubtedly continue doing so for many, many years to come.

The housekeeper had then nervously stated. "I didn't know what you were likely to think, m'lady. But we've hardly the staff—"

"You don't need to say anything more. As you must know, I manage a—a certain property in Lancashire and understand the difficulties involved when one is woefully understaffed. But please understand me that this is not an appropriate time to discuss the future."

Mrs. Diehl was all embarrassment as she assured Sophia that of course it was not fitting at all to speak of such things with the marquess so ill.

Sophia felt for the lady's awkward position and with a few more assurances left that good woman smiling.

The next day, Sophia returned home feeling happier than she had in years. Joel had come to her every night and performed his husbandly duty with a tenderness that was endearing her more closely to him every day. She stepped into the hall of

Woodbridge House, laughing at something Joel had said to her when she was greeted by Edwina and Nevil, their faces ashen, and Edwina holding a letter out to her.

"Caroline didn't think you would be returning so soon. They left not an hour ago. I found this on the mantel in the drawing room a few minutes ago. Oh, Sophy, I had no idea what was going forward. Nevil and I have been so busy with our own concerns that we didn't see it. I'm so sorry!"

Sophia shook her head, disbelieving the few disjointed suspicions that were running rampant in her head. She jerked the letter from Edwina's hand and read it through once quickly.

"No!" she cried, her hand flying to her mouth, her eyes filling with tears. "How could she! In love with Mark? Why didn't I see it!" She looked up at Edwina. "Are you saying they have eloped?"

Edwina nodded. "Yes. The butler said that when they left Caroline told him you had written begging them both to come to Yorkshire, that you and Joel had need of them. He said he thought there was something funny about the business but he felt he had no right to question Caroline, especially since he considered her to be such a sensible female."

Sophia shook her head, then looked up at Joel. "How could she have done this to me? Why did she feel she must elope? Did you know she was in love with Mark?"

He shook his head as well and took the letter from her. "A couple of times I saw that they had been tête-à-tête but I didn't think much of it. He always had the run of the house like a brother. What do you intend to do?"

"Why to follow them of course," Sophia said, "and to talk her out of this nonsense."

"If the skies didn't look laden with snow, I'd have my curricle harnessed. I could overtake them within a couple of hours. But not if it snows. We had best take my coach."

"You'll come with me?" she asked.

He lifted his brows. "As though I would permit my wife to be traipsing about the countryside in this kind of weather." He narrowed his eyes and with a half-smile said, "Besides, should the coach overturn with you in it, I don't know if I would trust any chance passerby."

For a moment, Sophia didn't know what he was talking about and then the memory came flooding back to her so swiftly that she burst out laughing. "What a thing to bring up at such a moment."

He smiled. "Isn't it better to laugh just a little? Besides, you know she is in capable hands. Mark is a good man."

"Mark Ingram is a mere tutor. He has no future and certainly not Caroline's best-interests at heart."

When no one stepped forward to agree with her, she glanced from Joel's face to Edwina's and Nevil's. She was stunned. "Do you mean to tell me you all think Mark a match for Caroline?" When Nevil and Edwina nodded, she glanced up at Joel, waiting to listen to his opinion.

"I want to hear and to see that he loves her," he said quietly.

"But how often is love a proper basis for a marriage?" she shot back.

He leveled his gaze squarely at her. "There is no other basis," he said.

Sophia didn't know what to make of this statement. She blinked at him and opened her mouth to speak but already he was in motion, ordering the butler to have fresh horses harnessed to the traveling chariot, hot bricks placed on the floor of the coach, and a basket of food packed for the journey since they had not eaten for several hours.

Having concluded that the couple was heading for Gretna Green, the decision to travel west toward Lancaster was an easy one. From Lancaster, a well-traveled northern road to Scotland had existed for centuries.

The snow started falling shortly after the coach wheels began grinding their way along the westerly route. Stops at Whalley, Billington and Langho all confirmed their belief the couple was heading to Gretna Green and that they were not far behind. The snow grew heavier as the postillion drew the horses into the

Wilpshire. A few inquiries at the local alehouse indicated that
the couple had been seen taking the road to Salesbury. At Salesbury, another inquiry set the couple a mere half hour ahead of
them.

By the time the coach reach Little Town, the snow was so
heavy that it seemed impossible that Mark would have permitted
any further travel. But a few questions posed to the local inhabitants of the hamlet settled the fact that he and Caroline had
pressed on. Of course the accompanying news that the lady
seemed most anxious to continue the journey spoke volumes
for why the attempt to reach Ribchester had occurred.

Ribchester, dating from Roman times, was ordinarily a delightful village encircled by lovely green hills and resting on a
curve of the swift-flowing River Ribble. The High Street was
a pleasant jumble of stone cottages in varying colors ranging
in a long row of twisting terraces. The presence of two alehouses, the White Bull and the Black Bull, made the discovery
of the couple an easy task especially since their coach was visible outside the Black Bull. But the early snow had cloaked the
village in a deep blanket of white, obscuring the pretty stone
houses and the lovely green hills. Night was descending over
the rooftops.

Sophia saw the coach and breathed a sigh of relief. She was
grateful beyond words to have found them so quickly and so
easily. Yet at the same time she was nearly fagged to death with
traveling. The bricks had lost their heat and her toes, fingers,
and nose were freezing with cold.

She entered the tidy alehouse and received the first rush of
warm air with a moan of gratitude.

"You're freezing, aren't you?" Joel asked as he drew up beside her and slipped a comforting arm about her shoulders.

Sophia nodded, drawing off her gloves and moving instantly
to the large, stone fireplace. She let the heat soak into her face
and her fingers and until the warmth penetrated her bonnet, her
cloak and her velvet gown, she refused to remove a single article
of clothing.

The landlord of the inn, startled by their arrival became aware instantly by the bearing and fashion of his guests that he was waiting upon as well-shod a pair as he had ever seen. He attended to them in quick, obsequious fashion, bowing over and over and promising a bowl of hot rum punch if they were of a mind, just to take the chill off, of course.

Sophia was of a mind. For the present, she thought she would drink anything steaming hot just to shake the chill from her bones. The taproom was not spacious and there was no evidence of her sister and Mark. She was about to inquire after them, when she heard her sister's laughter. A moment later, Caroline appeared in the doorway with Mark in tow, the laughter dying on her face and her rosy, contented complexion turning a chalky white.

"Sophy!" she cried. "What are you doing here?"

Mark's expression was no less ashen as he added, "You've found us? But how is that possible—" He broke off, a heat of embarrassment covering his cheeks as he met Sophia's stony gaze.

When the landlord appeared shortly after, bearing a steaming bowl, Joel immediately drew the pair into the room and jovially bid Caroline to take up a place by the fire. "Fancy meeting the pair of you here in Ribchester. We were heading for Lancaster ourselves when the snow forced us to stop."

Mark took up his hint and began speaking idly of their own journey from Woodbridge. "We had hoped, just as you must have, that the snows would ease up past Whalley. But they didn't, so here we are."

Joel then asked the landlord if there were rooms available and the good man said he would do all he could to find accommodations for them.

"If you could settle the ladies in a chamber, I'm sure Mr. Ingram and I could make ourselves comfortable here in the taproom for the night."

The landlord had a pinched expression on his face. Joel read his troubled mind and immediately took him aside and spoke to him in a low voice. Sophia watched the man's countenance lighten and afterward he disappeared into the nether regions.

"All is settled," Joel said quietly, addressing Mark. "A room for the ladies and a few blankets for us."

Mark nodded, his expression having grown solemn and pained.

Sophia, utterly fatigued by the journey and in despair over her sister's reprehensible and unnecessary conduct, could restrain herself no longer. "How could you!" she cried in a hoarse whisper, knowing the landlord was now out of earshot. "And what precisely did you tell that good man?"

Caroline lifted her chin and dropped into a chair by the fireplace. She had long since removed her bonnet and her dark brown curls were sadly flat. "That I am Mrs. Ingram, of course, which I would soon be anyway had you not arrived."

"Then it is Gretna Green?" Sophia asked hotly.

"Of course," Caroline answered coldly.

So many angry thoughts coursed through Sophia's mind that she could not speak for a while. She turned toward the fire and ground her teeth. She jerked the ribbons of her blue velvet bonnet apart and slid the bonnet from her dark curls.

Joel handed her a steaming cup of punch which she cradled in her hands and found not surprisingly that her fingers were trembling with rage. Slowly, she let the brew slide down her throat. She sipped and sipped again. Soon, the rum was having its affect, her trembling stopped, her bones began to grow warm and some of her rage disappeared.

The landlord returned bearing a platter of simple fare, stewed apples and prunes, slices of cold roast beef, bread and butter and a bottle of Madeira which he offered to Joel with obvious pride.

Sophia found that she had no words now, nor much of an appetite. She forced herself to eat, however, and swallowed the glass of wine Joel pressed on her. "You are very tired, my dear," he said, taking her hand and giving it a squeeze. "As we all are

Wouldn't any appropriate conversation be better conducted tomorrow?"

Sophia looked at him and saw nothing but compassion in his gray eyes. She nodded in agreement but could not bring herself to look at her sister.

The next morning, Sophia awoke to the sight of dull gray skies and a throbbing headache. She could hear the morning's activity in full force, the sweeping of the floors, the clanking of tankards and glasses, the moving of chairs, the stoking of fires. With her back to her sister, for they had shared a bed, she heard the steady rise and fall of Caroline's breathing. She still didn't understand how Caroline could have betrayed her so completely.

She thought back to her last interview with her sister and the missing parts of Caroline's intentions flooded her mind. Caroline had asked for a loan to begin a school, undoubtedly with Mark by her side. Many incidents returned to her, of Caroline addressing Mark with an inappropriate familiarity, even as far back as the months preceding the London Season. She had supposed the familiarity reflected Mark's brotherly place in all their lives. Never for a moment would she have thought or believed Caroline would have fallen in love with the penniless tutor.

But even if love was the order of the day, how could Caroline be so foolish as to allow sentiment to guide her judgment? Sophia had never done so, she had never been permitted to do so. From the moment she buried both parents, sentiment had not been permitted to be a factor in her life. Responsibilities had structured every thought and activity for years.

Yet Caroline was a sensible woman which made her conduct all the more incomprehensible.

Well, she wouldn't allow her intelligent, sensible sister to throw her life away on a mere tutor, without prospects, for something as silly as *love*. She rose from her bed and began to dress herself and to repair as best she could her weary hair. Caroline woke soon after, silent and sullen.

When Sophia was dressed, and her curls as presentable as

she could make them, she addressed her sister. "We'll return to
Woodbridge. I don't wish to discuss the matter until then." She
knew if she did, she would undoubtedly raise her voice and not
for the life of her would she permit the landlord of the Black
Bull Inn, or his wife, to hear the lectures she was longing to
pour on her recalcitrant sister's ears.

After breakfast, Sophia looked at Joel and asked, "I have
been curious about something. What did you tell the landlord
last night? He seemed terribly distressed about something."

Joel smiled. "He was afraid he would have to turn his wife
out of her bed to accommodate us. I understood his panic at
once. A lady who labors from morning 'til night will not soon
forgive a husband for pandering to a nobleman who will no
doubt never see her hearth-fires again."

For all her distress about Caroline's elopement, she could not
keep from laughing at the memory of the landlord's pinched
face. Joel continued, "I daresay she would have given his head
a washing he would not soon forget, which brings me to another
point—have you spoken with Caroline?"

Sophia shook her head as she drew on her gloves and prepared to depart. In a whisper, she said, "I have been too angry
to speak in moderation and have told her that I don't want to
discuss the matter until we return home."

Joel nodded. "Very wise. Then perhaps you and I can discuss
the matter on our way back."

"That won't be possible," Sophia said, frowning. "Or do you
think I intend to let them travel in the same carriage?"

Joel lowered his head slightly as though settling in for a battle. "I do," he responded curtly.

Sophia gasped. He was challenging her, a fact which caused
her temper to soar suddenly. "You have nothing to say in this
and if you think that I will permit them the intimacy of traveling
in the same carriage, you are greatly mistaken. You are not
thinking clearly."

Joel narrowed his eyes. "At least I have enough sense to see
that a heavy hand in this moment, will only cause the couple

o fly again as soon as they are away from the scrutiny of your eye, or do you imagine that either will acquiesce easily to your decision regarding their lives?"

Sophia was taken aback, but her temper was not assuaged in the least. He softened his voice and added, "Sophy, trust me a little in this. I have already spoken to Mark and he has agreed to see Caroline returned to Woodbridge—he has spoken a vow and as a gentleman will not break that vow. But he loves Caroline, as he put it, *to the point of madness,* which tells me that unless you want the scandal of a second elopement, you had best disarm the situation by letting them travel together. You only add wood to the fire by trying to keep them apart."

By the end of this speech, Sophia found herself in agreement with Joel. She wished it otherwise, but she knew that Caroline, in her stubbornness, would only become more resistant to the inevitable if she was forced to travel separately from Mark.

Within a few minutes, Sophia watched with failing heart as Mark and Caroline's coach bowled from the white-cloaked village. How could she trust either of them again, she wondered. Mark may have made a vow to Joel, but she had little faith in Mark's ability not to allow Caroline to persuade him into a second rash course of action.

As Joel settled himself beside her in their carriage, she heard him laugh. When he sat down, he slipped his arm about her shoulders and murmured, "Gentle, my love. We'll get them home safely."

She looked at him only dimly registering in her mind the endearing term with which he had addressed her. "I have never known Caroline to be so bird-witted."

"Perhaps she felt she had no choice."

"No choice to be sensible about her future? Has she learned nothing by my example?"

Joel took her hand and though he squeezed it gently, he said, "I'm afraid she's learned too much from your example."

Sophia didn't know what he meant and she was still far too anxious and too worn-out to try to decipher his meaning.

When they arrived back in Woodbridge, night had fallen once more.

Late the following morning, Sophia went to her sister's bedchamber to finally address her scandalous conduct. She found Caroline dressed in a high-waisted wool gown of a forest green hue, her expression somber. She had a book open on her lap, and when Sophia drew closer she could see it was a volume of the *Iliad,* in Greek.

Caroline looked up at her. "I love him, Sophy," she said simply.

Sophia felt oddly close to tears as she clasped her hands in front of her. "During the Season, when you spoke so eloquently on Edwina's behalf, prompting me to lower my expectations for her and permit her to become betrothed to Nevil Royce, I never thought I would have you turn against me like this. Do you understand how cruelly you've treated me?"

Caroline took a deep breath. "Yes," she responded. "But you gave me no choice."

"And what choices have you given me?" Sophia snapped. "As usual I am forced to play the dragon, with everyone eyeing me as though I breathe fire when I speak. Only tell me in what way you can possibly think that a marriage to a penniless tutor can be at all acceptable to any parent, guardian, or woman of sense? Explain this much to me, Caroline, and then I will acquiesce to your marriage.

"I know we shall not enjoy great financial comfort during our lives. But I don't need very much, as you ought to know by now, nor does Mark. We are high-minded in our ideals and in our purposes for our respective lives—"

"High-mindedness never put food in a child's stomach."

Caroline set her jaw. "In case you haven't noticed, Mark does have a profession. However poorly paying it might be, he earns enough in any year to enable us to keep a roof over our heads and food on the table sufficient for a growing family. And then is my dowry, which, if well-invested, will purchase us a home and the ability to keep at least two servants which is all I believe we will need once we are settled in Lancaster."

Sophia was horrified by the meagre description Caroline was presenting her. "I won't allow it. I won't allow you or your future children to suffer like this, not when it is so easily preventable."

"Why won't you understand that it is not your business to prevent my suffering any more than it is your responsibility to see to my happiness. These are my tasks, mine alone. I know the sacrifice I am making. When I refused Sanditon's proposal of marriage, I didn't do so without having given great consideration to the comfort such an alliance would mean for me. But more than anything in life, beyond seeing to the instruction of my own children, I wish to have a school. Mark and I have spoken at length about the kind of school we would sponsor."

"So you are back at this school business, believing it will answer all your difficulties. But you don't have any idea how hard it is to manage any business, nonetheless a school."

"I can learn," she retorted firmly. "Just as you learned."

"But I had a mentor in Bartholomew and a strong right-hand support in Ned Walcot."

"And why do you think I wouldn't search for knowledge or for someone to guide me in the business aspects of operating an academy?"

"You are too young, too naive to know what you are asking of life. Again, I tell you, I won't permit a marriage between you and Mark Ingram."

To Sophia's surprise, Caroline did not bat an eye nor did she try to argue further. Stubbornness and determination were written on every cool feature. Clearly, she felt she had no need of words.

Sophia turned on her heels and quit the room, but as she stepped into the cool hallway, she remembered Joel's warning, that the pair would likely attempt another elopement. For that reason she did the only thing she could do, she called Mark to the library and after giving him a letter of reference, dismissed him as tutor to her brother.

Though Mark was rather pale when she delivered the news to him, he accepted her decision and within the hour he was gone from Woodbridge House.

She was in her office when Joel threw the door open, his complexion high, and demanded to know if it was true.

"If what is true?" she asked, both angry that he would barge into her office without requesting admittance and frightened by the obvious anger on his face.

"You know damn well what I mean," he responded, closing the door behind him and moving to stand in front of the desk and glare down at her.

Sophia rose from her chair, disliking his intimidating stance. Straightening her shoulders, she said, "If you are referring to Mark's dismissal then yes, it is true, but I don't know why you feel you need to come in here and quarrel with me about the only reasonable decision I could make given the scandalous circumstances of his having eloped with my sister two days ago."

"He loves her, Sophy!" Joel cried. "Have you no heart! No feeling?"

Sophy was thunderstruck. "And when was I ever given the chance to act upon my feelings or the changeable whims of my heart? Never, and for that reason I expect no less from my siblings. I compromised once for Edwina's sake, but Nevil at least has a competence upon which he can support his bride in reasonable comfort. But Mark Ingram hasn't two pennies to rub together. I suggest he find a means of supporting Caroline and then he may come to me and beg for her hand, but not a moment sooner. I don't do this lightly, or to please myself. I hope you have more faith in me than that. I am looking toward the future, to the day when Caroline has not just herself to think of, of children as well which will surely follow their nuptials. She is not old enough to be thinking of such things. Were my father here, would he agree to such a wedding? I think not."

Joel did not respond right away but Sophia could see that

none of her words had changed his opinion of the situation for his gaze was still dark with anger. "How odd," he began at last, "to think that my father was so opposed to your being my wife, when you are just like him."

Sophia gasped and lifted her hand in a gesture of stunned protest. "You are greatly mistaken!" she cried.

But Joel only grimaced in disgust as he turned on his heel and left the room.

Sophia sank slowly to her chair, blinking in disbelief, her vision blurred as his words began to pound against her mind. *Like his father.* How could he have said such a thing to her when she was nothing like Lord Kennington. Had he forgotten already her compassion and concern following his father's dismissal of him from the sickroom? Why would he say such a cruel thing to her? She wasn't like the marquess. She wasn't!

She leaned her elbows on her desk and dropped her head into her hands covering her face. She felt sick at heart, suddenly, as though she was beginning to acknowledge a truth she had not wanted to see before.

But there was no truth to see except that the entire household had no understanding of her or her motives.

Suddenly she was on her feet, moving quickly from her office. She startled the butler in the foyer and asked him if he had seen Lord Leyburn.

"I—I do believe he's in t'drawing room, m'lady."

"Thank you," she answered crisply.

She found Joel standing by the window, one hand pushing aside the royal blue velvet drapes in order to see the snow on the hills behind Woodbridge House.

"How dare you!" she cried.

He looked back surprised, but unrelenting in his hostile expression.

"How dare any of you criticize me or the decisions I've made!" she continued. "Have you been willing to take all my burdens from me? Has Edwina or Caroline? Has God! Has Fate! I didn't ask for my life, my life was thrust on me by something I couldn't control, by the deaths of my parents. I never asked for the care and responsibility of my siblings, but so it was given to me. I have taken my responsibilities as seriously as any man or woman before me and I have done well by all of them. Have any of them wanted for food when the whole countryside is starving? Even you—you came to me only when you had need of my money and what was my return motive?—only to see that my brother and my sisters were well-established in this life and protected from as much of the harshness of this existence as possible. And what thanks do I get for it—a constant reminder that I am this great evil force at Woodbridge House, determined to ruin everyone's lives, determined to prevent everyone from being *aux anges* day and night, and determined only to have my own way regardless of the circumstances. Well all of you are fair and far off the mark, Lord Leyburn. If I could undo this I would. I should never have married you for the Season was wasted on my sisters and I can certainly see my brother into Oxford without your connections and your assistance."

She didn't give him time to respond, but left the drawing room, hastily brushing away angry tears. She ran up the stairs and sought the seclusion of her room, sitting on the side of the bed, her arms folded across her chest and rocking to and fro in an attempt to comfort herself.

But there was no comfort in the thought of how she had lost her temper and said things she hadn't wanted to say. At last she whirled around, threw herself on the bed, and gave herself over to a hearty bout of tears.

Sixteen

Over the next week, Sophia stayed mostly in her office, avoiding her family. Tensions were high in the house. Edwina had taken Caroline's side, Tristan was despondent over Mark's dismissal and Caroline was as stiff-jawed as ever. The only time the family was together was at dinner which Joel presided over with good grace and with a steadfast purposefulness in forcing the siblings to behave with good manners if not love and affection. He kept the conversation light and directed as much as possible on Edwina's approaching nuptials.

November had arrived with a vengeance. The snows were deep in the lanes about the wooded valley and a thick blanket on the nearby moorland. Joel had not come to her bedroom since their quarrel, nor had he tried to make amends. For herself, his opinion that she was just like his father, still rankled sorely.

She knew there was nothing more to be said, either to her husband or to Caroline. It was clear to her that none of them understood either her motives or the level of responsibility she bore. Several times she considered relenting, especially where Caroline was concerned, but all she had to do was look into the future and her opinions were confirmed yet again. Caroline held a far too romantic view of just what her life with Mark would be like and so long as Caroline was under her roof and her care, she would not allow her young sister to make such a horrendous mistake. She was convinced a little more experience of the world for Caroline was what was necessary to dispel the romance of both her wished-for marriage and her hope of opening a school.

To that purpose, she had set herself to finding just the right situation for her sister that would not only take her mind off of Mark but which would give her a taste of the kind of work she was intending to undertake. By mid-November she had found exactly the position she was looking for, a governess situation to two young girls in Carnforth north of Lancaster.

She called Caroline to her office the day her decision was made, and presented her plan to her astonished sister.

She gave Mrs. Marsett's letter to Caroline.

"You mean you would permit me to become a governess?"

Caroline cried, lifting her gaze from the letter to stare at Sophia in stunned disbelief.

"I am not the sapskull you believe me to be," Sophia replied. "Nor am I indifferent to you. My complaint about either an elopement or a marriage to Mark Ingram is that I am convinced neither of you understand precisely what your lives would be like. I realize you have an interest in opening a school—an idea I oppose wholeheartedly—but if you are to do so I want you to know just what it would be like to be responsible for the complete education of a young mind."

"I—I don't understand you, Sophy," Caroline said, giving her head a shake. Tears brimmed in her eyes.

Sophia eyed her sister worriedly. "You do not wish for the post, then?" she asked.

"Not wish for it?" Caroline cried. "I want for nothing more. I've been thinking a lot about my life since, well since you brought Mark and me back to Woodbridge House. It was wrong of me to have eloped with him, I know that, I just didn't feel you would support my goals. But this," she waved the letter in the air. "Now I can prove to you how serious I am."

Sophia leaned back in her chair. "You have every opportunity in the world available to you and yet you would choose to become a governess? Why?" She saw the enthusiasm in her sister's face and was truly dumbfounded. When she had concocted the scheme of procuring a position for Caroline she had supposed that her sister would have fought the idea tooth and nail, but here she was appearing as though Sophia had given her gift of great price.

"Why?" Caroline reiterated. "How could I not want to be a governess? I never asked you about it because I was convinced you would have opposed me entirely. But this! Now I can earn a wage and after a time, Mark and I will be able to open our school." These last words, spoken in the heat of her excitement, brought a blush of embarrassment to Caroline's cheeks.

Sophia asked gently, "Have you heard from him?"

Caroline lifted her chin slightly, "He has procured a teaching position in Lancaster. I—I have written to him a dozen times."

"Yes, I know."

Caroline opened her eyes wide. "But how?"

Sophia smiled. "Because I am not blind. I see you at your writing desk everyday, completely oblivious to everything around you. Who else would you be writing to so lost in thought."

Caroline bit her lip. "I know we haven't spoken, you and I, about what happened. The truth is, Mark didn't want to elope. From the first he was completely opposed to the idea."

"I supposed as much," Sophia said quietly.

Caroline lifted her brow. "You did? But I thought you blamed him."

"He shouldn't have given in to your strong will, Caroline, and you might want to think about that before you marry him."

Again, she had stunned her sister. "Are you saying you will give me permission to marry Mark?"

Sophia laughed lightly. "I have refused to consider it because you are not even eighteen. But there will come a time, not too far in the future, when you will be of age and any man of the cloth will be willing to marry you. I want what's best for you and for the present that means that I want you to have a little experience of the path you seem so set upon before you make a commitment you will both come to regret in the future."

"I could never regret becoming Mark's wife and nothing will change my mind about opening a school."

"Only time will tell."

Caroline met her eye to eye, her expression challenging. "You'll see, Sophy. You'll see."

"I hope I will," she responded. "And now you had best write to Mrs. Marsett and accept the post."

Caroline rose quickly to her feet. A bloom of excitement was on every feature which faded only a little as she reached the door and turned back to Sophia. "I can't believe I'm saying this to you, but by the time we'd reached Wilpshire, I was regretting the elopement but I didn't know how to get out of it. I had been so headstrong and then when you arrived I was torn between sheer relief and my horrid pride."

"You were?" Sophia cried.

Caroline smiled wryly. "Why do you think I didn't run off with him again? We didn't lack for opportunities."

"No, I suppose you didn't," she realized.

The sisters stared at one another for a long moment. Finally, Caroline smiled. "Thank you, Sophy." Tears again brimmed in her eyes. "Look! I've become a watering pot!" She laughed, and afterward disappeared through the doorway.

At dinner that night, with the news of Caroline's new post the topic of much stunned yet enthusiastic discussion, the tensions in the house dissipated entirely. Edwina kept shaking her head and crying out, "How can you think of teaching spoiled little girls their alphabets and stitches! I would rather die!"

When she had said it for the third time, Caroline told her to stubble it, which didn't offend Edwina in the slightest. The twins were as different as night and day and where Edwina had always found schooling of any kind to be a horrible burden to bear, Caroline had always thrived in the classroom.

At one point during the dinner, she realized Joel was staring at her with a warm expression in his eye. And while Caroline and Edwina were engaged in a discussion of how many gowns Edwina should take on her honeymoon, Joel lifted his wineglass to her in an approving salute. Perhaps she shouldn't have been so very pleased, but the knowledge that her husband approved of how she had chosen to resolve the situation, meant more to her than she would have thought possible.

She thought back to his last recrimination of her, and she wondered for the first time if his stinging accusation that she was like his father had been part of the reason she had sought a position as a governess for Caroline. She realized with a start that it had been. She would never have considered such a course of action a year or even a month ago. But knowing that Joel and his father's relationship had been severed by a stubborn insistence that obedience be the only rule of the day, she had been forced to examine every aspect of the situation and to address the real issue—her fear that Caroline would suffer for her decision.

In the end, the choice to give Caroline a practical, first-hand experience at the life and occupation she was seeking, seemed the best route to take. After all, if Caroline truly was a teacher at heart, then nothing would keep her from her calling anyway. To remain stridently opposed to her teaching ambitions would therefore keep her in the same role with Caroline that Lord Kennington had assumed with his son, a role that had cost both Joel and his father a loving relationship.

She lifted her wineglass to Joel in return and smiled. She murmured, "Thank you."

Sophia returned her attention to the table and noticed for the first time that Tristan hadn't eaten very much and that he was pushing his peas around his plate with his fork. He sat next to her so she was able to express her concern without drawing attention to him.

Tristan immediately took a bite of the peas and insisted that he was fine, that he was just a little tired from having gone out riding that afternoon. "I went a little too far. The road leading to the highway was free of snow for the first time in a couple of weeks and I couldn't resist. Now I ache from head to foot."

Sophia looked at him closely and saw that his eyes were encircled with shadows and a suspicion formed quickly in her brain. "You aren't—that is, Tristan, I hope you've not been to any meetings of late."

He glanced quickly toward her then his gaze slid away just as quickly. He shrugged. "Of course I haven't," he said, but he didn't look at her. "What could I do anyway to make a difference?" He laughed almost bitterly. "After all, my sister owns the mill."

"Are you still distressed that the steam-factory is almost complete?"

At that, he dropped his fork and turned to stare at her, his gaze hard. "I can't believe you said that," he responded with another bitter laugh. He then pushed himself away from the table and said, "If you don't mind, I'm going to bed. I—I'm not feeling well."

Sophia could see that he wasn't and given his irritability, she thought he ought to seek his bed. "Very well," she said. "Perhaps we can talk in the morning."

He nodded, again without looking at her, and left the dining room with his lips pressed tightly together.

Sophia watched him go, her brows knit into a frown of concern. They had quarreled a week earlier about Mark's dismissal, and about her intentions to proceed with the steam-powered factory. He had placed his arguments against both circumstances with more force than she had ever seen him previously display. She had reiterated, yet again, the difficulties she was facing—that the only way she could keep up with the competition was by opening the factory. His final argument of you just don't understand, failed utterly to move her in her opinions which had left Tristan exasperated and sullen.

His responses she had set down to his youth and she had left him to work out his feelings by himself.

After dinner, Caroline excused herself to write a letter to Mark, and Nevil and Edwina stole off to the library to work out more of the details of their wedding. If Sophia thought it likely that more than wedding plans were being discussed, she only smiled and thought it a good thing the wedding would take place very soon. She then wondered if perhaps tonight Joel would come to her room.

When she found herself alone with him in the drawing room, she was trying to think of some way of inviting him to do so, when he brought forward a different subject altogether.

"I was mistaken about you, Sophy," he began solemnly. "I

should never have said you were like my father. I was angry at the time. Will you forgive me?"

Sophy, seated on the blue velvet sofa by the glowing fire, nodded. "Of course I will. But I ought to tell you that your words had something to do with the post I secured for Caroline. A few months ago I would never have permitted a sister of mine to work in such a menial capacity. So I think it a great irony that a nobleman would have to teach me a little of not being a snob. Do you have any reservations about the post?"

He took up a seat in Bartholomew's chair and shook his head. "Not a bit, but I must say until I married you I wouldn't have believed I would hold all the opinions I do now."

"What do you mean?"

"The circles in which I traveled before I married you were so insular, so constricting. I didn't see that until I accompanied Tristan on a couple of his expeditions in London. My world has been broadened in a wonderful way. Tristan wants me to invest in the Coke Gas and Light Company," he chuckled. "And I'm considering it! Sometimes I even wonder what it would be like to operate a factory like yours, whether I could succeed at it, as you've done here."

Sophia stared at him in amazement.

He smiled. "I see that I've shocked you." He was silent apace then frowned slightly. "But I've been thinking of late that Tristan might be right about the steam-factory. Perhaps you ought to reconsider postponing."

"I can't," she said simply. "If we can't compete with the other textile mills, we'll be out of business within a couple of years."

"I understand that. But there have been more machine-smashings and more predicted everywhere and you've already had one attack."

Sophia threw her hands wide. "But I had Ned explain our predicament to our workers and we gave out subsistence relief to those in need. I only wish we could give more, but I've already used up what I could have given freely—" she broke off, realizing what she had said.

"A bad bargain, eh?" he asked.

Sophia glanced at him and noted the wry expression on his face. "I've never said so," she began lamely.

"But right now you're thinking it," he said.

Sophia felt a blush rise on her cheeks. She was thinking something so different that she was afraid he would comprehend her true feelings. She didn't want him to know that never in her life had she spent so much money so well. She tried to still her suddenly fluttering heart. She could not bring herself to look at him.

"Is that how it is, then?" he asked, the tone of his voice strange.

She looked up at him and saw that his gray eyes had taken on a familiar, cold expression. "What do you mean?" she asked swallowing hard. She didn't want to be forced into admitting the truth of her feelings when she was convinced he didn't love her.

"You know very well what I mean. You think you've made a bad bargain, that you've spent your money poorly."

Why was he pressing her? "I don't think anything of the sort," she murmured, her voice barely above a whisper.

He rose to his feet. "For God's sake, Sophia, at least don't lie to me. I can see how you feel, the answer is written plainly on your beautiful face. I just thought, maybe, in time, you'd come to—" he paused. What had he meant to say? To love him? "Well, at least to find me an agreeable companion."

"But I do," she tried to assure him. "You've always been kind and considerate."

"But not the husband you wanted."

"Ours is a marriage of convenience," she said. "I wasn't thinking of you in any other way than that when we married."

He looked away from her, staring at the carpet by her feet. He looked as though he wanted to say more, but abruptly he turned on his heel and left the room.

Sophia placed a hand to her mouth. Her fingers were trembling and tears stung her eyes. She had offended him, badly. She hadn't meant to, yet it almost seemed to her as though he wanted her to tell him she loved him. Yet how could he want that from her when he had never said as much himself?

In the early hours of the morning, Sophia awoke to the sounds of a sharp rapping on her door. She sat up in bed and called out, "Who is it?"

At the same time, she became aware of feet running down the hall.

Her abigail opened the door and rushed in. "M'lady!" she cried. "The mill is burning. The Luddites have set t'new factory on fire! The blaze has lit up the whole countryside! His lordship is gone and Master Tristan was not found in his bed and the covers weren't even disturbed."

Fear shot through Sophia as though lightning had struck her. She fairly leapt from her bed. Rose helped her struggle into a warm shift, woolen stockings and a high-waisted gown of russet velvet. She threw a wool cape over her shoulders and a bonnet over her dark brown curls. She couldn't get her half-boots on quickly enough, but once they were on, she was running, following in the wake of all her servants who poured from the house. She saw that Nevil was with them and called to him.

Nevil was wild-eyed as she reached him, the cold, snowy air biting her cheeks.

"Is it another riot?" she cried. "Against my mill? How is this possible!"

He hooked his arm tightly about hers. "I don't know. There's been talk for weeks at the inn, but who would have believed it would come to this, when you've done so much more than any of the others!"

"These are hard times," she responded, walking quickly beside Nevil who several times kept her from slipping in the ice laden snow as they descended the hill to the factory.

The mills were ablaze, just as her abigail had told her, the flames dancing into the black night, and casting a bloody hue onto the snow all around.

"Where's Tristan?" she asked hoarsely. The freezing air was hurting her lungs as she hurried along.

"No one knows, Sophy. I'm sorry."

She gripped his arm tightly and felt him pat hers reassuringly in response. "I don't see Joel," she said.

"He left before me. Perhaps he's on the other side of the new steam-loom factory. Good God! Nothing can stop this inferno now! Not even a downpour."

He's right, Sophy thought. Only where was Tristan.

When she arrived at the entrance to the blazing factory, to her surprise she found several men from the village clustered nearby. She released Nevil's arm and approached them. "Was this your doing?" she cried. Gone was any thought of restraint. "Frawley, are you the one who has incited this horrible act? Where's Tristan?"

At her last question, she watched as several of the men shifted from looking at her to staring at the mill.

She looked back at the mill, smoke pouring from several broken windows and the doorway. This side of the mill was now engulfed as was the side facing Woodbridge House. "You can't mean to say he's inside?" she asked in a small voice.

A sense of hysteria rose up within her and without hesitation she ran toward the door only to find herself tackled and thrown to the packed snow. The impact caused her to bite her lip and she came up throwing her arms about wildly, trying to scramble to the front door. "Tristan!" she screamed. But someone was holding her waist and legs fast from behind, preventing her from moving.

She turned on her assailant, flipping herself over, and began beating at his face. She wasn't sure who had hold of her but she was enraged that he was stopping her from helping Tristan. She screamed and hit at him, until he pinned her in a tight, painful hug.

When she grew exhausted from struggling with her captor, only then did she recognize Nevil's voice. "Stop it, Sophy!" he cried. "There's nothing you can do. Either Joel will find him, or—easy now. Easy. That's better. You couldn't have done anything."

Sophy didn't even know she was crying until she felt her sobs racking Nevil's chest. She threw her arms tightly about him. He was right. But what a powerful instinct it had been to catapult herself toward the doorway. She was looking at the men, many of whom had crumpled into the snow and now sat with their heads bowed across folded arms.

Suddenly she realized Nevil had said something of Joel. Releasing her stranglehold on his neck, she pulled back and asked, "What of Joel? Oh, Nevil don't tell me he's in there, too? Shall I lose them both in one night? Oh, dear God, help me."

Still holding tightly to him, she turned sufficiently toward the building and stared blindly at the flaming monster that had devoured those she loved. Disbelief flooded her. She became suddenly numb, almost as though she wasn't even seeing a burning building.

"Take me home," she murmured. "I'll leave here and never come back."

Just as Nevil turned her toward the path back to Woodbridge, Joel burst through the doorway, a man slung over his back. He threw the figure into the snow, doubled over and began coughing and wheezing. Sophia and Nevil ran to them both, but the fire was near and growing hotter by the second so that all four of them were in danger now. Just as before, she felt herself grabbed only this time dragged backward. Joel and Tristan were surrounded by men who were lifting them up and carrying them away into the snowbanks fifty feet from the building.

A roar quickly followed as the top floor was engulfed and then Sophia watched as the whole factory collapsed into itself, shuddering and roaring as the entire edifice fell to the earth. Had the men not moved them, they would all have been killed.

That night, Sophia moved from one bedroom to the other,

watching over the sufferings of the men. The smoke of the fire had injured both Tristan and Joel. Tristan was burned on his neck and some of his hair was singed off. Joel's hands were badly burned. Tristan's clothes had caught fire and Joel had instinctively dampened the fire with his hands. Neither man could speak. The doctor kept them dosed with laudanum for the pain.

In the hallway between their rooms, she spoke with him. "Will my brother and, and my husband be all right?"

The doctor settled his hand on her shoulder. "A bit scarred up, but yes, they'll both survive to give you a great deal more grief."

Sophy had never heard such wonderfully comforting words in her entire life and she fell on the doctor's chest. He enfolded her in his arms and patted her gently until her tears had subsided. When he recommended a sleeping draught for her as well, she refused. She would not leave either her brother or Joel tonight.

Later, she knelt beside Joel's bed, and placed a gentle hand on his arm. He was breathing in small shallow breaths, his brow creased even in his sleep. "I love you, Joel." she whispered. "I was afraid to tell you how I felt before. You see, I was so afraid you didn't love me. As for the debt I settled on our marriage, you are worth a hundred such debts to me. I keep thinking how, after tonight I might never have been able to tell you as much. It would seem I'm a bit of coward, after all."

She heard Joel moan and looked up to find that he was watching her and smiling. His lips were moving, but she couldn't hear him. She moved close to him. "Did you hear what I said?" she asked. "I thought you were sleeping." She brushed away a tear which had slid down her cheek.

"I love you, too," came the raspy reply.

"Oh, Joel," she cried, placing her cheek against his. "I love you so very much. You've no idea." She felt his arms encircle her, even though his hands were heavily bandaged.

He spoke again. "But—you're not—a coward," he whispered brokenly.

Tears flooded her eyes now. She had to draw back to wipe them all away. Her life suddenly made complete sense to her as she blew her nose and smiled at the man she loved. Her marriage of convenience was no more and in its stead was a proper marriage, just as Joel had said—a marriage based on love.

Two weeks later, Sophia was carrying a tray of food to Tristan's bedchamber, when she found his bed empty. Edwina, who was straightening the bedcovers, looked up at her entrance and said, "He's visiting Joel."

"What?" she cried, startled. She didn't wait for an answer, or even expect one since the general consensus of the entire household was that she was coddling the men far too much. Setting the tray down on a table by the door, she left the room.

Sophia found Joel and Tristan laughing together. How could they laugh at all, she thought, grimacing a little and remembering the doctor's warning that both of them would live to give her more grief.

"Why are you out of bed?" she called to Tristan. "I've brought your nuncheon to your room and Edwina said you'd come in here. Go back at once, or I shall have the doctor prescribe a purging draught for you."

Tristan laughed outright then immediately bid Joel good-bye. His slow gate and his thinness were not lost on Sophia. The ordeal of recovering from inhaling so much smoke, and from the burns on his neck, was proving more difficult than he wished for.

Sophia approached Joel's bedside and took up her place beside him. She sat in a red velvet winged chair and said, "Shall I read to you, my love?"

He reached over and took her hand in his bandaged paw.

"No, not just now," he said. "There's something I want to say to you that I've been putting off."

Sophia was surprised, a sense of panic striking her heart. They had talked a lot during the past two weeks about the future, about Tristan, about the mill. She had thought they had come to a meeting of the minds. For one thing, she would not rebuild right away even though she would be receiving insurance monies because of the fire. She had concluded, belatedly, that she needed to let her plans rest especially given the fact that more and more machine-smashings and fires were being reported in the newspapers as winter began setting in heavily on the starving midland and northern counties. For another thing, Joel had advised her to counsel her brother to attend Oxford after all, even if he was to take over management of the mill one day. Joel had persuaded him that he could take advantage of all his associations from University as the years wore on, since many of these men would be the future leaders in the House of Lords and in the House of Commons and would direct the financial policies of the nation which would invariably affect his mill.

Sophia felt this argument was very sensible and that in her own anxiety to make certain her brother had a good future, she had missed this most obvious point of fact. The compromise gave her an assurance that his education and his future would not be neglected and at the same time helped her to accept that Tristan would one day own the mill and more than likely build more factories.

What then did Joel need to say to her now? Some confession she didn't want to hear?

"What is it?" she asked nervously.

"I should have told you the truth the day we were married," he said.

Now her heart began to pound in her chest, in her neck and in her head. What terrible thing was he going to confess to her? "Yes?" she asked, her mouth dry.

"I've loved you from the first," he said, his voice still somewhat hoarse. "But I knew you were proud and that I had offended you on that first night, in Chester, and that it was likely you would always despise me for that. You have never behaved cowardly, but I have. When we were together at my father's house, I knew you wanted me to tell you I loved you, I could sense as much each time you touched me. But I was a coward, I was afraid you didn't love me and I was unwilling to speak the words first. You were always straight with your opinions of me and I was afraid you'd tell me that your heart could never be engaged by me."

Sophia was dumbfounded. "You have loved me, for so many months, and never said a word? Joel, you're not a coward, you're a bacon-brained idiot!"

Joel began to laugh and Sophia joined him. "But if you've been bacon-brained," she conceded, "then I've been bird-witted. All this time, when you were being so loving toward my sisters and my brother, so considerate of the time I needed to spend with Ned Walcot, so convivial in the evenings, I thought you were merely doing your duty."

He smiled warmly at her. "And did you believe I was only doing my duty at my father's house?"

Sophia remembered the sweetness of his love-making and knowing now that he had loved her all along, somehow made the memories of his touch, of his embraces, of his kisses, more endearing than ever. "I should have known something was amiss," she said lightly. "We were together for hours. I have never known a more wonderful time in my life."

"Then I had better recover quickly," he said, his gray eyes intense. "For I want to be with you again more than anything in the world."

Edwina's wedding was a turning point for the family. For the first time in their lives, Sophia realized, the siblings would not be together as a family. Edwina's happiness made the parting both joyous and poignant, but welcome. Life was moving forward in its relentless way.

Caroline left Woodbridge House a week later to take up her post in Carnforth. Sophia still couldn't believe that her sister actually wanted to become a teacher, but at least now she no longer struggled with this fact. Now, she could let each of her siblings be who they were without being so fearful of the future.

Joel had changed that in her, she realized. He had given her ability to judge a measure of balance it had hitherto lacked. She was better able to let her brother and her sisters make their own mistakes and at the same time take pleasure in the results of those decisions that brought them success.

Tristan got a new tutor, one Joel recommended to prepare him in his weaker subjects for the more rigorous studies at Oxford. Tristan would never be a scholar, just as Joel had said, but now Sophia was assured that his future in business would never be hindered by a lack of education or connections.

The primary instigator of the mill-burning was transported to the colony in New South Wales. Those who had aided him were each given prison sentences of two-years. All of these judgments were light for not one of them, under the law, was undeserving of hanging. But Sophia spoke on their behalf and on behalf of the sufferings of so many who have taken the brunt of Parliamentary policies inflicted on the common people without the ability on any level for redress. In other communities and counties, hangings for machine-smashings that winter were not uncommon.

By Christmas, Sophia knew she was carrying Joel's child and the event served to give their lives a new turn. They decided to leave Woodbridge House and spend the remainder of the holidays with Lord Kennington who was failing steadily. Joel was determined to be with his parent on his deathbed, for his own sake. He didn't know if reconciliation would be possible, but he knew that no matter what happened he wanted to be with his father at his only possible time of farewell.

Sophia began to take up her responsibilities at the great house in Yorkshire with a concern, dedication and purpose that set the staff at ease. The first change she made was in the sick-chamber, which Lord Kennington had ruled. She was rarely far from his room, and regardless of his fits of ill-temper directed toward her, she saw the chamber freshened with pine branches, she saw his linens changed more frequently and the draperies drawn back from the windows so that the dark room was flooded with light.

He grumbled and complained, but after a week, she saw that he was a great deal more comfortable and more resigned to her presence. She read him the daily newspapers, *The Times* and the *Morning Post*, then left him alone with his son.

After three weeks, when January was stiff on the Yorkshire moors, Joel stopped her just as she collected the morning papers for her father-in-law. He was smiling and said that though his father still bellowed about "that woman"—the only appellation by which he addressed Sophia—he knew that his father was softening toward his wife.

"He said you were devilishly persistent and he didn't like your high-handed manners one whit!"

"Sounds like a compliment to me," Sophia said, smiling.

He caught her up in his arms, the swell of her stomach sweetly between them, and kissed her soundly on the mouth. "I love you, my darling Sophy."

Sophy accepted his embraces for a moment, then drew back, blushing. "You can't be forever catching me up in the hallways like this. You will have all the servants gaping and gossiping."

Joel smiled down at her. "Well it would be a terrible thing to have them know that I love you," he responded facetiously.

"You know that's not what I mean."

"I want them to know that I love you and that from now on this will be a house full of sunshine and love and—forgiveness."

Sophia looked at him and realized he was being very specific. Besides, he had a peculiarly pleased expression on his face. All of a sudden she knew what had happened. "He's forgiven you!" she cried.

Joel nodded, his gray eyes suddenly full of tears. She threw her arms about his neck and he danced her in circles until they were both laughing and dizzy.

"Then we can want for nothing more," she said, but only after she could keep herself upright without feeling like she was going to fall over.

"Nothing, except a dozen more of these." He patted her stomach affectionately. "Thank you, Sophy, so much, for everything."

Again he kissed her and this time she made no protest, not caring that footsteps could be heard on the stairs nearby nor that a door snapped shut and a giggling could be heard from an undermaid down the hall.

She loved and she was loved and for the present nothing else mattered, not even Lord Kennington's shouting, "Where the devil is *that woman* with my newspapers!"